tender

Also by Sofia Samatar

A Stranger in Olondria
The Winged Histories

tender:
stories
Sofia
Samatar

Small Beer Press
Easthampton, MA

This is a work of fiction. All characters and events portrayed
in this book are either fictitious or used fictitiously.

Small Beer Press
150 Pleasant Street #306
Easthampton, MA 01027
smallbeerpress.com
weightlessbooks.com
info@smallbeerpress.com

Distributed to the trade by Consortium.

Library of Congress Cataloging-in-Publication Data

Names: Samatar, Sofia, author.
Title: Tender : stories / Sofia Samatar.
Description: First edition. | Easthampton, MA : Small Beer Press, [2017]
Identifiers: LCCN 2016059748| ISBN 9781618731265 (hardback : alk. paper) |
  ISBN 9781618731272 (ebook)
Subjects: | BISAC: FICTION / Fantasy / Short Stories. | FICTION / Science
  Fiction / Short Stories. | FICTION / Short Stories (single author).
Classification: LCC PS3619.A4496 A6 2017 | DDC 813/.6--dc23
LC record available at https://lccn.loc.gov/2016059748

First edition 1 2 3 4 5 6 7 8 9

Text set in Centaur 12pt.

Printed on 30% recycled paper by the Maple Press in York, PA.
Author photo © 2016 by Scott Jost.
Cover image: *Kirkes Handbook of Physiology*, W. Morrant Baker & Vincent Dormer Kirkes Harris, 1892.

For Isabel and Nico

Tender Bodies

Tender Landscapes

tender
bodies

Selkie Stories Are for Losers

I hate selkie stories. They're always about how you went up to the attic to look for a book, and you found a disgusting old coat and brought it downstairs between finger and thumb and said, "What's this?", and you never saw your mom again.

I work at a restaurant called Le Pacha. I got the job after my mom left, to help with the bills. On my first night at work I got yelled at twice by the head server, burnt my fingers on a hot dish, spilled lentil-parsley soup all over my apron, and left my keys in the kitchen.

I didn't realize at first I'd forgotten my keys. I stood in the parking lot, breathing slowly and letting the oil-smell lift away from my hair, and when all the other cars had started up and driven away I put my hand in my jacket pocket. Then I knew.

I ran back to the restaurant and banged on the door. Of course no one came. I smelled cigarette smoke an instant before I heard the voice.

"Hey."

I turned, and Mona was standing there, smoke rising white from between her fingers. "I left my keys inside," I said.

Mona is the only other server at Le Pacha who's a girl. She's related to everybody at the restaurant except me. The owner, who goes by "Uncle Tad," is really her uncle, her mom's brother. "Don't talk to him unless you have to," Mona advised me. "He's a creeper." That was after she'd sighed and dropped her cigarette and crushed it out with her shoe and stepped into my clasped hands so I could boost her up to the window, after she'd wriggled through into the kitchen and opened the door for me. She said, "Madame," in a dry voice, and bowed. At least, I think she said "Madame." She might have said "My lady." I don't remember that night too well, because we drank a lot of wine. Mona said that as long as we were breaking and entering we might as well steal something, and she lined up all the bottles of red wine that had already been opened. I shone the light from my phone on her while she took out the special rubber corks and poured some of each bottle into a plastic pitcher. She called it "The House Wine." I was surprised she was being so nice to me, since she'd hardly spoken to me while we were working. Later she told me she hates everybody the first time she meets them. I called home, but Dad didn't pick up; he was probably in the basement. I left him a message and turned off my phone.

"Do you know what this guy said to me tonight?" Mona asked. "He wanted beef couscous and he said, 'I'll have the beef conscious.'"

Mona's mom doesn't work at Le Pacha, but sometimes she comes in around three o'clock and sits in Mona's section and cries. Then Mona jams on her orange baseball cap and goes out through the back and smokes a cigarette, and I take over her section. Mona's mom won't order anything from me. She's got Mona's eyes, or Mona's got hers: huge, angry eyes with lashes that curl up at the ends. She shakes her head and says: "Nothing! Nothing!" Finally Uncle Tad comes over, and Mona's mom hugs and kisses him, sobbing in Arabic.

After work Mona says, "Got the keys?"

We get in my car and I drive us through town to the Bone Zone, a giant cemetery on a hill. I pull into the empty parking lot and Mona rolls a joint. There's only one lamp, burning high and cold in the middle of the lot. Mona pushes her shoes off and puts her feet up on the dashboard and cries. She warned me about that the night we met: I said something stupid to her like "You're so funny" and she said, "Actually I cry a lot. That's something you should know." I was so happy she thought I should know things about her, I didn't care. I still don't care, but it's true that Mona cries a lot. She cries because she's scared her mom will take her away to Egypt, where the family used to live, and where Mona has never been. "What would I do there? I don't even speak Arabic." She wipes her mascara on her sleeve, and I tell her to look at the lamp outside and pretend that its glassy brightness is a bonfire, and that she and I are personally throwing every selkie story ever written onto it and watching them burn up.

"You and your selkie stories," she says. I tell her they're not my selkie stories, not ever, and I'll never tell one, which is true, I never will, and I don't tell her how I went up to the attic that day or that what I was looking for was a book I used to read when I was little, *Beauty and the Beast*, which is a really decent story about an animal who gets turned into a human and stays that way, the way it's supposed to be. I don't tell Mona that Beauty's black hair coiled to the edge of the page, or that the Beast had yellow horns and a smoking jacket, or that instead of finding the book I found the coat, and my mom put it on and went out the kitchen door and started up her car.

One selkie story tells about a man from Mýrdalur. He was on the cliffs one day and heard people singing and dancing inside a cave, and he noticed a bunch of skins piled on the rocks. He took one of the skins home and locked it in a chest, and when he went back a girl was sitting there alone, crying. She was naked, and he gave her some clothes and took her home. They got married and had kids. You know how this goes. One day the man changed his clothes and forgot to take the key to the chest out of his pocket, and when his wife washed the clothes, she found it.

"You're not going to Egypt," I tell Mona. "We're going to Colorado. Remember?"

That's our big dream, to go to Colorado. It's where Mona was born. She lived there until she was four. She still remembers the rocks and the pines and the cold, cold air. She says the clouds of Colorado are bright, like pieces of mirror. In Colorado, Mona's parents got divorced, and Mona's mom tried to kill herself for the first time. She tried it once here, too. She put her head in the oven, resting on a pillow. Mona was in seventh grade.

Selkies go back to the sea in a flash, like they've never been away. That's one of the ways they're different from human beings. Once, my dad tried to go back somewhere: he was in the army, stationed in Germany, and he went to Norway to look up the town my great-grandmother came from. He actually found the place, and even an old farm with the same name as us. In the town, he went into a restaurant and ordered lutefisk, a disgusting fish thing my grandmother makes. The cook came out of the kitchen and looked at him like he was nuts. She said they only eat lutefisk at Christmas.

There went Dad's plan of bringing back the original flavor of lutefisk. Now all he's got from Norway is my great-grandmother's Bible. There's also the diary she wrote on the farm up north, but we can't read it. There's only four English words in the whole book: *My God awful day.*

You might suspect my dad picked my mom up in Norway, where they have seals. He didn't, though. He met her at the pool.

As for Mom, she never talked about her relatives. I asked her once if she had any, and she said they were "no kind of people." At the time I thought she meant they were druggies or murderers, maybe in prison somewhere. Now I wish that were true.

One of the stories I don't tell Mona comes from *A Dictionary of British Folklore in the English Language*. In that story, it's the selkie's little girl who points out where the skin is hidden. She doesn't know what's going to happen, of course, she just knows her mother is looking for a skin, and she remembers her dad taking one out from under the bed and stroking it. The little girl's mother drags out the skin and says: "Fareweel, peerie buddo!" She doesn't think about how the little girl is going to miss her, or how if she's been breathing air all this time she can surely keep it up a little longer. She just throws on the skin and jumps into the sea.

After Mom left, I waited for my dad to get home from work. He didn't say anything when I told him about the coat. He stood in the light of the clock on the stove and rubbed his fingers together softly, almost like he was snapping but with no sound. Then he sat down at the kitchen table and lit a cigarette. I'd never seen him smoke in the house before. *Mom's gonna lose it*, I thought, and then I realized that no, my mom wasn't going to lose anything. We were the losers. Me and Dad.

He still waits up for me, so just before midnight I pull out of the parking lot. I'm hoping to get home early enough that he doesn't grumble, but late enough that he doesn't want to come up from the basement, where he takes apart old T.V.s, and talk to me about college. I've told him I'm not going to college. I'm going to Colorado, a landlocked state. Only twenty out of fifty states are completely landlocked, which means they don't touch the Great Lakes or the sea. Mona turns on the light and tries to put on eyeliner in the mirror, and I swerve to make her mess up. She turns out the light and hits me. All the windows are down to air out the car, and Mona's hair blows wild around her face. *Peerie buddo*, the book says, is "a term of endearment." "Peerie buddo," I say to Mona. She's got the hiccups. She can't stop laughing.

I've never kissed Mona. I've thought about it a lot, but I keep deciding it's not time. It's not that I think she'd freak out or anything. It's not even that I'm afraid she wouldn't kiss me back. It's worse: I'm afraid she'd kiss me back, but not mean it.

Probably one of the biggest losers to fall in love with a selkie was the man who carried her skin around in his knapsack. He was so scared she'd find it that he took the skin with him everywhere, when he went fishing, when he went drinking in the town. Then one day he had a wonderful catch of fish. There were so many that he couldn't drag them all home in his net. He emptied his knapsack and filled it with fish, and he put the skin over his shoulder, and on his way up the road to his house, he dropped it.

"Gray in front and gray in back, 'tis the very thing I lack." That's what the man's wife said, when she found the skin. The man ran to catch her, he even kissed her even though she was already a seal, but she squirmed off down the road and flopped into the water. The man stood knee-deep in the chilly waves, stinking of fish, and cried. In selkie stories, kissing never solves anything. No transformation happens because of a kiss. No one loves you just because you love them. What kind of fairy tale is that?

"She wouldn't wake up," Mona says. "I pulled her out of the oven onto the floor, and I turned off the gas and opened the windows. It's not that I was smart, I wasn't thinking at all. I called Uncle Tad and the police and I still wasn't thinking."

I don't believe she wasn't smart. She even tried to give her mom CPR, but her mom didn't wake up until later, in the hospital. They had to reach in and drag her out of death, she was so closed up in it. Death is skin-tight, Mona says. Gray in front and gray in back.

Dear Mona: When I look at you, my skin hurts.

I pull into her driveway to drop her off. The house is dark, the darkest house on her street, because Mona's mom doesn't like the porch light on. She says it shines in around the blinds and keeps her awake. Mona's mom has a beautiful bedroom upstairs, with lots of old photographs in gilt frames, but she sleeps on the living-room couch beside the aquarium. Looking at the fish helps her to sleep, although she also says this country has no real fish. That's what Mona calls one of her mom's "refrains."

Mona gets out, yanking the little piece of my heart that stays with her wherever she goes. She stands outside the car and leans in through the open door. I can hardly see her, but I can smell the lemon-scented stuff she puts on her hair, mixed up with the smells of sweat and weed. Mona smells like a forest, not the sea. "Oh my God," she says, "I forgot to tell you, tonight, you know table six? That big horde of Uncle Tad's friends?"

"Yeah."

"So they wanted the soup with the food, and I forgot, and you know what the old guy says to me? The little guy at the head of the table?"

"What?"

"He goes, *Vous êtes bête, mademoiselle!*"

She says it in a rough, growly voice, and laughs. I can tell it's French, but that's all. "What does it mean?"

"*You're an idiot, miss!*"

She ducks her head, stifling giggles.

"He called you an idiot?"

"Yeah, *bête*, it's like *beast*."

She lifts her head, then shakes it. A light from someone else's porch bounces off her nose. She puts on a fake Norwegian accent and says: "*My God awful day.*"

I nod. "Awful day." And because we say it all the time, because it's the kind of silly, ordinary thing you could call one of our "refrains," or maybe because of the weed I've smoked, a whole bunch of days seem pressed together inside this moment, more than you could count. There's the time we all went out for New Year's Eve, and Uncle Tad drove me, and when he stopped and I opened the door he told me to close it, and I said, "I will when I'm on the other side," and when I told Mona we laughed so hard we had to run away and hide in the bathroom. There's the day some people we know from school came in and we served them wine even though they were under age and Mona got nervous and spilled it all over the tablecloth, and the day her nice cousin came to visit and made us cheese-and-mint sandwiches in the microwave and got yelled at for wasting food. And the day of the party for Mona's mom's birthday, when Uncle Tad played music and made us all dance, and Mona's mom's eyes went jewelly with tears, and afterward Mona told me: "I should just run away. I'm the only thing keeping her here." My God, awful days. All the best days of my life.

"Bye," Mona whispers. I watch her until she disappears into the house.

My mom used to swim every morning at the YWCA. When I was little she took me along. I didn't like swimming. I'd sit in a chair with a book while she went up and down, up and down, a dim streak in the water. When I read *Mrs. Frisby and the Rats of NIMH*, it seemed like Mom was a lab rat doing tasks, the way she kept touching one side of the pool and then the other. At last she climbed out and pulled off her bathing cap. In the locker room she hung up her suit, a thin gray

8

rag dripping on the floor. Most people put the hook of their pad-lock through the straps of their suit, so the suits could hang outside the lockers without getting stolen, but my mom never did that. She just tied her suit loosely onto the lock. "No one's going to steal that stretchy old thing," she said. And no one did.

That should have been the end of the story, but it wasn't. My dad says Mom was an elemental, a sort of stranger, not of our kind. It wasn't my fault she left, it was because she couldn't learn to breathe on land. That's the worst story I've ever heard. I'll never tell Mona, not ever, not even when we're leaving for Colorado with everything we need in the back of my car, and I meet her at the grocery store the way we've already planned, and she runs out smiling under her orange baseball cap. I won't tell her how dangerous attics are, or how some people can't start over, or how I still see my mom in shop windows with her long hair the same silver-gray as her coat, or how once when my little cous-ins came to visit we went to the zoo and the seals recognized me, they both stood up in the water and talked in a foreign language. I won't tell her. I'm too scared. I won't even tell her what she needs to know: that we've got to be tougher than our moms, that we've got to have different stories, that she'd better not change her mind and drop me in Colorado because I won't understand, I'll hate her forever and burn her stuff and stay up all night screaming at the woods, because it's stupid not to be able to breathe, who ever heard of somebody breath-ing in one place but not another, and we're not like that, Mona and me, and selkie stories are only for losers stuck on the wrong side of magic—people who drop things, who tell all, who leave keys around, who let go.

Ogres of East Africa

Catalogued by Alibhai M. Moosajee of Mombasa
February 1907

I. Apul Apul

A male ogre of the Great Lakes region. A melancholy character, he
eats crickets to sweeten his voice. His house burned down with all of
his children inside. His enemy is the Hare.

[My informant, a woman of the highlands who calls herself only
"Mary," adds that Apul Apul can be heard on windy nights, crying
for his lost progeny. She claims that he has been sighted far from his
native country, even on the coast, and that an Arab trader once shot
and wounded him from the battlements of Fort Jesus. It happened
in a famine year, the "Year of Fever." A great deal of research would
be required in order to match this year, when, according to Mary, the
cattle perished in droves, to one of the Years of Our Lord by which
my employer reckons the passage of time; I append this note, therefore, in fine print, and in the margins.

"Always read the fine print, Alibhai!" my employer reminds me
when I draw up his contracts. He is unable to read it himself; his eyes
are not good. "The African sun has spoilt them, Alibhai!"

Apul Apul, Mary says, bears a festering sore where the bullet
pierced him. He is allergic to lead.]

2. Ba'ati

A grave-dweller from the environs of the ancient capital of Kush. The ba'ati possesses a skeletal figure and a morbid sense of humor. Its great pleasure is to impersonate human beings: if your dearest friend wears a cloak and claims to suffer from a cold, he may be a ba'ati in disguise.

[Mary arrives every day precisely at the second hour after dawn. I am curious about this reserved and encyclopedic woman. It amuses me to write these reflections concerning her in the margins of the catalogue I am composing for my employer. He will think this writing fly-tracks, or smudges from my dirty hands (he persists in his opinion that I am always dirty). As I write I see Mary before me as she presents herself each morning, in her calico dress, seated on an overturned crate.

I believe she is not very old, though she must be several years older than I (but I am very young—"Too young to walk like an old man, Alibhai! Show some spirit! Ha!"). As she talks, she works at a bit of scarlet thread, plaiting something, perhaps a necklace. The tips of her fingers seem permanently stained with color.

"Where did you learn so much about ogres, Mary?"

"Anyone may learn. You need only listen."

"What is your full name?"

She stops plaiting and looks up. Her eyes drop their veil of calm and flash at me—in annoyance, in warning? "I told you," she says. "Mary. Only Mary."]

3. Dhegdheer

A female ogre of Somaliland. Her name means "Long Ear." She is described as a large, heavy woman, a very fast runner. One of her ears is said to be much longer than the other, in fact so long that it trails upon the ground. With this ear, she can hear her enemies approaching from a great distance. She lives in a ruined hovel with her daughter. The daughter is beautiful and would like to be married. Eventually, she will murder Dhegdheer by filling her ear with boiling water.

[My employer is so pleased with the information we have received from Mary that he has decided to camp here for another week. "Milk her, Alibhai!" he says, leering. "Eh? Squeeze her! Get as much out of her as you can. Ha! Ha!" My employer always shouts, as the report of his gun has made him rather deaf. In the evenings, he invites me into his tent, where, closed in by walls, a roof and a floor of Willesden canvas, I am afforded a brief respite from the mosquitoes.

A lamp hangs from the central pole, and beneath it my employer sits with his legs stretched out and his red hands crossed on his stomach. "Very good, Alibhai!" he says. "Excellent!" Having shot every type of animal in the Protectorate, he is now determined to try his hand at ogre. I will be required to record his kills, as I keep track of all his accounts. It would be "damn fine," he opines, to acquire the ear of Dhegdheer.

Mary tells me that one day Dhegdheer's daughter, wracked with remorse, will walk into the sea and give herself up to the sharks.]

4. Iimū

Iimū transports his victims across a vast body of water in a ferry-boat. His country, which lies on the other side, is inaccessible to all creatures save ogres and weaverbirds. If you are trapped there, your only recourse is to beg the weaverbirds for sticks. You will need seven sticks in order to get away. The first two sticks will allow you to turn yourself into a stone, thereby escaping notice. The remaining five sticks enable the following transformations: thorns, a pit, darkness, sand, a river.

["Stand up straight, Alibhai! Look lively, man!"

My employer is of the opinion that I do not show a young man's proper spirit. This, he tells me, is a racial defect, and therefore not my fault, but I may improve myself by following his example. My employer thrusts out his chest. "Look, Alibhai!" He says that if I walk about stooped over like a dotard, people will get the impression that I am shiftless and craven, and this will quite naturally make them want to kick me. He himself has kicked me on occasion.

It is true that my back is often stiff, and I find it difficult to extend my limbs to their full length. Perhaps, as my employer suspects, I am growing old before my time.

These nights of full moon are so bright, I can see my shadow on the grass. It writhes like a snake when I make an effort to straighten my back.]

5. Katandabaliko

While most ogres are large, Katandabaliko is small, the size of a child. He arrives with a sound of galloping just as the food is ready. "There is sunshine for you!" he cries. This causes everyone to faint, and Katandabaliko devours the food at his leisure. Katandabaliko cannot himself be cooked: cut up and boiled, he knits himself back together and bounces out of the pot. Those who attempt to cook and eat him may eat their own wives by mistake. When not tormenting human beings, he prefers to dwell among cliffs.

[I myself prefer to dwell in Mombasa, at the back of my uncle's shop, Moosajee and Co. I cannot pretend to enjoy nights spent in the open, under what my employer calls the splendor of the African sky. Mosquitoes whine, and something, probably a dangerous animal, rustles in the grass. The Somali cook and headman sit up late, exchanging stories, while the Kavirondo porters sleep in a corral constructed of baggage. I am uncomfortable, but at least I am not lonely. My employer is pleased to think that I suffer terribly from loneliness. "It's no picnic for you, eh, Alibhai?" He thinks me too prejudiced to tolerate the society of the porters, and too frightened to go near the Somalis, who, to his mind, being devout Sunnis, must be plotting the removal of my Shi'a head.

13

In fact, we all pray together. We are tired and far from home. We are here for money, and when we talk, we talk about money. We can discuss calculations for hours: what we expect to buy, where we expect to invest. Our languages are different, but all of us count in Swahili.]

6. Kibugi

A male ogre who haunts the foothills of Mount Kenya. He carries machetes, knives, hoes, and other objects made of metal. If you can manage to make a cut in his little finger, all the people he has devoured will come streaming out.

[Mary has had, I suspect, a mission education. This would explain the name and the calico dress. Such an education is nothing to be ashamed of—why, then, did she stand up in such a rage when I inquired about it? Mary's rage is cold; she kept her voice low. "I have told you not to ask me these types of questions! I have only come to tell you about ogres! Give me the money!" She held out her hand, and I doled out her daily fee in rupees, although she had not stayed for the agreed amount of time.

She seized the money and secreted it in her dress. Her contempt burned me; my hands trembled as I wrote her fee in my record book. "No questions!" she repeated, seething with anger. "If I went to a mission school, I'd burn it down! I have always been a free woman!"

I was silent, although I might have reminded her that we are both my employer's servants: like me, she has come here for money. I watched her stride off down the path to the village. At a certain distance, she began to waver gently in the sun.

My face still burns from the sting of her regard.

Before she left, I felt compelled to inform her that, although my father was born at Karachi, I was born at Mombasa. I, too, am an African.

Mary's mouth twisted. "So is Kibugi," she said.]

7. Kiptebanguryon

A fearsome yet curiously domestic ogre of the Rift Valley. He collects
human skulls, which he once used to decorate his spacious dwelling.
He made the skulls so clean, it is said, and arranged them so prettily,
that from a distance his house resembled a palace of salt. His human
wife bore him two sons: one which looked human like its mother, and
one, called Kiptegen, which resembled its father. When the wife was
rescued by her human kin, her human-looking child was also saved,
but Kiptegen was burnt alive.

[I am pleased to say that Mary returned this morning, perfectly calm
and apparently resolved to forget our quarrel.

She tells me that Kiptegen's brother will never be able to forget
the screams of his sibling perishing in the flames. The mother, too,
is scarred by the loss. She had to be held back, or she would have
dashed into the fire to rescue her ogre-child. This information does
not seem appropriate for my employer's catalogue; still, I find myself
adding it in the margins. There is a strange pleasure in this writing and not-writing, these letters that hang between revelation and
oblivion.

If my employer discovered these notes, he would call them impu-
dence, cunning, a trick.

What would I say in my defense? "Sir, I was unable to tell you.
Sir, I was unable to speak of the weeping mother of Kiptegen." He
would laugh: he believes that all words are found in his language.

I ask myself if there are words contained in Mary's margins: stories of ogres she cannot tell to me.

Kiptebanguryon, she says, is homeless now. A modern creature,
he roams the Protectorate clinging to the undersides of trains.]

8. Kisirimu

Kisirimu dwells on the shores of Lake Albert. Bathed, dressed in
barkcloth, carrying his bow and arrows, he glitters like a bridegroom.

His purpose is to trick gullible young women. He will be betrayed by song. He will die in a pit, pierced by spears.

[In the evenings, under the light of the lamp, I read the day's inventory from my record book, informing my employer of precisely what has been spent and eaten. As a representative of Moosajee and Co., Superior Traders, Stevedores and Dubashes, I am responsible for ensuring that nothing has been stolen. My employer stretches, closes his eyes, and smiles as I inform him of the amount of sugar, coffee, and tea in his possession. Tinned bacon, tinned milk, oat porridge, salt, ghee. The dates, he reminds me, are strictly for the Somalis, who grow sullen in the absence of this treat.

My employer is full of opinions. Somalis, he tells me, are an excitable nation. "Don't offend them, Alibhai! Ha, ha!" The Kavirondo, by contrast, are merry and tractable, excellent for manual work. My own people are cowardly, but clever at figures.

There is nothing, he tells me, more odious than a German. However, their women are seductive, and they make the world's most beautiful music. My employer sings me a German song. He sounds like a buffalo in distress. Afterward, he makes me read to him from the Bible.

He believes I will find this painful: "Heresy, Alibhai! Ha, ha! You'll have to scrub your mouth out, eh? Extra ablutions?"

Fortunately, God does not share his prejudices.

I read: *There were giants in the earth in those days.*

I read: *For only Og king of Bashan remained of the remnant of giants; behold, his bedstead was a bedstead of iron.*]

9. Konyek

Konyek is a hunter. His bulging eyes can perceive movement far across the plains. Human beings are his prey. He runs with great loping strides, kills, sleeps underneath the boughs of a leafy tree. His favorite question is: "Mother, whose footprints are these?"

❧

[Mary tells me that Konyek passed through her village in the Year of Amber. The whirlwind of his running loosened the roofs. A wise woman had predicted his arrival, and the young men, including Mary's brother, had set up a net between trees to catch him. But Konyek only laughed and tore down the net and disappeared with a sound of thunder. He is now, Mary believes, in the region of Eldoret. She tells me that her brother and the other young men who devised the trap have not been seen since the disappearance of Konyek.

Mary's gaze is peculiar. It draws me in. I find it strange that, just a few days ago, I described her as a cold person. When she tells me of her brother she winds her scarlet thread so tightly about her finger I am afraid she will cut it off.]

10. Mbiti
Mbiti hides in the berry bushes. When you reach in, she says: "Oh, don't pluck my eye out!" She asks you: "Shall I eat you, or shall I make you my child?" You agree to become Mbiti's child. She pricks you with a needle. She is betrayed by the cowrie shell at the end of her tail.

["My brother," Mary says.

She describes the forest. She says we will go there to hunt ogres. Her face is filled with a subdued yet urgent glow. I find myself leaning closer to her. The sounds of the others, their voices, the smack of an axe into wood, recede until they are thin as the buzzing of flies. The world is composed of Mary and myself and the sky about Mary and the trees about Mary. She asks me if I understand what she is saying. She tells me about her brother in the forest. I realize that the glow she exudes comes not from some supernatural power, but from fear.

She speaks to me carefully, as if to a child.

She gives me a bundle of scarlet threads.

She says: "When the child goes into the forest, it wears a red necklace. And when the ogre sees the necklace, it spares the child." She says: "I think you and my brother are exactly the same age."

My voice is reduced to a whisper. "What of Mbiti?"

Mary gives me a deep glance, fiercely bright.

She says: "Mbiti is lucky. She has not been caught. Until she is caught, she will be one of the guardians of the forest. Mbiti is always an ogre and always the sister of ogres."]

11. Ntemelua

Ntemelua, a newborn baby, already has teeth. He sings: "Draw near, little pot, draw near, little spoon!" He replaces the meat in the pot with balls of dried dung. Filthy and clever, he crawls into a cow's anus to hide in its stomach. Ntemelua is weak and he lives by fear, which is a supernatural power. He rides a hyena. His back will never be quite straight, but this signifies little to him, for he can still stretch his limbs with pleasure. The only way to escape him is to abandon his country.

[Tomorrow we depart.

I am to give the red necklaces only to those I trust. "You know them," Mary explained, "as I know you."

"Do you know me?" I asked, moved and surprised.

She smiled. "It is easy to know someone in a week. You need only listen."

Two paths lie before me now. One leads to the forest; the other leads home.

How easily I might return to Mombasa! I could steal some food and rupees and begin walking. I have a letter of contract affirming that I am employed and not a vagrant. How simple to claim that my employer has dispatched me back to the coast to order supplies, or to Abyssinia to purchase donkeys! But these scarlet threads burn in my pocket. I want to draw nearer to the source of their heat. I want to meet the ogres.

"You were right," Mary told me before she left. "I did go to a mission school. And I didn't burn it down." She smiled, a smile of mingled defiance and shame. One of her eyes shone brighter than the other, kindled by a tear. I wanted to cast myself at her feet and beg her forgiveness. Yes, to beg her forgiveness for having pried into her past, for having stirred up the memory of her humiliation.

Instead I said clumsily: "Even Ntemelua spent some time in a cow's anus."

Mary laughed. "Thank you, brother," she said.

She walked away down the path, sedate and upright, and I do not know if I will ever see her again. I imagine meeting a young man in the forest, a man with a necklace of scarlet thread who stands with Mary's light bearing and regards me with Mary's direct and trenchant glance. I look forward to this meeting as if to the sight of a long-lost friend. I imagine clasping the hand of this young man, who is like Mary and like myself. Beneath our joined hands, my employer lies slain. The ogres tear open the tins and enjoy a prodigious feast among the darkling trees.]

12. Rakakabe

Rakakabe, how beautiful he is, Rakakabe! A Malagasy demon, he has been sighted as far north as Kismaayo. He skims the waves, he eats mosquitoes, his face gleams, his hair gleams, his favorite question is: "Are you sleeping?"

Rakakabe of the gleaming tail! No, we are wide awake.

[This morning we depart on our expedition. My employer sings— "Green grow the rushes, o!"—but we, his servants, are even more cheerful. We are prepared to meet the ogres.

We catch one another's eyes and smile. All of us sport necklaces of red thread: signs that we belong to the party of the ogres, that we are prepared to hide and fight and die with those who live in the forest, those who are dirty and crooked and resolute. "Tell my brother his house is waiting for him," Mary whispered to me at the end—such an honor, to be the one to deliver her message! While she continues walking, meeting others, passing into other hands the blood-red necklaces by which the ogres are known.

There will be no end to this catalogue. The ogres are everywhere. Number thirteen: Alibhai M. Moosajee of Mombasa.

The porters lift their loads with unaccustomed verve. They set off, singing. "See, Alibhai!" my employer exclaims in delight. "They're made for it! Natural workers!"

"O, yes sir! Indeed, sir!"

The sky is tranquil, the dust saturated with light. Everything conspires to make me glad.

Soon, I believe, I shall enter into the mansion of the ogres, and stretch my limbs on the doorstep of Rakakabe.]

Walkdog

This paper is in response to the assignment "Know Your Environment."
In this paper I will discuss an animal called Walkdog which is native
to my local environment which is South Orange, New Jersey. First I
will describe the animal ("Brief Description"), then I will write about
it's origin and habits ("Research"), then I will conclude with why I
chose to write about this animal and why its important ("Conclusion"). Thesis statement: *Even though not much has been written about it,
Walkdog is an important part of North American wildlife* .

I. Brief Description

What is Walkdog? Well Mrs. Patterson you probably know better
than me. However, I am writing this paper and not you, because I
need the grade as you know very well, so here is what I know.

Walkdog contrary to it's name is not a dog. It is more like a
beaver or large rat. It lives mostly in sewers but also creeks and rivers.
It is nocturnel and believed to eat fish and also, excuse me, excrament.[1]

---

1   The reason Walkdog is supposed to eat excrament is simply common sense,
because what kind of fish is it eating in the sewer? Also we can assume that
Walkdog has a seriously powerful gut and high-level immune system because eating random fish out of Jersey creeks will kill you. If Walkdog can eat bugged-out

Walkdog when walking is said to be about 5 feet long, including the tail, but when it stands up it looks taller than a man. Its fur is black and oily. Its a great swimmer and can stay underwater for 3 days without coming up for air.

Other names for Walkdog: Grimdog, Grimwolf, The Dog that Walks Men, The Dog that Walks Hisself, Jumpy Leg, Conjure Dog, Canewolf.

Some people also call it Growldog, but this is stupid because Walkdog doesn't growl. It has no voicebox.[2]

2. Research

One thing you will notice when you start researching Walkdog is that not much has been written about it at all. It gets mentioned in a sentence here and there but you won't find a book about it or even a Wikipedia page which is weird, don't you think? Its like its hiding from everything with some kind of magic. Probably the person who knows most about Walkdog is your nephew, Andrew Bookman, the most hopeless dork in this school you'll excuse me for saying, because you know its a fact and facts as you say are the Building Blocks of Research.[3]

From Andy I learned that the origins of Walkdog are, as he put

---

radioactive fish it would probably consider excrament a healthy snack.

2   Marjorie Wilson, "Sounds of the Jersey Night," in *Voices of Nature*, ed. Steven Wilkins, Rutgers University Press, 1980, p. 115. "Then there is the Walkdog, a creature without a voicebox, known only by its footstep and its splash."

3   Facts about Andrew: fat (nickname: "Bubble-Butt"), glasses, always reading (and his last name is Bookman!), started calling himself "Andy" when he started highschool, which anybody should of known that was a stupid thing to do, he should of just stuck with Andrew, even Drew would be cooler, but no, he had to be Andy. Also, his aunt is a teacher (you) which does not help anybody I am sorry to tell you. The cloud of nerd gas surrounding Andy is so strong it could make your eyes water. People only go near him to mess with him. As a teacher you probably know this unless you are unbelieveably clueless.

it, "obscure." There are three main theories on the origins of Walkdog:

a) indigenous animal related to otter
b) came over from Europe or Asia with immigrants
c) came over from Africa on slave ship[4]

In other words, the origins of Walkdog are the origins of just about everybody. This is why I describe it as a native animal. I mean I consider myself a New Jersey native, what else would I be, even though I'm African and German and Spanish and God knows what else.[5]

Now for the habits of Walkdog. These habits are not what you would call nice. Walkdog steals kids (another name for it is The Child Thief). It does not steal them to eat, as stated above, it eats fish and

---

4 Source: private conversation with Andrew Bookman. Andy's personal favorite of these theories was #3. Mostly because of the name "Canewolf" which must mean sugarcane which is something we don't have a lot of here in Jersey. Andy's grandmother, who I guess was possibly a relative of yours, died and left him what he says is a mat made of Walkdog hair. His grandma called it her "conjure mat." This mat supposedly came from the Caribbean somewhere which Andy also says supports his theory. He kind of lost me at that point—he talks really fast when he gets going, and his face, which is already oily, starts getting oilier than ever, I mean really impossibly shiny, which is distracting—but it was something about slave routes and stopping points and getting from Angola or somewhere to Charleston. I don't know. Poor Andy. He had on a white button-down shirt. Big sweat stains under the arms. It was like he didn't *want* to be normal.

5 This note is not exactly related to the above, I just want to clarify the previous note in which I named my source as a private conversation with Andrew Bookman, but I also said earlier that people only go near him to mess with him. I want to be clear that I myself never messed with your nephew in any way, also I did not go near him at school because to be frank I did not want to get contaminated by his nerd gas. I went to Union Market on the weekend because as you must know that is where Andy goes every Saturday to run a coin swap booth with his parents.

Andy's parents are also terrible nerds, his dad in combat boots, his mom in a red wig, both of them obsessed with antique coins. Their super nice which just makes it worse. I guess you know that though. You certainly didn't stop by their booth while I was there.

excrament mainly, but it steals them at night and then *it takes them for walks.*

It takes them for walks. It just takes them around with it. I want you to think about what that's like. Imagine your a normal kid asleep in your normal bed. Don't imagine yourself as Andy Bookman, because that kid is not normal *at all*, but imagine you're somebody regular like me. Me, Yolanda Price. I would say I'm pretty normal. I'm not popular, in fact I generally have to keep my head down, just smile at the right times and keep my mouth shut, because I am almost on the edge of nerd, I only manage to do all right because I can sing. If you have a cool talent like that and are not stupid you'll be okay. I'm not saying that singing could of saved Andrew Bookman. Your nephew I am sorry to say was a grade-A world class nerd and singing probably would of just made things worse for him. Do you know he told everybody that after graduation he was going to go eat strawberries in Denmark? Who *says* that? Strawberries and new potatoes and the grave of Hans Christian Andersen. People called him The Little Mermaid for weeks. Bubble-Butt, your too ugly to get into another country. Did you notice? Were you afraid that defending him would make things worse? If so you were probably right. It was best to just ignore it. There are places that once you step in, you can't get out.

So, you're me, Yolanda, lying in bed. There's a tap at the window. Tap tap tap. Annoying. You think its a tree branch on the glass. You get up and open the window, even if its winter you would open it to break off the branch and get rid of that awful tapping. So you open the window, lets say its winter like now, February, the worst time of year, with no holidays in sight except Valentines Day a.k.a. National Torture Day, and not being able to sleep is just the last straw, so you open the window and theres a small black shape looking at you from the yard. You stand there, because what is it? Too big for a cat or even a racoon. And then it rears up. It hauls itself up and its tall, its snuffling at the window, and its eyes are small red lights and it says in this voice that comes from no voicebox, this voice in your head, it says Come on girl lets get walking.

Where are we going?

Down to the creek.

I don't want to.

It laughs: Eee, eee, eee.[6]

I don't want to. But your already putting your knee on the sill. Walkdog reaches its paws up and catches you as you fall out. It smells like drains. It puts you down on the ground and crouches on all fours. Bam, just like that, its small again. It sets off walking over the snow, and you follow. Your sliding down the slope at the end of the yard. Now you're on Varsity Ave. It's all dark out. I don't know if you're crying. Would you cry? Some of the stars are gold, the same color as the streetlights.

Now you are going to walk for a long time.

You might walk as far as the Wolf-Boy, Carlton O'Neill. Just trying to get back home again. I know for a fact you could walk to Indiana easy, like in the song "Indiana Morning" by Blueswoman Maisie Oates. [7]

---

6   This is the sound of the Walkdog laugh as you hear it in your head. Carlton O'Neill who was abducted by Walkdog when he was nine years old and let go again for some reason when he was thirty-six described the sound for the *Star Ledger*. "It sounded like a kid locked up and crying or a train whistle far away." "'Wolf-Boy' Found in Livingston Reservation," *The Star Ledger*, August 14 2005, p. I. Carlton O'Neill was skinny and a mess when he was found. He said he'd been to Canada and the farthest tip of Argentina. All on foot. They gave him a pen to write down who he was and when he remembered how to write his name he fainted.

Andy who was a Walkdog fanatic had this newspaper article tacked to his bulletin board. He also had Carlton O'Neill's signature on an index card. He had actually tracked the guy down and gotten his autograph. Carlton lived with his mother in East Orange at that point. I don't know where he is now.

7   *Indiana morning, I'm as low as I can be.*
            Indiana morning, I'm as low as I can be.
            Went to walk my hound dog, but now he's walking me.

This song is from the album *Indiana Morning* by Blueswoman Maisie Oates. I heard it at Andy's house which is also where I read the article about Carlton O'Neill, and also I may as well say since its part of my Research that I saw and

Walking and walking. You'd see a lot. Maybe you'd like it since you are such a fan of Research. You could do all the Research you wanted, walking up and down the country. I think you'd be cold though. You'd sleep in ditches and drains. Curled up against Walkdog for warmth. Walkdog's voice in you murmuring, Time to get up.

3. Conclusion

In this conclusion I will write about why I chose Walkdog for this assignment and why its important.

I chose Walkdog because I heard about it from Andy. What happened is two boys who you definitely know so I won't repeat their names slammed into Andy in the hall and sent his papers flying. This happened on a daily basis. *Every day.* You have to ask yourself why Andy was always carrying stuff in his arms when he also wore a backpack. Why not keep everything in the backpack and then when people banged into him he would fall but his stuff would not be all over the hallway. Theres a sign above your desk that says "Nobody is Unteachable,", but Mrs. Patterson I beg to disagree. In this matter Andy was 100% Unteachable. So there his papers went as usual and these two boys enjoyed kicking them and leaving footprints on them. One of the papers slid over to me and almost touched my foot. I didn't pick it up, because unlike Andy I am Teachable, but I glanced down at it. There was a drawing of something black and blobby with red eyes and underneath it it said Walkdog.

---

touched the "conjure mat" Andy inherited from his grandma. I am wondering if you know anything about this mat? Have you ever seen it? Its gray and hairy and about as big around as those things you put on the table under hot dishes. I said I thought it would be black and Andy said he doesn't know why its gray, he thinks maybe since its cut off the Walkdog its lacking essential oils. That was in his room which is like Nerd Heaven, full of action figures and model planes. You can't touch anything or Andy starts freaking out. Obviously I would not be caught dead going in the front door at Andy's house. I went in the back. He opened a window.

You could say that that was when I got the idea for this assignment even though you had not given it to us yet. I got curious about Walkdog. It seemed like such a weird thing to draw, even for Andy. I asked my parents about it at dinner and they'd never heard of it. Sounds like an urban legend, my mom said later, when I told her about my Research. Mm-hm, said Dad. Mom did remember when Carlton O'Neill got found in the reservation. That poor man, she said, God bless him. She said that's probably where Walkdog got started, and poor wandering Carlton is the only Walkdog there ever was. I asked how she would explain the song "Indiana Morning" which was recorded back in 1955. Oh that's just a metaphor she said, and I said, a metaphor for what? She looked uncertain. Alcoholism?[8]

When you gave us this assignment I went to the Union Market and found Andy at his parent's booth and asked him about his picture that said Walkdog, and whether it was something that would be good for a paper on "Know Your Environment," and he said it would be awesome. Andy was always saying things were awesome, and he meant it. He beamed at me from under the leaves of a plant being sold in the stall next to his. He didn't even think that I might of come out there to mess with him or make fun of him even though that was the most likely scenario. Mrs. Patterson, Andy was special. I know you know that. I know you saw him getting picked on every day. When he

---

8   This is Mom's explanation for most bad things. It is based on personal experience because my grandfather (her dad) drank himself to death. In my opinion this is the reason she married a security guard (my dad) who works at the same bank where Mom is a teller. Security is her thing. This is my parent's week: Bank, Bank, Bank, Bank, Bank, Groceries, Church. After graduation I am going to Rutgers and my mom assumes I will major in Accounting. Accounting is a good secure choice. I want to major in Music. The only person I have told this to (besides you) is Andy Bookman. It was after we listened to "Indiana Morning." He said I should do Music if I want, maybe I should even go to an arts school instead of Rutgers. I never thought of that, I said. I felt like such an idiot. But Andy didn't laugh. He looked calm and thoughtful. Its hard to get started, he said. Its hard to get going by yourself. He was looking at my boots, which I'd left by the window. Snow melting off them on the floor.

raised his hand in class all it took was for somebody to shout *Bookman!* and the whole class would burst out in these awful little giggles. They didn't even have to use his nasty nickname. Imagine how it would feel if just your name made other people laugh. You never batted an eye, you just said Yes, Andy? like it was all normal and like I said before it was probably the right thing to do. And then Andy would say whatever he was going to say, always something smart, while people made fart noises and snickered or whatever. You know Mrs. Patterson, this school is actually hell. I don't know why everyone acted shocked when Andy got beat up the way he did. Special assembly and Principal Reed on the stage with his voice all wobbly. He said we must realize we are becoming men and women. He's right about that. But that doesn't mean we're changing. It just means we're bigger now, big enough to put somebody in the hospital.[9]

It's true. People act like highschool students are kids and need to be taken care of all the time but we are actually adults. If this was the Middle Ages we'd all be married or in wars and you, Mrs. Patterson, you'd be considered a very old lady. And the truth is, you are a very old lady. The day after Andy got beat you looked so frail. You had that old lady's look of being lost in the world. The truth is, Mrs. Patterson, that a lot of us kids are married and a lot of us are in wars. Andy was both.[10]

---

9 They cornered him down by the creek. Behind the fucking police station. I am sorry, I don't care that I'm swearing in my paper. Why did he have to walk that way? Why couldn't he have gone down South Orange Ave. like everyone else? Why didn't I invite him to my house? Do you think Andy Bookman has gotten invited anywhere since seventh grade? They cornered him down by the creek. They yanked off his backpack and threw it in the water. They broke his nose. They broke three of his ribs. They stepped on his wrist and broke that too. They kicked him all over, those same two boys that I won't repeat their names. Nice boys that everybody knows. All they got was suspended because they're sorry. Right behind the police station. Where were the police? Where was fucking Walkdog when Andy needed him? I went to the hospital after and Andy's father was crying in the hall.

10 His bed was so saggy. He'd probably slept there since he was six years old. It seemed too small. He had the best smile, a perfect dimple on either side. Long

Now when I think about why I chose Walkdog, I think I really chose Andy. I think I chose him even before I knew it. That black, bulky shape on the paper was just an excuse. I wish I could end my paper there and say that getting to know Andy was getting to know my environment. You might give me an A for a paper like that, or you might give me an F, but I wouldn't care because I would be going over to Andy's after school, or I would have invited him over to my house, and on National Torture Day we would have watched dumb horror movies in my basement and laughed. My head on his shoulder oh God Mrs. Patterson where do you think he is ? Is he still alive? Is he with Walkdog? Is that it? Is he walking around? Is he going to appear in thirty-some years in the forest like Carlton O'Neill and are people going to start calling him another Wolf-Boy? I went to look for Carlton, you know, after Andy disappeared, but I couldn't find him, he's not at his mother's house anymore. I found his mother and she blew a ton of cigarette smoke in my face and said He gone for a walk and shut the door on me. Is that where Andy is? Just gone for a walk? If I'd known I never would have gone back to his house for the conjure mat like he asked me. Yes, I went back for it. He told me where to find the spare key and I went into his house and got the mat from his room. His stupid action figures staring at me in their creepy way. The mat was on top of the filing cabinet. It felt prickly and weird in my hand. I put it in a plastic bag that used to have my lunch in it and stuck it in my purse and went back to the hospital. Maybe I should of known something was wrong, but I just wanted to make Andy happy for once, and I could tell the flowers I'd brought him weren't doing

---

eyelashes that brushed my cheek. I don't want to ruin anything, I said, and he said what? and I said I don't want to mess up your trip to Denmark. I was already hoping he'd cancel and stay with me because even if I had my own money my parents would never let me to go Europe with a boy, not even a boy like Andy who was so sweet, its not secure, even though there is no place more secure than Andy's arms. He laughed and kissed me. Your not ruining anything. I love you. Model plane wings turning, shadows on the wall. Snow outside and the windows all blue. He hugged me and I just sank. There are places that once you step in, you can't get out.

anything. He just sat in the bed and stared at nothing. White bandages over his nose, white light everywhere. He looked really drained there, drained and small. I didn't know how to touch him, he looked so hurt. I was crying but he didn't seem to notice. He just said in this muffled voice: Get me the conjure mat. Okay, I said, still crying. Andy's parents were outside. Are you a friend? his mom asked, and I said, I'm his girlfriend.

Some girlfriend, right?

I never went anywhere with him. Never went in his front door. Never, ever walked home with him from school.

I should have walked home with him. I should have. *I should have walked him home.*

So now you know why I couldn't finish my solo at the service they held in his honor. Praying for news of the missing Andrew Bookman. The choir kept going and I just stopped. I saw you out there in a pew, looking at me, so sad. I couldn't keep going. My voice was just gone, cut off, there was nothing but air, like I was all full of dust, like I didn't have a voicebox .

Mrs. Patterson this is my thesis statement: *Even though not much has been written about it, Walkdog is an important part of North American wildlife.* I hope you can see why Walkdog is important. I hope you can help me. The fact is I think your nephew conjured up Walkdog using the conjure mat. I think he felt so alone, so abandoned by everybody, including you and me, that he did something drastic, he summoned up Walkdog and Walkdog came. I want you to tell me if I'm right. Did you know that conjuring grandmother? What was she like? Did she leave you anything? Did she tell you the counterspell?

I want you to tell me that yes, you know a spell, or you have your own conjure mat. I want you to tell me how to find Andy. I need him. Mrs. Patterson this hound dog is walking me and he's walking me hard. Everywhere I go I hear his footstep and his splash.

If you can't give me a spell then I want you to tell me that Walkdog is not a devil or anything scary but that its a helper and a friend. I want you to tell me that Andy's not scared right now and not alone.

He's just walking. He's doing Research, which is another kind of Nerd Heaven. Maybe he's walked to Indiana by now. Maybe he'll get to Denmark. Maybe he'll swim with Walkdog who can stay underwater for three days. I see this boy in the waves, he's holding onto Walkdog's small black ears and heading out to where its strawberry season. I always see him in his hospital gown, the way he was the last time, the way I imagine he got up one night, his conjure mat in his hand, and walked through the hospital in the ghostly light and opened the doors and there was Walkdog waiting, black and low to the ground. Come on lets get walking. I want you to tell me that Andy's not going to come back all skinny and beat-up like Carlton O'Neill. I want you to tell me that he's not cold. Somebody's always with him. He's got protection. No one will ever hurt him again. [11]

---

[11] To complete my Research here is the rest of the song "Indiana Morning."

If you got a dollar, why don't you give me half.
If you got a dollar, come on and give me half.
The stories I could tell you, they'd make a preacher laugh.

When I had a good man, the sun shone every day.
When I had that good man, the sun shone every day.
Now I need this whiskey to take the pain away.

Budworm in the cotton, beetle in the corn.
Budworm in the cotton, beetle in the corn.
Feel like I been walking since the day that I was born.

Hear that hound dog. Day that I was born.

Olimpia's Ghost

My Dear S.,

Emil says you will not come to Freiberg this year; but Mother says you will. Who is right? We all know you hate Vienna with a passion; that is, Mother and Emil know it, and I know it through them, for Mother reads your letters aloud, and sometimes Emil, too, shares a few lines. Pray do not be angry! It is such a little thing, to hear of your successes, and it makes me very happy. And then, your sallies on your masters are so droll, and your remarks on Vienna—St. Stephen's steeple like a "great rolled-up umbrella"—Mother can hardly read for laughing.

I am sure you will not begrudge me this diversion, my dear S. On the days when there is no letter from you, life continues just as usual. The weather has been fine. There is fruit on the peach trees. In the long twilight, while Emil reads, I go up and down, up and down the stairs.

A few days ago I did have a new amusement: a marionette theater sprang up overnight in the square, like a white mushroom. I watched the marionettes for several hours, even though a light rain was falling, and the children screamed mercilessly. I suppose you would not have liked the noise, or the look of the dirty little boy who came around afterward, hat extended to gather our coins. As I left I saw him sharing a cigar behind the theater with the puppet-master, a rough, disreputable-looking fellow, undoubtedly his father. Oh, but the marionettes were so beautiful! The little Pierrot had a spangled coat, and two great tears shone under his eyes. He wore his heart on the outside, like any fool. As for Columbine, she carried a hand mirror that reflected her lavender hair.

I looked for them today, but they are gone.

I try not to be restless. Emil dislikes what he calls my "thumping." Tonight I will try to read. A volume by E.T.A. Hoffmann has been discovered in the library, and we think it must be yours, for it is certainly not ours. As I read, I will imagine that you are here again, seated in your chair by the window, teasing Mother as she chuckles over her knitting, and that you turn, with your hair lit up all reddish by the sunset through the window, and speak to me kindly.

Your
Gisela

My Dear S.,

I have had the most marvelous dream! And I believe I have you to thank for it—for it came directly out of the pages of Hoffmann.

I dreamt that I was entering the door of a very large eating-house, rather like a restaurant in the Prater. The door was of glass, with gilt lettering; I could not make out what it said, but I remember a large O with twisting vines. Inside everything shone: the glasses and tableware, the chandeliers, and the jewels and curled hair of the fine people at the tables. The walls were all covered with mirrors. I saw myself moving among the tables: I wore a mauve dress and, strangely enough, a powdered wig. I was not at all nervous, though the restaurant was very imposing. I went on walking, for I felt vaguely that I was supposed to be meeting someone. Then a young man caught my eye. He wore an old-fashioned frock coat and was talking earnestly to his companion, a lady in a powdered wig.

It was Hoffmann's Nathanael! I knew him at once: his thin face, very handsome if somewhat sickly; his black eyes; the trembling of his hands. He was precisely like the hero of that bewitching story, "The Sandman," which I had finished just before going to bed. And who do you suppose the lady was? Olimpia, of course! As I passed behind her chair, she made a wheezing mechanical sound, and then cried out "Ah! Ah!" It was she—Spalanzani's exquisite doll, so lovely and lifelike that Nathanael fell wildly in love with her. I knew I had stumbled into the part of the story that tells of their courtship. It is difficult to describe the elation I felt upon this discovery. To be in a story! All the chandeliers seemed to blaze more brightly, and I hurried around the table to look at Olimpia's face.

What do you think? She looked exactly like me!

Well, all but her eyes—these were quite fixed and strange, and glittered only when she nodded her head. This she did regularly, and then her eyes reflected the lights of the restaurant, creating an effect that was almost human. Poor Nathanael was smitten with her. I circled the table to look at him again, but just as he glanced at me, I woke up.

I suppose it should have been frightening—to see oneself as a doll. But it wasn't, not in the least! I woke up feeling rested and full of life. Indeed, I feel better than I have done for weeks. Both Mother and Emil commented on my color, and said I looked very well. "The summer has reached you at last," said Mother. You know she often calls me her "arctic chick"—a silly name, for I am not at all cold-natured. If I have been subdued lately, it is only because it makes me melancholy to think you will not come to see us.

Your

Gisela

S.:

So, you think I ought not to read Hoffmann? I am "too sensitive" for his art?

Then why could you not write to me yourself? Think how humiliating it was for me to be taken aside by Emil, like a child! He could hardly look at me; he knew himself it was wrong. "Don't be angry," he pleaded—as if I could help it! I felt myself growing hard and stony, absolutely petrifying with rage. When he left me, and I moved at last, raising my hand to smooth my hair, my own shadow startled me, shifting on the wall.

I have given the book to Emil. My dreams are my own.

I have been there again, you know. To the restaurant. I have walked between the smooth white tablecloths. No one seems to notice me there—except him. He sees me! Nathanael— he sees me. The first time he looked at me, he started like a hare. I was standing behind Olimpia, just at her shoulder, and Nathanael glanced at me and then down at his beloved and then up at me again, a potent horror dawning in his eyes. I realized then how disconcerting it must have been for him. Here was a second idol standing behind the first, and this one ever so much more alive than the seated one, more human, with vivid eyes aglow beneath the lights! He looked wildly at the mirrors, to find that I was also there. It was clear that no one else in the restaurant could see me. A waiter walked past me, brushing my arm. Nathanael paled; his hair went lank with sweat; I feared to see him faint.

I smiled at him, with the idea of calming his nerves. He flung his arm up before his face.

That made me hesitate. I watched him grope for his glass. He gulped the wine greedily. He was looking at Olimpia now, with a different kind of terror in his eyes. Of course, he believed her to be human. He was desperately in love, and would not wish to act like a madman in front of her. He straightened himself and smoothed his coat, and said something to her in a strange, shrill voice—a silly, drawing-room question about music.

Music: had she been studying it long?

It was—*comical.*

When he glanced at me again, I could not help baring my teeth. Just a little bit, to see what would happen. He shuddered and blanched more violently than before. It was as if he were a fish, and the hook had pierced his lip.

I winked at him. Very vulgar—but it was a dream! He danced at the end of the line, gasping for air. "Nathanael," I said. Great drops stood on his brow. "Nathanael!" I repeated. He babbled of Mozart, grapes, and handkerchiefs while his clockwork darling answered, "Ah! Ah!"

Such a ridiculous scene—I woke up laughing!

But I am not laughing now. Dear S., why could you not write to me directly? I would so love a letter from you, even a scolding one! If only you would reply, I would not ask to read E. T. A. Hoffmann or anyone else. And don't say "propriety"—you know I hate the sound of the word. We all hated it together when we were children, don't you remember? The Hochwald, and how you flung your hat into the weeds. You said hats were never worn in paradise. Can we not go there?

Your

Gisela

Dear S.—Dear Master,

Do you remember how we used to call you that? I suppose you think me too young to remember myself; but I recall every detail of your visits here, even the first year, when you wore a penknife on a chain, and the blackberries were so plentiful. I used to trail behind when you and Emil walked to the Hochwald. You talked of Cervantes and the noble Castilian tongue; you called each other "Don," and the two of you tied me to a tree by my apron strings and left me alone for half an hour. The sky grew dark, and the whole wood sighed. I twisted against my apron, trying to move my left arm, which was closest to the knot. The cloth pressed into my abdomen, the rugged bark scraped my forearm, and I closed my eyes as a cold wind shook the bracken. The first drop of rain struck my brow with such violence I thought it was an acorn. Then I heard voices calling me through the trees. "Gisela! Gisela!" You had lost me. I writhed harder against my taut apron, saying nothing, and then you crashed through a thicket and almost toppled into me. "Why didn't you answer? And what have you done?" you cried, having untied me to discover my arm rubbed bloody by the tree. "Why, Gisela?" Your eyes were dark with fear, your lips so close I could see the dim sheen on them, their texture of cranberry skins.

The family opinion that I am "strange" and "cold" dates from that visit. You knew better. Didn't you ask permission to bring my milk upstairs? I remember your face in the light of my little candle, the warmth of my heated blankets, the storm outside blowing as if it would knock the house down. You were too large for my room; you made it shrink. "You must tell me everything," you said, "everything, even if it makes you afraid. *Especially* if it makes you afraid." Such urgency in your voice. I was happy for the slight sting in my arm; without it, I might have thought I was dreaming.

Did you not say, dear Master, that the life of dreams is real?

I follow Nathanael through Hoffmann's streets. When he goes to the opera, I am there, in a great fur the color of horn. When he buys tobacco I am there, turning over some postcards. My favorite amusement is to run beside him when, in the evenings, he goes out to settle his nerves with a bit of air. He runs faster, and I run faster—my feet are so light, so light! I can hear him whimpering, and even praying in a low voice. His fear is so strong! I breathe it in, like the odor of aqua vitae. He is rather beautiful, his brown hair cut long, his face pale as a lamp with suffering. These days he has grown somewhat shabby: his coat is stained, and a faint beard blurs his cheeks. I wish he looked more like you.

G.

My Dear Master,

My dreams are so lovely, they really ought to be turned into something—perhaps an opera. Yes, why not? I should call it *Olimpia's Ghost*. Perhaps you and I could write it together: I would provide the dreams, and you the poetry. Let me know if you would like me to send you some notes. Like this: *Evening. A dark garret. NATHANAEL, a young man of gloomy aspect, paces between the window and the fire.* That was how I found him last night. When I entered, he crossed himself and sank to his knees, his upraised face capturing all the poor light in the room.

"Who are you? Who are you?" he whispered.

I said: "You know."

"No!" he said. "You are not she."

"But I am, Nathanael," I told him gently. "I am her soul."

He shook his head, recoiling toward the wall. "Never! I know my Olimpia's pure soul: it looks at me out of her tranquil eyes."

Well, I laughed at that. He covered his face. He cannot bear my laughter: Olimpia never laughs. "Come, show some spirit," I said, prodding him with my foot. He began to strike his head against the wall, and when he seized the poker, determined to do himself a mischief, I decided to leave the room.

Outside, the streets were lightly dusted with snow. Winter is coming early to the dream city, just as it is coming here. Walking beside the dream canal, I hummed a snatch of tune which, now that I come to think of it, might become an aria for *Olimpia's Ghost*. I think I should call it "The Hidden Life of Dolls." It will be sung by the Ghost herself, of course. The tune is similar to "Ach, du lieber Augustin." I am only really happy with two lines:

See! the midnight clock is shining brightly.
It is the dolls' moon.

Is it not rather fine? Perhaps it is not exactly poetry; but you will take care of that. I remember a golden day, so long it seemed nearly endless, and the strawberries in the meadow, and you told us a fortune-teller had predicted you would become a cabinet minister. Emil said it was possible; he might become one too, why not; you might both have distinguished careers, for being Jewish was hardly a handicap nowadays. You stared at him in amazement. "A cabinet minister! Is that what you envision for me? Boiled beef at dinner, and speech-writing afterward? Thank you very much!"

I understood you perfectly. I said: "Sigmund will be a poet."

You looked at me, grateful and sunburned, your shirt open at the neck. "There!" you said, triumphant. "Gisela knows me best, after all." And we both laughed at Emil, you and I together.

Then, of course, he blushed, and claimed he was only joking, and that he would be a painter. But he will do no such thing. He will inherit the dye-works.

What of you, dear Master?

This morning my eyes were crusted shut, as if I had slept for many days. The Sandman has been here!
G.

My Dear Master,
Last night I pursued him into a church. I wore a barometer at my waist like a reticule. Clumps of candles shone here and there in the huge dark sanctuary, tiny and far apart, like autumn crocuses in a plain of mud.

These lines, I notice, make me sound rather restless and unhappy. Be sure that I am nothing of the sort. My health is splendid: Mother has had to let out all of my dresses, and my hair has grown so thick I can scarcely grasp it in both hands. It is true that I go up and down the stairs more frequently than ever, but only because it is too wet to go out. I must tire myself somehow, and nobody likes my moving about so much, either in the house or in the dye-shop. And so: to the stairs. The old carpeting is almost all worn away, and the polished wood underneath gleams beautifully, rich as fat. I hurry down, for I get the most relief from climbing up again, toward the little hall window that frames a patch of sky.

I begin to be frightened for him. When I entered the church his shock and horror were so great that he collapsed in the aisle, foaming at the lips. The priest and the other good people there took him away to a back room, where I hovered anxiously until he regained consciousness. He looked very thin, very frail, like a glass angel. I slipped away before he noticed me. I could hear him weeping as I went out of the church. What if he should die? I am haunted by the awful conclusion to Hoffmann's tale.

Dear Master! I write because you said "tell me everything." G.

And two years ago, the last time you came, you rushed past the house just as you were, all grimy from the journey, and you ran off into the meadow, and I ran after you, like a lunatic Mother said later, and we kicked through the grass, releasing a green, bruised odor, and you threw yourself into the arms of the cypress tree, the most somber tree in the meadow, certainly more funereal than the ones in Italian pictures, and perhaps there is something about our northern clime that makes them grow that way, almost black, absorbing all the light, not reflecting it at all, or perhaps it is only the paler light here, the paler sky against which they stand like sentries, and you seized a branch in your teeth and chewed it savagely, and I too pressed my face to the needles and bit, and you muttered *Freiberg Freiberg*, and I imagined that you were repeating my name.

My Dear Sigmund,

So, you persist in your silence. This is no more than I expected. Emil assures me that you will certainly not come now. Your zoology examination, it appears, is set for the end of the month. Well! I wish you success; though it is clear you need no encouragement from me.

You are resolved, he says, to become a man of science.

Perhaps you are thinking of my Nathanael, and wondering if he lives? Please do not distress yourself. Nathanael is quite well. Only last week I observed him consuming cakes on a balcony with his Olimpia. She, of course, ate nothing. It seems she is conscious of her figure. I peered at them from under my parasol, and walked on. I try not to let Nathanael see me these days. I imagine he and his darling will marry, and produce a line of human children with wooden hearts.

Sigmund, I know the secret.

Emil took me out this morning, at Mother's urging. The air was raw, the streets a rough mixture of frost and mud. To my amazement, the marionettes were again dancing in the square, before a paltry audience of mostly poor children. Pierrot's little face was so hard and sad, it brought the tears to my eyes. Columbine's hand mirror, I realized, is a lorgnette. She peered at me with an eye as gray as a clam. Her gaze quite went through me; but the magnification also revealed a great crack in her plaster forehead.

Thanks to the improved health I have enjoyed recently, I am very nimble and strong. I tore away from Emil and dashed behind the theater. The dirty little boy was sitting there, quite comfortable on an overturned pail, blowing vigorously on his gloveless hands. I could only see his father, the puppet-master, from the waist down: a pair of baggy trousers tucked into hobnailed boots. The boy stood, but I pushed past him and tugged the puppet-master's shirt. He lifted the spangled curtain and glared at me.

"What is it, miss?"

On the other side of the theater, the children had begun to roar their disapproval at the sudden collapse of the show. Emil rushed up behind me. The puppet-master, breathing white fog from his black beard, told us to be off, using a vulgar expression. "I know the secret," I told him. Emil had seized me now, and was pulling me away. He gave me a terrible lecture all the way home. I did not mind. Every time I raised my hand, as if sprinkling sugar, a host of swallows rose into the sky.

To climb. To climb.

This morning my eyes were crusted shut again. When I rubbed them, my fingers came away covered with brown flakes. Has the cold weather caused it somehow, or is it blood?

Now that I am avoiding Nathanael, I have had the chance to explore more of the dream city. I often find myself in black, narrow, odorous, humid streets: the streets where I used to chase him in merrier days. There is a certain alley that reminds me of the one behind the smithy in Freiberg, the one with a plaque commemorating the burning of witches. I always feel nervous in that dark dream street—yet at the same time I am drawn to the place. Last night, as I wandered there, a curious scraping echoed from the walls. A slow, uneven, tortured sound, the groan of an object moving with great difficulty over the slimy stones.

I paused. There was very little light—the buildings on either side shut out the moon—but the stones of the alley themselves possess a strange, greenish radiance. In that eldritch light, a figure came toward me, dragging itself painfully, a towering thing with an outline like a crag.

Closer, closer! I watched, frozen to the spot. For the first time in that place, I was terrified. The creature lurched toward me on heavy, jointless legs. I saw it was made of wood. And not just wood, but a wild patchwork of wood, painted pieces fixed haphazardly together. It was as if a crazed puppeteer had taken all the pieces left over from building his marionettes, and constructed one fabulous, horrible puppet, a creature taller than a man, its shoulders built up like buttresses, its sad face hanging down upon its chest. For it had a sad face, Sigmund, such a sad face! A face of flesh, very pale, the face of an invalid. Bloody tear-tracks descended from its eyes. I knew at once that it was the Sandman. It raised a clumsy arm and pointed toward the sky.

To climb. To climb.

The last time I saw you: Vienna, New Year's Eve. Your mother was distressed, as your father had not yet arrived. She kept running out to the landing to see if he had come. The parlor was hot from our dancing. I wore a white holiday dress and a black velvet ribbon. I had decided that there would be no more shyness on my part, no pretense. The flavor of bitter cypress was in my mouth. I had tucked a sprig of it inside the bosom of my dress, to bring you, there in the city, the delirious freshness of Freiberg. When we danced, I pressed close to you so that you would smell it. You pushed me back with a cold look. Later that night I heard you talking in the kitchen. "As for Gisela Fluss," you said, "once she was a decorous doll, and now she has become an indecorous flirt."

A doll, a flirt. But I shall become an artist. And you: you will be a man of science.

The Sandman jerked his arm, signaling to me. I realized that he was pointing to the single lighted window in the dismal tenement above the street. There, at a table, a man sat writing.

His brown hair was tied in a pigtail. His coat was not clean. I thought, astonished, that this must be my Nathanael. Then he raised his head and looked out the window, eyes narrowed, pencil against his teeth, and I saw that he was an entirely different person. With his mobile face and pensive, furrowed brow, he looked more like the Sandman than Nathanael. He was, of course, the double of them both. Father, devil, puppeteer: he was Hoffmann. I glanced at the Sandman, who gestured eagerly at the drainpipe on the wall.

I am no fortune-teller, Sigmund. But I will make you a prediction. I predict that one day you will regret your choice. I predict that you will try to go back, to find your way to the dream city and the winding streets that might have made you a poet. You will search for Hoffmann, and you will not find him. It will not be your destiny to embrace him and kiss him on the mouth. Nor will it be your destiny to wind your apron string about his neck, and set free his collection of wooden birds.

The Sandman gestured to me, weeping blood.

I went to the wall and examined the drainpipe. Now I could no longer see Hoffmann in his room. The edge of the lighted window shone like frost.

I handed the Sandman my wig, grasped the pipe in both hands, and began to climb.

The Tale of Mahliya and Mauhub and the White-Footed Gazelle

This story is at least a thousand years old. Its complete title is "The Tale of Mahliya and Mauhub and the White-Footed Gazelle: It Contains Strange and Marvelous Things." A single copy, probably produced in Egypt or Syria, survives in Istanbul; the first English translation appeared in 2015. This is not the right way to start a fairy tale, but it's better than sitting here in silence waiting for Mahliya, who takes forever to get ready. She's upstairs staining her cheeks with antimony, her lips with a lipstick called Black Sauce. Vainest crone in Cairo.

She leaves her window open for the birds to fly in and out. If you listen closely, you'll hear the bigger ones thump their wings against the sash. The most famous, of course, is the flying featherless ostrich. A monstrous creature, like something boiled. Mahliya adores it. She lets it eat out of her mouth.

While we're waiting, why don't I tell you the Tale of the White-Footed Gazelle? I'm only a retainer, but I do know all the stories, for that's the definition of a servant, especially one in my position, the head servant, and indeed, in these lean times, the only one. Once I presided over a staff of hundreds; now instead of directing many people, I direct many things: I purchase shoes and bedding, I keep up with all the fashions, with advances in medicine, tax laws, satellite TV. If your purpose, as you say, is to produce a monograph on the newly translated *Tales of the Marvelous and News of the Strange*, including versions of the stories as told by people who experienced them, why not begin with me? I am perfectly familiar with the Tale of the White-Footed Gazelle, which lies enclosed in the Tale of Mahliya and Mauhub. You will be familiar with this narrative structure from *A Thousand and One Nights*, a collection of tales whose fate has been very different from that of Mahliya's story. One might ask: Why? Why should *A Thousand and One Nights* rise to such prominence, performed on stages in Japan and animated by Disney, while the very similar collection containing the Tale of Mahliya and Mauhub has moldered in a library for centuries? Well! No doubt all that is about to change. Just close the window for me, if you would; my bald head feels every draft. When I was a younger man—but that's not the story you came to hear! Listen, then, and I shall spin you a marvelous tale.

THE TALE OF THE WHITE-FOOTED GAZELLE

I have condensed it for you because you are a researcher. In this story you will find:
1. Haifa', daughter of a Persian king, also a gazelle
2. The White-Footed Gazelle, also a prince of the jinn
3. Ostrich King
4. Snake King
5. Crow Queen
6. Lion

A love story. Haifa' and the White-Footed Gazelle fall in love, then separate, then move toward each other again, then apart, as if in a cosmic dance. We learn that the Ostrich King unites hearts while the

Crow Queen divides lovers. These movements of attraction and repulsion also characterize the Tale of Mahliya and Mauhub.

An animal story. A prince of the jinn takes the form of a white-footed gazelle to follow Haifa' into her secluded garden. When he abandons her due to a misunderstanding (he thinks she's divulged his true nature), she tracks him through a country of marvelous beasts. In a wild green valley, ostriches graze in the shadow of the Obsidian Mountain that marks the border of the land of the jinn. The Ostrich King herds his flock with a palm branch, flicking their tails with the spikes. That night, as Haifa' takes shelter with him, the Snake King passes with his retinue. A noisy party, jostling and laughing, quaffing great goblets of smoke. They ride upon snakes and wear snakes coiled round their heads like turbans. "Have you seen the White-Footed Gazelle?" Haifa' asks. "No," says the Snake King, flames flashing up in his mouth. "Ask the Queen of the Crows."

To reach the Crow Queen, Haifa' flies on a smooth-skinned, featherless ostrich, which covers a two-year journey in a single night. The Crow Queen is a scowling old woman with ten jeweled bracelets on each arm, ten anklets on each leg, and ten rings on each finger. She wears a golden crown studded with gems, carries an emerald scepter, spits on the floor, and has never shown pity to anyone. Fortunately, Haifa' bears a letter from the Ostrich King, and the Crow Queen owes him a debt. She reunites Haifa' with her beloved.

The story doesn't end there. Haifa' pines for her own country, and her new husband agrees to a visit as long as they both go as gazelles. Unfortunately, they are captured: Haifa' the Gazelle by Mauhub, and the White-Footed Gazelle by Mahliya. When we meet Haifa', she's just been turned back into a woman by a priest of Baal. Weeping, she tells Mauhub her story. Mauhub is astounded, but not as much as you might think. He's an animal intimate himself: as a child, he was suckled by a lion.

A few more interesting points about this story:

1. Feet

The White-Footed Gazelle is named for his feet and also seems to have a foot fetish. When he first transforms himself into a man in front of Haifa', he declares his love and immediately kisses her feet. In between kisses he speaks to her in a pure and elegant language, more delicious than honey and softer than clarified butter. "He said I was like a shoot of sweet basil. He kissed my feet and sucked them and by God I felt my heart fly into my throat."

2. Shivering

The gazelle shivers and turns into a woman. She tells the story of the White-Footed Gazelle, which shivered and turned into a man. A weird sort of shudder seems to precede transformation. The strangest thing, though, is the seizure suffered by our heroine's father. This happens early in the story, when Haifa' is living with her lover in an exquisite idyll: he's her pet gazelle by day, her lover in a locked room at night. Then one night Haifa' wakes to a cry of alarm: "The king! The king!" Terrified for her father, she rushes out half-dressed, leaving the door open. The White-Footed Gazelle doesn't wake up—perhaps he's a heavy sleeper, or perhaps, being a jinni, he's deaf to human sorrow. Whatever the reason, he only wakes at dawn. Finding himself alone, the door open, he thinks Haifa' has betrayed him and exposed their secret.

Out the window he goes on mist-white feet. Haifa' will come back soon, having left her father sleeping peacefully. She'll cry out over the empty bed. She'll dash out into the garden, slapping her face in her grief. She will begin her quest.

How strange that the source of the error that parts these lovers should be a seizure. An excess of trembling.

To shiver is to move rapidly from one place to another and back. From prince of the jinn to white-footed gazelle, from beloved to enemy. I think of this whole story as a long shudder.

3. Lion

I did say there was a lion, didn't I! Haifa' the Gazelle meets him shortly before she's captured by Mauhub. The lion has scraped out a hole in the ground and he's squatting in it and crying. "Dark-eyed gazelle, fair as the moon, I, the red lion, have suffered a great sorrow . . ." The story sort of drops him there. Later, of course, he'll turn out to be the long-lost mate of the lioness who suckled Mauhub. This fact won't redeem the lion, who remains throughout the story the same dirty, sniveling creature we meet in this scene. Forget about him. He's an asshole.

I think I hear Mahliya's feet on the stairs. It's either that or the shuffling and crowding of the birds on the perches in her bedroom. Mahliya's feet are so light they sound like wings. You'll notice, in a few moments, how graceful and regal she is, an incredible thing at her age. Even I, who have attended her for more years than I care to remember, and have therefore had many occasions to be annoyed with her tricks, admit this. Her queenly poise never shatters. During the revolution, while others cowered indoors, she watched the crowds from her balcony, smoking a water-pipe.

Really, it's too bad that a foreign researcher like yourself, the first to visit her, should be kept waiting so long! If you like, I can tell you a version of her story myself. Just keep in mind that Mahliya will tell it differently.

THE TALE OF MAHLIYA AND MAUHUB
or
THE PORTRAIT

My story begins with a portrait. The Egyptian princess Mahliya fell in love with a portrait of Mauhub that was painted on the wall of a church in Jerusalem, as was customary for princes of Mauhub's line. The painting was fresh, the oil still gleaming; it was adorned with red gold and its eyes were a pair of topazes. Beside it glimmered a picture of a lioness suckling the infant Mauhub. A crystal candle filled with jasmine oil illuminated both paintings. Mahliya was enchanted. She embarked at once on a love affair conducted entirely under the sign of the portrait.

Portrait One: Mahliya as a Young Man

When Mahliya first met Mauhub, she was disguised as a young man. She introduced herself as Mukhadi', Mahliya's vizier. We must suppose she did this in order to increase Mauhub's interest in the real Mahliya, who was sending him gifts and letters at the same time. A frantic existence: by day, hunting trips and conversation with her beloved, seizing each chance to give him a brotherly punch in the arm; by night, tender yet formal letters, the preparation of splendid packages, sighs, poetry, fainting spells, and tears. You will have noticed the shudder in this story, the same trembling motion that shapes the Tale of the White-Footed Gazelle. Back and forth, back and forth. Incidentally, it's a wonder Mauhub didn't suspect Mahliya's pretty young vizier. Mukhadi' means Impostor.

Portrait Two: Mahliya as Mirror

On their last hunting trip together, Mauhub caught Haifa' in her gazelle form and Mahliya caught the White-Footed Gazelle. It was Haifa', restored to human shape, who informed Mauhub that his hunting companion was also the mysterious princess who kept sending him gifts and letters. Mauhub rushed to Mahliya's tent. They spent one glorious night together before their fathers recalled them to their respective kingdoms. The lovers continued to communicate through gifts, the most magnificent of which was certainly Mahliya's mirror.

This mirror was enchanted so that when Mauhub looked into it, he saw Mahliya sitting beside him. "Nothing was missing," the story tells us, "except the lady herself." Such an odd phrase; if she was missing, surely nothing else mattered.

I see Mauhub contorting himself, one eye on the mirror, embracing a lady who only appears to be there.

When Mahliya heard of the beauty of Haifa', who was staying with Mauhub, she got so furiously jealous she sent an eagle to snatch the mirror away.

Portrait Three: Mahliya as Anchorite

For the crime of arousing Mahliya's suspicions, Mauhub had to be punished. Mahliya tortured his messengers, crushed his armies, beguiled him across the sea with a magic bird. At last, worn thin from travel and near-starvation, ugly with suffering, he stumbled to a hermitage on swollen feet. An anchorite peered down from the window, radiant in black wool. She made Mauhub swear to serve her, forced him to write the promise on his arm. All this so that when he reached the city, Queen Mahliya, in her true form at last, could yank up his sleeve and expose his inconstancy.

A love story. She forgave him.

An animal story, teeming with life. Mahliya's army of buffaloes tramples Mauhub's army of lions. Her army of wildcats destroys his army of elephants. She builds him a fortress in the land of the jinn, a place swarming with snakes and lizards. Above each door of this fortress, a brass falcon whistles in the wind. When the lovers have passed many years in delight, a sorceress transforms Mauhub into a crocodile. Mahliya recognizes him by his pearl earrings. She knows him, although he never recognized her: neither as Mukhadi' the vizier nor as the beautiful anchorite. He didn't know. He didn't know me. Of course it was me, what's the matter with you? Why are people so stupid? You're like Mauhub: rather than the real person in an unexpected shape, you prefer the magic mirror, which gives you the image you wish to see, although it leaves you grasping nothing but air.

THE WONDER CURSE

Now that we're being honest, let me ask you something. (A photograph? All right. Here, I'll blow some smoke. That's an old moviestar trick. It'll make my mouth a delectable little beak, smooth my wrinkles, and impart an air of nostalgia.) My question is this: Why are you people so hungry for marvels? I mean here you are, braving a twelve-hour journey from JFK, one of the world's worst airports, plus a taxi ride through the afternoon traffic, only to sit in an elderly woman's apartment and listen to a story. Really, I felt I had to trick you to make it worth your while! (Hand me my wig, will you? It's under your chair. You'll want another photograph now, I suppose!) Of course there's a venerable tradition of marvel tales here, a tradition that harbors my own story. But lately it seems to me that there is such a thing as a *wonder curse*, like the literary version of a resource curse. As if, having once tasted the magic of the East, visitors become determined to extract it at any cost.

The link between marvels and money is quite clear. Fabulous tales, astronomical wealth: both are forms of fortune. Perhaps the story is a kind of treasure map. But there is more than one map of the world, my friend. Consider what this tale contains and what it does not:

This Tale Contains:
Yellow silk, red leather, white marble, red onyx, gilded copper, ambergris, topaz, emerald, amber, musk, ebony, gold, carnelian, camphor, Indian aloes, Bactrian camels, pearls, rubies, Chinese steel, silver, sandalwood, slaves.

This Tale Does Not Contain:
Airports, cigarettes, internet cafés, "Shipsy" potato chips in tiny packets, pineapple-flavored "Fairuz" soft drinks, soap operas based on the works of Naguib Mahfouz, traffic jams, copy shops, subway trains shrieking down long black tunnels, subway trains so crowded you can't

get in, schoolgirls fanning themselves with exercise books, schools, radios, the knife-grinder's cry, wedding parties on barges, street murals of Umm Kulthum with her iconic glasses and handkerchief, the light through the windows of Mari Mina Church at precisely 5:45 pm, broken china, makeshift tents, outdoor barbers, street musicians, street protests, cell phones, pictures of bruises taken with cell phones, barricades, security police, rooms where the lights are never turned on, tear gas, pamphlets, bullets, peaceful activists shot down on the street, a poet shot down on the street, the poet who wrote of the streets, who trembled, bleeding, her body transformed into something else, but what? There is no gazelle.

THE LION'S TALE

There is, however, a lion. There's always a lion. This is his story:

The lion weeping in the dust was reunited with his mate, Mauhub's wetnurse. He promised to be faithful to her, as Mauhub had promised Mahliya. But just as Mauhub betrayed Mahliya by swearing to serve the lovely anchorite, even going so far as to write her name on his arm, the lion betrayed the lioness. Tempted by some delicious roasted game, he agreed that if the old woman cooking it would give him a taste, he would marry her daughter.

For the sin of inconstancy he was turned over to devils in human shape who docked his tail and cauterized the stump with fire. His nose and ears were cut off, his whiskers shaved, his body smeared with dung, his neck encircled by an iron ring. Fairy tales are inexorable, their ferocity divine. When the lion returned to his mate, he was so hideously deformed she wouldn't have him. His howls of anguish curl about the story, creating a beautiful border, a frame for Mauhub and Mahliya's wedding portrait.

Yes, it was Mahliya—that is, it was I—who sent the old woman to tempt the lion. You may suppose I did so in order to spare my beloved, to transfer his crime onto another body through which I could then enjoy, without suffering myself, all the pleasures of vengeance. Think what you like. Somebody has to pay. There's always an animal, a wonderfully absorbent material, capable of sopping up an ocean of cruelty. Go visit the Alexandria Zoo sometime—you'll see lions panting in a concrete hole, surrounded by mounds of trash.

THE CROW QUEEN'S TALE

Things don't always work out in life. Somebody has to pay. This is my song.

Oh, come. You must have known I was also the Crow Queen. Didn't you read the story? Look how Mahliya holds back from Mauhub, hides from him, tricks him, fights him. She is the Queen of the Crows, who separates lovers.

In the end, it's true, I stayed with him. He died quietly in my arms. He had grown so small by the end, so shriveled, I could carry him like a child. The day before he died I flew with him over the tombs of Giza. He was half-blinded by cataracts, but he loved the air.

Sometimes I still can't believe I cast my lot with human beings. It's humiliating. Of Mahliya the story says: "Iblis captured her heart." It's true, I was captured and I was defeated. I can save a man who has been turned into a crocodile, but not a man who is growing old.

"Are you near or far, living or dead?" sings Mahliya in the story. "Oh that I were a cross hung around his neck, that I might taste his scent." She sings that she wants to cover his mouth with hers, trace the gaps between his teeth with her tongue. "Oh that I were a sacrifice, mingled with his spit." A love story, an animal story. All these animals in love. I understand the White-Footed Gazelle's desire for his beloved's feet. There is a place where we are all animal, even you. We flicker in and out of it. We can be terribly hurt there, but also comforted.

The Queen of the Crows falls from her window at dusk. She catches the air. An old woman, languid. She glides down Ramses Street toward Masarra. She doubles back toward the river. Masr al-'Adima. Everything's pink. In the gardens of Maadi they are hosing down the paths.

I am the spirit of ruined utopias and unrequited love. It's not my fault. You didn't recognize me—do you think I recognize myself? No! That face in the mirror: that's not me. I see myself only in motion, smoking, gripping my windowsill in the instant before flight. I only recognize the wings that flap. God, I loved Mauhub so much. He was a descendant of Nebuchadnezzar, you know—the king who lost his mind and ate grass like an ox, whose hair grew long like an eagle's feathers and his nails like an eagle's claws.

It's growing late. The Crow Queen always feels restless at this hour. She longs for flight. Tonight, however, she has a guest, a foreign researcher. The Crow Queen squawks like an impresario, preens before the camera. The photographs will show a bald old lady with snapping kohl-rimmed eyes.

I have cast my lot with human beings, even knowing what I know: that things don't always work out, that somebody has to pay. I'll rise or fall with them. Dear beasts! Instead of scribbling down notes, why don't you let me fly you over the square tonight? You can ride the featherless ostrich if you prefer, though I warn you he's very slow these days, his belly scarred by rubber bullets. We'll weave through the ghostly lights around the Mugamma al-Tahrir and watch the city flicker like a broken bulb. In that stuttering glow the square is like a dirty yellow mirror, a magic mirror reflecting even the ones who are missing. Yes, even the lions. I call it my palace, for these beasts are my true subjects. Look at me: I can't stop shaking.

Honey Bear

We've decided to take a trip, to see the ocean. I want Honey to see it while she's still a child. That way, it'll be magical. I tell her about it in the car: how big it is, and green, like a sky you can wade in.

"Even you?" she asks.

"Even me."

I duck my head to her hair. She smells fresh, but not sweet at all, like parsley or tea. She's wearing a little white dress. It's almost too short. She pushes her bare toes against the seat in front of her, knuckling it like a cat.

"Can you not do that, Hon?" says Dave.

"Sorry, Dad."

She says "Dad" now. She used to say "Da-Da."

Dave grips the wheel. I can see the tension in his shoulders. Threads of gray wink softly in his dark curls. He still wears his hair long, covering his ears, and I think he's secretly a little bit vain about it. A little bit proud of still having all his hair. I think there's something in this, something valuable, something he could use to get back. You don't cling to personal vanities if you've given up all hope of a normal life. At least, I don't think you do.

"Shit," he says.

"Sweetheart . . ."

He doesn't apologize for swearing in front of Honey. The highway's blocked by a clearance area, gloved hands waving us around. He turns the car so sharply the bags in the passenger seat beside him almost fall off the cooler. In the back seat, I lean into Honey Bear.

"It's okay," I tell Dave.

"No, Karen, it is not okay. The temp in the cooler is going to last until exactly four o'clock. At four o'clock, we need a fridge, which means we need a hotel. If we are five minutes late, it is not going to be okay."

"It looks like a pretty short detour."

"It is impossible for you to see how long it is."

"I'm just thinking, it doesn't look like they've got that much to clear."

"Fine, you can think that. Think what you want. But don't tell me the detour's not long, or give me any other information you don't actually have, okay?"

He's driving faster. I rest my cheek on the top of Honey's head. The clearance area rolls by outside the window. Cranes, loading trucks, figures in orange jumpsuits. Some of the slick had dried: they're peeling it up in transparent sheets, like plate glass.

Honey presses a fingertip to the window. "Poo-poo," she says softly.

I tell her about the time I spent a weekend at the beach. My best friend got so sunburned, her back blistered.

We play the clapping game, "A Sailor Went to Sea-Sea-Sea." It's our favorite.

Dave drives too fast, but we don't get stopped, and we reach the hotel in time. I take my meds, and we put the extra in the hotel fridge. Dave's shirt is dark with sweat, and I wish he'd relax, but he goes straight out to buy ice, and stores it in the freezer so we can fill the cooler tomorrow. Then he takes a shower and lies on the bed and watches the news. I sit on the floor with Honey, looking at books. I read to her every evening before bed; I've never missed a night. Right now, we're reading *The Meadow Fairies* by Dorothy Elizabeth Clark.

This is something I've looked forward to my whole adult life: reading the books I loved as a child with a child of my own. Honey adores *The Meadow Fairies*. She snuggles up to me and traces the pretty winged children with her finger. Daffodil, poppy, pink. When I first brought the book home, and Dave saw us reading it, he asked what the point was, since Honey would never see those flowers. I laughed because I'd never seen them either. "It's about fairies," I told him, "not botany." I don't think I've ever seen a poppy in my life.

> *Smiling, though half-asleep,*
> *The Poppy Fairy passes,*
> *Scarlet, like the sunrise,*
> *Among the meadow grasses.*

Honey chants the words with me. She's so smart, she learns so fast. She can pick up anything that rhymes in minutes. Her hair glints in the lamplight. There's the mysterious, slightly abrasive smell of hotel sheets, a particular hotel darkness between the blinds.

"I love this place," says Honey. "Can we stay here?"

"It's an adventure," I tell her. "Just wait till tomorrow."

On the news, helicopters hover over the sea. It's far away, the Pacific. There's been a huge dump there, over thirty square miles of slick. The effects on marine life are not yet known.

"Will it be fairyland?" Honey asks suddenly.

"What, sweetie?"

"Will it be fairyland, when I'm grown up?"

"Yes," I tell her. My firmest tone.

"Will you be there?"

No hesitation. "Yes."

The camera zooms in on the slick-white sea.

By the time I've given Honey Bear a drink and put her to bed, Dave's
eyes are closed. I turn off the TV and the lights and get into bed.
Like Honey, I love the hotel. I love the hard, tight sheets and the
unfamiliar shapes that emerge around me once I've gotten used to
the dark. It's been ages since I slept away from home. The last time
was long before Honey. Dave and I visited some college friends in
Oregon. They couldn't believe we'd driven all that way. We posed in
their driveway, leaning on the car and making the victory sign.

I want the Dave from that photo. That deep suntan, that wide
grin.

Maybe he'll come back to me here, away from home and our
neighbors, the Simkos. He spends far too much time at their place.

For a moment, I think he's back already.

Then he starts shaking. He does it every night. He's crying in
his sleep.

"Ready for the beach?"

"Yes!"

We drive through town to a parking lot dusted with sand. When
I step out of the car the warm sea air rolls over me in waves. There's
something lively in it, something electric.

Honey jumps up and down. "Is that it? Is that it?"

"You got it, Honey Bear."

The beach is deserted. Far to the left, an empty boardwalk whit-
ens in the sun. I kick off my sandals and scoop them up in my hand.
The gray sand sticks to my feet. We lumber down to a spot a few yards
from some boulders, lugging bags and towels.

"Can I take my shoes off too? Can I go in the ocean?"

"Sure, but let me take your dress off."

I pull it off over her head, and her lithe, golden body slips free.
She's so beautiful, my Bear. I call her Honey because she's my sweetheart, my little love, and I call her Bear for the wildness I dream she
will keep always. Honey suits her now, but when she's older she might

want us to call her Bear. I would've loved to be named Bear when I was in high school.

"Don't go too deep," I tell her, "just up to your tummy, okay?"

"Okay," she says, and streaks off, kicking up sand behind her.

Dave has laid out the towels. He's weighted the corners with shoes and the cooler so they won't blow away. He's set up the two folding chairs and the umbrella. Now, with nothing to organize or prepare, he's sitting on a chair with his bare feet resting on a towel. He looks lost.

"Not going in?" I ask.

I think for a moment he's going to ignore me, but then he makes an effort. "Not right away," he says.

I slip off my shorts and my halter top and sit in the chair beside him in my suit. Down in the water, Honey jumps up and down and shrieks.

"Look at that."

"Yeah," he says.

"She loves it."

"Yeah."

"I'm so glad we brought her. Thank you." I reach out and give his wrist a squeeze.

"Look at that fucked-up clown on the boardwalk," he says. "It looks like it used to be part of an arcade entrance or something. Probably been there for fifty years."

The clown towers over the boardwalk. It's almost white, but you can see traces of red on the nose and lips, traces of blue on the hair.

"Looks pretty old," I agree.

"Black rocks, filthy gray sand, and a fucked-up arcade clown. That's what we've got. That's the beach."

It comes out before I can stop it: "Okay, Mr. Simko."

Dave looks at me.

"I'm sorry," I say.

He looks at his watch. "I don't want to stay here for more than an hour. I want us to take a break, go back to the hotel and rest for a bit. Then we'll have lunch, and you can take your medication."

"I said I'm sorry."

"You know what?" He looks gray, worn out, beaten down, like something left out in the rain. His eyes wince away from the light. I can't stand it, I can't stand it if he never comes back. "I think," he tells me, "that Mr. Simko is a pretty fucking sensible guy."

I lean back in the chair, watching Honey Bear in the water. I hate the Simkos. Mr. Simko's bent over and never takes off his bathrobe. He sits on his porch drinking highballs all day, and he gets Dave to go over there and drink too. I can hear them when I've got the kitchen window open. Mr. Simko says things like *Après nous le déluge* and "Keep your powder dry and your pecker wet." He tells Dave he wishes he and Mrs. Simko didn't have Mandy. I've heard him say that. "I wish we'd never gone in for it. Broke Linda's heart." Who does he think brings him the whiskey to make his highballs?

Mrs. Simko never comes out of the house except when Mandy comes home. Then she appears on the porch, banging the door behind her. She's bent over like her husband and wears a flowered housedress. Her hair is black fluff, with thin patches here and there, as if she's burned it. "Mandy, Mandy," she croons, while Mandy puts the stuff down on the porch: liquor, chocolate, clothes, all the luxury goods you can't get at the Center. Stuff you can only get from a child who's left home. Mandy never looks at her mother. She hasn't let either of the Simkos touch her since she moved out.

"I'm going down in the water with Honey," I say, but Dave grabs my arm. "Wait. Look."

I turn my head, and there are Fair Folk on the rocks. Six of them, huge and dazzling. Some crouch on the boulders; others swing over the sea on their flexible wings, dipping their toes in the water.

"Honey!" Dave shouts. "Honey! Come here!"

"C'mon, Hon," I call, reassuring.

Honey splashes toward us, glittering in the sun.

"Come *here!*" barks Dave.

"She's coming," I tell him.

He clutches the arms of his chair. I know he's afraid because of the clearance area we passed on the highway, the slick.

"Come here," he repeats as Honey runs up panting. He glances at the Fair Folk. They're looking at us now, lazy and curious.

I get up and dry Honey off with a towel. "What?" she says.

"Just come over here," says Dave, holding out his arms. "Come and sit with Daddy." Honey walks over and curls up in his lap. I sit in the chair next to them and Dave puts his hand on my shoulder. He's got us. He's holding everyone.

Two of the Fair Folk lift and ripple toward us through the light. There seems to be more light wherever they go. They're fifteen, twenty feet tall, so tall they look slender, attenuated, almost insect-like. You forget how strong they are.

They bend and dip in the air: so close I can see the reds of their eyes. "It's okay," Dave whispers.

And it is, of course. We've got each other. We're safe.

They gaze at us for a moment, impassive, then turn and glide back to their comrades. Honey waves at them with both hands. "Bye, fairies!"

On my first visit to the clinic, I went through all the usual drills, the same stuff I go in for every two weeks. Step here, pee here, spit here, breathe in, breathe out, give me your arm. The only difference the first time was the questions.

Are you aware of the gravity of the commitment? I said yes. Have you been informed of the risks, both physical and psychological? Yes. The side effects of the medication? Blood transfusions? Yes. Yes. The decrease in life expectancy? Everything: yes.

That's what you say to life. *Yes.*

"They chose us," I told Dave. Rain lashed the darkened windows. I cradled tiny Honey in my lap. I'd dried her off and wrapped her in a towel, and she was quiet now, exhausted. I'd already named her in my head.

"We can't go back," Dave whispered. "If we say yes, we can't go back."

"I know."

His eyes were wet. "We could run out and put her on somebody else's porch."

He looked ashamed after he'd said it, the way he'd looked when I'd asked him not to introduce me as "my wife, Karen, the children's literature major." When we first moved into the neighborhood he'd introduce me that way and then laugh, as if there was nothing more ridiculous in the world. Children, when almost nobody could have them anymore; literature when all the schools were closed. I told him it bothered me, and he was sorry, but only for hurting me. He wasn't sorry for what he really meant. What he meant was: *No.*

That's wrong. It's like the Simkos, hateful and worn out with saying *No* to Mandy, saying *No* to life.

So many people say no from the beginning. They make it a virtue: "I can't be bought." As if it were all a matter of protection and fancy goods. Of course, most of those who say yes pretend to be heroes: saving the world, if only for a season. That's always struck me as equally wrong, in its own way. Cheap.

I can't help thinking the absence of children has something to do with this withering of the spirit—this pale new way of seeing the world. Children knew better. You always say yes. If you don't, there's no adventure, and you grow old in your ignorance, bitter, bereft of magic. You say yes to what comes, because you belong to the future, whatever it is, and you're sure as hell not going to be left behind in the past. *Do you hear the fairies sing?* You always get up and open the door. You always answer. You always let them in.

The Fair Folk are gone. I'm in the ocean with Honey. I bounce her on my knee. She's so light in the water: soap bubble, floating seed. She clings to my neck and squeals. I think she'll remember this, this morning at the beach, and the memory will be almost exactly like my own memory of childhood. The water, the sun. Even the cooler, the crumpled maps in the car. So many things now are the way they were when I was small. Simpler, in lots of ways. The things that have disappeared—air travel, wireless communication—seem dreamlike, ludicrous, almost not worth thinking about.

I toss Honey up in the air and catch her, getting a mouthful of saltwater in the process. I shoot the water onto her shoulder. "Mama!" she yells. She bends her head to the water and burbles, trying to copy me, but I lift her up again. I don't want her to choke.

"My Bear, my Bear," I murmur against the damp, wet side of her head. "My Honey Bear."

Dave is waving us in. He's pointing at his watch.

I don't know if it's the excitement, or maybe something about the salt water, but as soon as I get Honey up on the beach, she voids.

"Christ," says Dave. "Oh, Christ."

He pulls me away from her. In seconds he's kneeling on our towels, whipping the gloves and aprons out of the bag. He gets his on fast; I fumble with mine. He rips open a packet of wipes with his teeth, tosses it to me, and pulls out a can of spray.

"I thought you said it wasn't time yet," he says.

"I thought it wasn't. It's really early."

Honey stands naked on the sand, slick pouring down her legs. Already she looks hesitant, confused. "Mama?"

"It's okay, Hon. Just let it come. Do you want to lie down?"

"Yes," she says, and crumples.

"Fuck," says Dave. "It's going to hit the water. I have to go make a call. Take this."

He hands me the spray, yanks his loafers on and dashes up the beach. There's a phone in the parking lot, he can call the Service. He's headed for the fence, not the gate, but it doesn't stop him, he seizes the bar and vaults over.

The slick is still coming. So much, it's incredible, as if she's losing her whole body. It astounds me, it frightens me every time. Her eyes are still open, but dazed. Her fine hair is starting to dry in the sun. The slick pours, undulant, catching the light, like molten plastic.

I touch her face with a gloved hand. "Honey Bear."

"Mm," she grunts.

"You're doing a good job, Hon. Just relax, okay? Mama's here."

Dave was right, it's going to reach the water. I scramble down to the waves and spray the sand and even the water in the path of the slick. Probably won't do anything, probably stupid. I run back to Honey just as Dave comes pelting back from the parking lot.

"On their way," he gasps. "Shit! It's almost in the water!"

"Mama," says Honey.

"I know. I tried to spray."

"You sprayed? That's not going to do anything!"

I'm kneeling beside her. "Yes, Honey."

"Help me!" yells Dave. He runs down past the slick and starts digging wildly, hurling gobs of wet sand.

Honey curls her hand around my finger.

"Karen! Get down here! We can dig a trench, we can keep it from hitting the water!"

"This is scary," Honey whispers.

"I know. I know, Hon. I'm sorry. But you don't need to be scared. It's just like when we're at home, okay?"

But it's not, it's not like when we're at home. At home, I usually know when it's going to happen. I've got a chart. I set up buckets, a plastic sheet. I notify the Service of the approximate date. They come right away. We keep the lights down, and I play Honey's favorite CD.

This isn't like that at all. Harsh sunlight, Dave screaming behind us. Then the Service. They're angry: one of them says, "You ought to be fucking fined." They spray Honey, right on her skin. She squeezes my finger. I don't know what to do, except sing to her, a song from her CD.

> *A sailor went to sea-sea-sea*
> *To see what he could see-see-see*
> *But all that he could see-see-see*
> *Was the bottom of the deep blue sea-sea-sea.*

At last, it stops. The Service workers clean Honey up and wrap her in sterile sheets. They take our gloves and aprons away to be cleaned at the local Center. Dave and I wipe ourselves down and bag the dirty wipes for disposal. We're both shaking. He says: "We are not doing this again."

"It was an accident," I tell him. "It's just life."

He turns to face me. "This is not life, Karen," he snarls. "This is *not life.*"

"Yes. It is."

I think he sees, then. I think he sees that even though he's the practical one, the realist, I'm the strong one.

I carry Honey up to the car. Dave takes the rest of the stuff. He makes two trips. He gives me an energy bar and then my medication. After that, there's the injection, painkillers and nutrients, because Honey's voided, and she'll be hungry. She'll need more than a quick drink.

He slips the needle out of my arm. He's fast, and gentle, even like this, kneeling in the car in a beach parking lot. He presses the cotton down firmly, puts on a strip of medical tape. He looks up and meets my eyes. His are full of tears.

"Jesus, Karen," he says.

Just like that, in that moment, he's back. He covers his mouth with his fist, holding in laughter. "Did you hear the Service guy?"

"You mean, 'You ought to be fucking fined'?"

He bends over, wheezing and crowing. "Christ! I really thought the slick was going in the water."

"But it didn't go in the water?"

"No."

He sits up, wipes his eyes on the back of his hand, then reaches out to smooth my hair away from my face.

"No. It didn't go in. It was fine. Not that it matters, with that giant dump floating in the Pacific."

He reads my face, and raises his hands, palms out. "Okay, okay. No Mr. Simko."

He backs out, shuts the door gently, and gets in the driver's seat. The white clown on the boardwalk watches our car pull out of the lot. We're almost at the hotel when Honey wakes up.

"Mama?" she mumbles. "I'm hungry."

"Okay, sweetie."

I untie the top piece of my suit and pull it down. "Dave? I'm going to feed her in the car."

"Okay. I'll park in the shade. I'll bring you something to eat from inside."

"Thanks."

Honey's wriggling on my lap, fighting the sheets. "Mama, I'm *hungry.*"

"Hush. Hush. Here."

She nuzzles at me, quick and greedy, and latches on. Not at the nipple, but in the soft area under the arm. She grips me lightly with her teeth, and then there's the almost electric jolt as her longer, hollow teeth come down and sink in.

"There," I whisper. "There."

Dave gets out and shuts the door. We're alone in the car.

A breeze stirs the leaves outside. Their reflections move in the windows.

I don't know what the future is going to bring. I don't think about it much. It does seem like there won't be a particularly lengthy future, for us. Not with so few human children being born, and the Fair Folk eating all the animals, and so many plant species dying out from the slick. And once we're gone, what will the Fair Folk do? They don't seem able to raise their own children. It's why they came here in the first place. I don't know if they feel sorry for us, but I know they want us to live as long as possible: they're not pure predators, as some people claim. The abductions of the early days, the bodies discovered in caves—that's all over. The terror, too. That was just to show us what they could do. Now they only kill us as punishment, or after they've voided, when they're crazy with hunger. They rarely hurt anyone in the company of a winged child.

Still, even with all their precautions, we won't last forever. I remember the artist in the park, when I took Honey there one day. All of his paintings were white. He said that was the future, a white planet, nothing but slick, and Honey said it looked like fairyland.

Her breathing has slowed. Mine, too. It's partly the meds, and partly some chemical that comes down through the teeth. It makes you drowsy.

Here's what I know about the future. Honey Bear will grow bigger. Her wings will expand. One day she'll take to the sky, and go live with her own kind. Maybe she'll forget human language, the way the Simkos' Mandy has, but she'll still bring us presents. She'll still be our piece of the future.

And maybe she won't forget. She might remember. She might remember this day at the beach.

She's still awake. Her eyes glisten, heavy with bliss. Large, slightly protuberant eyes, perfectly black in the centers, and scarlet, like the sunrise, at the edges.

How I Met the Ghoul

The poet Ta'abbata Sharran met the ghoul in the fifth century and composed a poem about it known as "The Short Poem Rhyming in Nūn." He says he struck the ghoul with his sword, and she told him to strike again, but he refused, by which we are to understand that the man was no fool, because of course if you strike a ghoul twice it won't die until you strike a thousand more blows: you have to kill it with one blow or one thousand and two. So instead of striking again Ta'abbata Sharran lay on the ghoul all night. He doesn't say exactly what was going on with that. In the morning he looked at her and saw *"two eyes in a hideous head, like the head of a split-tongued cat / legs of a misshapen fetus, back of a dog, clothes of striped cloth or skin."*

I met the ghoul in 2008. She agreed to give me half an hour in the airport. We sat at the back of a restaurant where we could watch the planes take off. I was too wound up to feel like eating, but I ordered some onion rings for show. The ghoul had the Hungry High-flyer Special with curly fries and cream of mushroom soup.

She also ordered a Coke, and I guess I gave her a look because she said: "What?"

"Nothing," I said. She had eyes like illustrated pages, one larger than the other. There was a mark on her temple, probably made by one of God's meteors, but she'd done a good job covering it with makeup.

I asked her if it was easy for her to travel, if she ever got held up at customs or anything. She asked if I was a real reporter or just some small-time blogger. One of her ears was like a dead mine-shaft, the other like a window in some desolate bed-and-breakfast of the plains.

"Look," she said, "I go everywhere. You could say it's in my blood."

I asked if she really had blood, and she picked up her fork like she was going to jam it into her arm.

"Don't!" I yelped.

People looked at us then, and she put the fork down and laughed. She had a nice laugh, like an electric mixer making cake in a distant apartment.

Our food came. I asked if she missed the desert. She said: "Where do you think you are?" She seemed to be having trouble fitting into her T-shirt. My guess is that this was a deliberate effect, like the whirl of her postage-stamp eyes. The T-shirt was red; I think it said something about Cancún.

"What is your favorite book?" I asked.

"Al-Maarri's *Epistle of Forgiveness.*"

"Favorite film?"

"*Titanic.*"

"Favorite food?"

"Reporters. Kidding! I don't know, maybe duck?"

"Have you given many interviews?"

"No. This is my very first. I chose you because you're special, and I will never forget you."

She drank the last of her Coke and belched. Her hair grew all over the wall. She said she liked planes, she didn't make many of them go down. Mostly she liked to look out the window. When everyone was asleep, she'd put her eye to the window and grow her eyeball until it covered the glass.

"What are you looking for?"

"Other planes to wink at. Lightning. Lightning is useful, like string. And I look for things to remember later. Burnt cities. Ruins."

She admitted she also looked for her brother the Qutrub, a demon in the shape of a cat. She didn't think she'd ever find him. For this reason, cats made her sad.

To take her mind off it, and to make sure I got the question in before the end of the interview, I asked about Ta'abbata Sharran.

"Sixty hells, not him again."

"My readers are interested."

She rolled her eyes. One escaped across her forehead, but she caught it.

"What do you want to know? What exactly he meant by 'lay upon her'?"

"No," I lied. "But can you tell me anything about his name?"

Ta'abbata Sharran is a nickname; it means "He Carried Evil Under His Arm." There are several stories explaining how he got the name, but no one knows for sure. The ghoul said it wasn't her fault if I wanted to ask questions a ten-year-old could answer. "He stank, all right?"

"The poet stank?"

"To the moon and back."

She took out a pack of cigarettes, and I reminded her there was no smoking. I asked if her body functioned like that of a human being.

"No," she said. She ate one of her cigarettes.

I asked if it was true that she existed mainly to cause harm to travelers.

"Define 'mainly.'"

Afterward people asked me what she was like. When I said "I can't say," they called it a cop-out. So now I try to break her down and describe her in pieces. Her upper lip was like a broken roof, her lower lip like a beached canoe. It made me feel good when she took my onion rings.

I asked her if modern development had made things harder for ghouls. She said there were more waste places in the world than ever before. I asked her if she was worried about climate change, and she said it was basically a ghoul's dream. She was optimistic about the future.

After a while her hair came down and curled up on her shoulder, and she picked up her bag and slid out of her seat while I paid for lunch. She wouldn't let me walk her to her gate. I asked for her autograph and she said um no, she wasn't born yesterday, but in a nice way.

"Do you think you'd let me interview you again?"

She wavered in the air, and nausea filled me up like breathing. *They are known by name*, I thought in a daze, *but not by shape*. I tried to focus on her: it was like staring into an April dust-storm, electric blackness blotting out the sky. Buried cities whirled in the chaos, broken dishes, bones, syringes, words without meaning, fingernails, so much hair. More paper than you could cover in your life. All of it pulled in, animated, fierce and beating like a heart.

I closed my eyes. *Nothing is wasted.*

The ghoul heard my thought, and snorted. "Everything is wasted." I opened my eyes, and she was stable again, her arms crossed. Her smile was vast and white and kind and a little bit detached, like the ceiling of a room where you have woken up with head trauma.

"So I guess that's a 'no,'" I said. "About the interview."

She laughed her electric-mixer laugh. We didn't shake hands. I watched her until she disappeared in the crowd. It didn't take long: as she turned away, she was already changing shape, on her way to the next brief shelter, the next campsite, the next ruin.

Those

". . . how is this nonsense possible, that the enemies of Kush are copies of the Kushite enemies of Pharaonic Egypt?"
— L. Török, "Kush and the External World"

Sarah sets the kettle on the hob. She bends and fans the fire, her face aglow for a moment, molten bronze. When she stands up, her color fades in the gloom of the little house with its high windows, that house built like a ship. Tight and trim as a yacht stands the little house, and the wind beats hard against the high windows, and Sarah's father with a blanket over his knees, her father the old seafarer with a black-bordered card grasped tight in one hand, draws his chair to the fire and clears his throat.

"Poor George, poor George! Well, he would keep his vow, he said; and so he has; we shall never meet again in this life. Poor fellow! Listen, my girl, when you go out, just stop by the Widow Cobb's, you know the place, at the end of the lane, and see if she has any lilies. We'll send them over to George's poor wife. It's kind of her to remember me after all these years—'remember' in a manner of speaking—we never met. George must have spoken of me to her, and kept my address among his papers . . . my God, Sally, but Man is a curious beast!

73

"I'll tell you a strange thing. The first time I was struck by the mystery that is Man, this same George Barnes, whose death has just been announced, was at my side. It was in the Sudan, at Meroe, and the two of us were making our way north to Cairo for a bit of a holiday. We were young and hardy then, but even so, our recent misadventures in the forests had brought us both down—George was so green about the gills, he was practically silver—and we longed for entertainment and pleasure. There was little of either in the dusty villages we passed on our way up the Nile, but the tombs of Meroe promised a diversion. At the time, I considered myself an amateur archaeologist, and it was with great excitement that I packed our Spartan picnic of bread and dried fish. There was also a jug of the native beer called *merissa*, which George wrapped in a towel as if it had been an infant. I can still see him astride his donkey, his long legs dangling comically on either side, his head swathed in a turban of blinding whiteness . . .

"He was a child, you know. Little more than a child. His father, whom George described as a 'holy terror,' had sent him to sea at the age of twelve, and George, whose nose had been permanently flattened by the fist of this same father, had set off gladly enough. The sea washed him to and fro for a number of years, with its cruelties and privations, the worst of them brought about by the men he served on ship after ship—for sea life is unkind to the small and weak, as I know from experience, though I was twenty when I left home for the waves. I was twenty, and tall, and broad, and George was a slip of a creature with gingery hair, and when we met years later in the Congo forest, natives of the same city, employees at the same plantation, I was thirty and solid as an anvil, and George, though the same age, was still a child. Was it because he'd been robbed of his childhood? Perhaps some men never grow old. What pleasure he took in our excursion to the tombs! He named his donkey Annabelle. He could whistle like a lark—it was his crooked teeth, he said. To think that George, even young George, is dead."

❧

The kettle sings. Sarah takes it off the fire and brews the tea. Soft steam, delicate fragrance, while the wind blows. She fetches her father's pipe from the shelf and helps him to light it. He grunts his thanks, a hollow rumble deep in his wintry throat. She takes the black-bordered card from his hand and reads it beneath a window. If there are lilies, she will take them to this address. She knows the street, a poor but respectable street much like her own. She'll wear her large bonnet. She will knock at the tradesman's door.

"Good afternoon, ma'am. Lilies. For the funeral."

For a moment, she will look into the woman's face. Perhaps she will catch it before the expression twists, before it becomes like all the others, molded by the same stamp, indistinguishable. Every day, every hour, this fog.

"Thank you, my dear. Would you help—just a little closer—yes, now I feel the warmth at last. I shan't scorch my beard, don't worry! Now George, as I was telling you . . . George who's laid in a box, God rest him! I suppose it ought to make us grateful we can still feel the nip of this blasted autumn . . . George was a merry lad, for all he'd been kicked about the globe like a stone in an alley. Down where we worked, at the teak plantation, the natives gave him a name I can't pronounce—your poor mother could tell you, if she weren't in Heaven—but it meant, as far as I understood it, a type of squirrel. And he was just like that, a gingery leaping squirrel with keen black eyes. I remember once at Christmas, when we were invited to dine with the plantation owner, Vermeiren, a bloodless Belgian with fangs like a mastiff, he had a bit of fun with George over that nickname. 'You do realize,' he drawled, 'that the natives eat these squirrels?'

"'Ha, ha! They are funny fellows,' laughed George.

"I laughed too, as would any man who had lived all year on millet porridge, and now found himself at the Belgian's table facing a guinea fowl poached in French wine. I laughed, I tell you; I opened my mouth and howled.

"Vermeiren showed his fangs. 'Oh yes,' he went on softly (and George and I both cut our laughter off short, so as not to drown him out), 'that little animal is quite popular with our dusky friends. Its stomach, I have been told, is full of oil. They prick the stomach— so!—collect the oil, and serve it to the chief.'

"When he said 'So!', he poked his finger in the air, toward George's midriff. His nail was long and yellow, his hand elegant and, for the tropics, marvelously clean. I noticed George turn pale, and felt a little unsteady myself.

"'They eat all sorts of disgusting things,' said George, with an effort. 'Monkeys. Grubs.'

"'So they do!' answered Vermeiren, with ghastly cheer. He addressed himself to his fowl, sawing his knife against the plate, red wine sauce mingling bloodily with the cassava that served us for potatoes. 'And men, of course!' he went on. 'You will have noticed how they file their teeth. Personally I would find it perturbing to have the name of a squirrel. I would find it most unlucky to have this name. As for me, they call me One Gun. Because of my Juliette. This satisfies me.'

"He pricked up a quivering, reddish bit of meat with his fork, and motioned with his eyes toward the rifle hanging on the wall. This was his hunting gun, called Juliette after his wife, who resided at Marseilles, where, to judge from his furnishings, she embroidered quantities of tablecloths.

"I do not know why the Belgian chose to rattle George in this manner. Perhaps he was trying, in his rough way, to put some backbone into the lad: for George was Vermeiren's overseer, charged with ensuring the productivity of the farm, and meting out punishment as required. In the early days of our employment, Vermeiren had often grumbled that George was too soft. On one occasion, I recall, the Belgian had actually brought forward, as evidence, a recently disciplined native called Francisco, and, exposing the native's back crisscrossed with small welts, demanded if *this* was what George called lashes? George protested that he had lashed the black soundly, as anyone could see, and Vermeiren retorted that a native's back was as insensible as teak, certainly impervious to George's paltry strokes, and that if George dared shirk again, he would be taught a lesson in lashing upon his own person. So perhaps Vermeiren's mockery that Christmas was meant to strengthen George's arm. If so, it was hardly necessary, for George had taken his first lesson to heart, and routinely exhausted himself in his exertions with the whip, even putting the same Francisco—apparently an habitual malingerer—into the infirmary at the Catholic Mission.

"But perhaps Vermeiren had other reasons. Perhaps he was simply possessed by that devil which leads men to tear at each other in a small space. I have often encountered this devil on board a ship; and in that house, the only white men for miles, were we not as three sailors launched on a Stygian sea? The darkness, Sally, the closeness of the place! I can scarce describe it. The windows were sheathed in white netting against the mosquitoes, and not a breath of air came through: the flames of the candles on the table stood up as straight and motionless as pikes. After dinner, George attempted to lighten the atmosphere with a carol. His voice faltered reedily into the massy night. I joined him for a few bars, but soon stopped from depression of the spirits, and he went on alone. *I gave my love a cherry.*

"The suffocating loneliness, the density of the forest. You couldn't see more than five yards in any direction. It weighed on you. It's the reason we felt so lighthearted on that trip up the Nile, the trip I was telling you about, to Meroe . . . But the forest, my God: sickness and heat and work. I kept the accounts in an office with a tin roof, so hot I'd feel my brains boiling by ten o'clock. That heat! And George stood in it all day. It took its toll on him. His fevers were terrible, enough to break your heart.

"'Get back, get it away.' That's what he said the night your mother came to see us. She wasn't your mother then, of course, just a nurse from up the river. I'd sent word to the nuns at the Mission to rush somebody down to us, for I was sure George could not live another day. 'Easy, George,' I told him. 'This is a nurse from the Catholics come to make you well.' All the same I had to hold him down on the bed.

Weak as he was, he thrashed in my arms like a seal. 'Get it away, oh God,' he moaned. And your mother bent over him in her white dress."

White, like a lily.

Sarah fingers the silver crucifix at her throat. This is her inheritance from her mother, who died when she was three years old. This, and a few dresses, and two pairs of shoes. She has let out the dresses, but she cannot wear the shoes, which are too small. She keeps them lined up underneath her bed. When she was very young, she used to bring them into bed with her. She gave them names: one was called "Maiyebo." To remember this now, this naming of the shoes, causes the heat of shame to slip up her neck.

She can no longer recall her mother's face.

Her father gestures with his pipe, and she fills it. He has told her the sweet smoke does him good. She helps him light the pipe, then tucks the blanket more snugly around his wasted legs. She remembers a dream, a song.

If only it were possible to control one's dreams!

If it were, she would dream the same dream every night. A dream that has only come to her a few times. Fragments of glittering color and a dry, delicate scent. A dream of swinging. A dream of a structure of light.

Light. Sharp pieces of radiance. No fog. A snatch of song in a lost language. *Maiyebo.* The name of a mushroom? A comical song. Someone bounces a baby on her knee. *Mi a bi nga ro berewe te.* "I'll never see you again."

"You're not . . . you're not too lonely, are you, Sal? Well, I know, but I can't help worrying. I think sometimes that we ought to have stayed in the forest. That I ought to have raised you there, among . . . But after we lost your mother, it was too difficult for me, taking care of a child alone. I didn't know what to do with you, and there was your aunt, too, writing to me about my Christian duty, and the life you might have here. And, of course, there was George. Passing me like a stranger, day after day. Three years like that. Without a word. I suppose a part of me thought that after your mother was gone . . . but no. He kept his vow. 'If you do this thing,' he told me, the night before my wedding, 'if you enter into—*that*—you're dead to me.'' He was trembling, white, as if in the grip of one of his fevers. I thought he'd get over it.

"I thought he was still shaken up from the scare we'd had on the farm that year, and that he'd soften and come around in time. It must have affected him more deeply than I thought. I should have known, now that I think of it. I should have recognized the signs. The way he pounded on my door that night. 'Come out, come out!' That high-pitched scream. I tell you, I thought the house was on fire. I rolled out of bed and stumbled across the room, and when I opened the door he practically fell into my arms.

"'Get your gun,' he cried hoarsely. He had his own rifle, and a lighted torch in the other hand. As I stared, our employer Vermeiren slouched into the circle of light, casually carrying Juliette over his shoulder.

"'Stir yourself, if you please,' he said pleasantly enough. 'It seems we must make a little show of strength.'

"'For God's sake, get your gun,' repeated George, looking over his shoulder. I obeyed, donning boots, a shirt, and trousers for good measure.

"I joined them outside and locked the door behind me, and was immediately struck by the peculiar silence. There used to always be a little noise on the farm, voices of the native families, and lights, too, from their fires. Now the place was entirely deserted.

"'What's happening?' I asked softly.

"'A little fuss from our savage friends,' said the Belgian. 'Not to worry.'

"George stood so close to me, I could tell he wanted to seize my arm, though he couldn't, being encumbered by his gun and torch. His teeth were chattering. 'Look here,' I said, alarmed by his evident panic, 'do we want to carry a light about, and make ourselves a target?'

"'By God, you're right!' cried George, and, looking at his own light in horror, he made as if to fling it to the ground.

"The Belgian snatched his wrist. 'Don't be stupid. We must not appear to be hiding. In our position, a show of fear would be catastrophic. Instead—stand up straight, little squirrel! Are you indeed a squirrel, or a caterpillar?—we must appear calm, and above all, we must shoot accurately, and to kill.'

"'Shoot at what?' I exclaimed. 'It's black as Hades.'

"Before us stretched the teak grove, like a columned ruin in the faint starlight, and beyond that, invisible to us, the damp tangle of the forest.

"'Only wait,' said the Belgian, and a spark flared as he lit his pipe.

"And so we waited. And waited. And whether it was the sound of George muttering prayers at my shoulder, the way his voice went up and down, full of little sobs, or the smell of fear that rose from him, thick and hot, I cannot say . . . Whether it was the darkness and silence around us, or the brooding, hostile forest, or the soft black of the sky in which no moon hung . . . I cannot say, Sally, why it was, but I felt something close around my heart, squeezing tight like a devil's vise. Tighter and tighter it squeezed, and my head grew light, and my body cold, and I thought of your mother, and was glad that she was away at the Catholic mission, where the nuns had given her thread, she said, to embroider a wedding veil. I clung to the thought of her face, as if it would save me . . . And perhaps, you know, it did save me. I held to that face, the face of my own Maria, as something began to happen in the dark. The darkness itself seemed to ripple, to stretch itself like a long snake. 'Ah,' breathed Vermeiren. 'Now it comes.'

"You were so little when we left the plantation, Sally. I wonder if you remember the soldier ants? George and I called them *siafu*, as the Belgian did, though among your mother's people they had another name. Black they were, a black and moving river, and when that river came across your path, you had best get out of the way. They'd appear after the rains, long streams of them crisscrossing the earth, and none could say whence they came or where they went. Their determination was terrible. They used to march up the walls of the house, under the roof, and straight through, across our parlor floor. I had an old Turkish *kilim* there, purchased at Istanbul in my merchant-seaman days, and where the *siafu* crossed it, they'd leave a swath clean as the noonday sky. Your mother would always laugh and say the ants proved how dusty the *kilim* was, and she'd haul it outside and beat it with the broom. But the *siafu* were nothing to laugh at. They were voracious: if they bit you, they'd draw blood. They killed chicks in the nest, and even, I heard, human babies . . .

"'Quiet!' I heard myself say. I hadn't meant to speak, but George's whimpering was breaking down my nerve. He'd given up praying now, and was simply staring at the darkness saying '*No oh no oh no oh no oh no.*' His torch was pitching and bobbing in his grip like a ship's lantern, and his face in the light sweated pale as melting wax, and behind him that ice-blooded Belgian was saying something about the seasons, and how these native disturbances came up each year as regular as the rains. It made me remember the soldier ants, which appeared after the rainstorms. Still the darkness swelled and coiled among the trees. And suddenly George let out a scream, followed an instant later by the report of the Belgian's gun: '*What the hell is that?*'

"Such a cry, Sally! My legs gave way.

"I saw the darkness bulge. It was leaking toward us; it was coming out of the trees. It was coming like a vast ocean of *siafu*, intent and ruthless and obscure like that, with a deep and cold intelligence. The terrifying thing about *siafu* is their *will*. They are utterly united, utterly faithful to their purpose. Once, I tried to snatch a tomato out of their path in our kitchen, and three of the ants went up my arm like fire.

"The Belgian was cursing. The torch had gone out. I felt a kick in my ribs, the toe of Vermeiren's boot. I've never felt so grateful to be kicked. 'Get up,' he was shouting, calling us bloody cowards and other things I won't repeat in your presence.

"I realized George lay beside me on the ground. 'George, George, are you all right?'

"'I've got to get out of here,' he sobbed. 'I've got to get out.'

"Somehow, each supporting the other, we staggered to our feet. The Belgian had retrieved the torch and ignited it with his tinderbox.

"'See!' he said triumphantly.

"There, at the edge of the teak grove, a native lay dead, shot through the heart. The darkness was natural now, empty, no longer the sentient thing it had been.

"'But—but—,' stammered George, 'it is Francisco!'

"He had abandoned his gun, and clasped my arm—whether in terror or some other emotion, I cannot say.

"'Who?' inquired our employer with a frown.

"George seemed unable to speak; I explained, therefore, that Francisco was the native George had put in the infirmary.

"'Nonsense,' said the Belgian. 'As if you'd recognize him!'

"'Turn him over,' whispered George, finding his voice at last, 'and let me see his back.'

"The Belgian refused to indulge what he called my friend's 'womanish horrors'; George, to my surprise, insisted passionately; but the Belgian stood firm, finally exclaiming: 'What difference would it make? You've lashed the lot of them, as well you should.' These words seemed to throw George into a sort of frenzy. It was with difficulty that I persuaded him back to his room, and into bed. He kept repeating that Francisco commanded an army of shadow selves, which, now that their master was dead, had swarmed across the world. 'One is another,' he babbled. And though I knew he was not well—he was so broken down, indeed, that I successfully petitioned the Belgian for a holiday—I could not shake my own sense that the darkness among the trees was *multiple*, and that George ought to have shouted, not 'What the hell is that,' but *'What the hell are those?'*"

Sarah puts on her bonnet at the glass. Neat black silk, with a generous brim that casts her features into shadow.

The wind beats the high windows. Her father sighs. Sarah touches her mother's cross.

Tonight, she will dream of tiny black eyes. A river of tiny black eyes. They're coming toward her. She lies on the grass, unable to rise. She's writhing and weeping. The eyes advance.

Waking, she will remain motionless in bed, her limbs icy. She will listen to the beating of her heart.

She will get out of bed. She'll find the matches and light the candle before the glass. Her own face will bloom toward her out of the dark. The same face that now regards her from the parlor glass, a face she has searched so often for a hint of her mother's ghost. This nose, this curving eyelid. Tonight she will take her candle and leave her room, she'll go to her father's room and shake him awake. "You called me an ant," she'll say. And he, sitting up, framed by wild white hair, "Why, Sally, what's come over you, are you mad?"

"I'm not an ant."

"But I never—"

"You said you saw her face."

"What?"

"You saw her face. In the forest. You said it saved you, the night the darkness came."

"Well, yes, I—"

"Was it the face of an ant?"

"What?"

"Did you see the face of an ant?"

And when he says nothing: "No. Of course not. An ant's face is too small."

He stares at her. White hair, white nightshirt, white wax from her candle dripping on the sheets. And his face in strange white motion. His skin quivers. She's never spoken like this to him before—has the disturbance, and the accusation, brought on some sort of attack? Gripped by remorse and terror—for how often has he told her, "You have no one but me, poor Sal"?—she leans to touch him, and realizes just in time that his arm is also trembling, his shirt is alive, a crowd of pale creatures swarms over his body.

Sarah steps back with a cry. She beats her hand against her night-dress, the hand that almost touched him. She is safe: her hand is dark and whole. She gazes at the thing in the bed, the thing in the shape of her father. It hisses softly, its tongue and teeth of small white bugs. "Help me." It arms make the motions of caressing something in its lap. A few red hairs protrude from the teeming pallor. "Help my baby," it hisses, before she wakes sweating in her bed again. "Help my little child. My baby boy."

"Yes, take a little extra with you, for the lilies. For poor George. Ah, I never told you about the trip to Meroe. Wait, before you go . . . this is what I meant to say, about that trip, the last time George and I were together as friends. Yes, the last time, for when we returned to the forest, I told him about my intention to marry, and he said those final words: 'You're dead to me.' He couldn't get over it, though I explained that your mother was a good woman, a trained nurse and a Christian convert . . . Well. But at Meroe we were quite happy. George clambered about on the ancient stones, whooping like a boy. I was afraid he'd get sunstroke, to tell the truth. We sat in the shade of a cracked mausoleum wall and ate our little picnic. George was cheerful, energetic, telling me all his plans. He was going to save enough to buy a cottage back home. Enough to marry a pleasant girl. You know I almost told him about my engagement then, but for some reason I held off . . . Ah, are you leaving? Well, bring me the big book on Kush before you go. That's the one. This is a treasure, my dear, bought for a song in Cairo, probably worth more than everything else in the house put together, remember that when I'm gone! Now look here. These are some of the paintings we saw in the tombs at Meroe. Marvelous, the way the desert air protects the color. In your poor mother's country these pictures would be eaten away by the damp. Look, here's the king, and under his feet, bound captives—a conquered people. Look how they fall beneath him in a line. And their arms and legs, twisted and broken, but repeated in the same pattern, as if with a stencil. Such precision! But the odd thing, you see, is that the same images appear in the tombs of Egypt. I recognized them as soon as I saw them, for I had visited the Valley of the Kings. As

I said, I thought of myself as a sort of archaeologist, and I remember I was very excited on that trip with George, thinking I might have made an important discovery. But when we got to Cairo, I found this book, and saw that the discovery had already been made. Egypt conquered Kush, you see, and the artists of Kush adopted Egypt's painting style. And generations later, these Kushite artists used these images, images of their own people, to depict their enemies! Isn't that odd? As if the images have no character at all. As if they are vessels that can be filled again and again. Simply the enemy. And what is required of the enemy's image? Only that the figures are identical, and that they are many."

Sarah goes out. She locks the door and tucks the key in her glove. She walks with her eyes fixed on an imaginary horizon. A pale face passes her, blurred. She senses a sneer, but does not see it. She allows it to pass her by like fog.

At the corner a man growls something at her. She steps aside quickly, avoiding his lunge. He shouts at her back. Muffled by her bonnet, his voice is the honk of a goose.

There are lilies at the Widow Cobb's. Sarah buys a dozen. She will not look at the Widow Cobb's pinched, resentful face. Let it blend into fog. She takes the flowers, but she does not go to the address on the black-bordered card. She goes to the harbor.

She sits on a bench. A cold wind blows from the water.

Sarah sets the lilies beside her and takes off her bonnet.

Cold. And the sound of the gulls. She never takes off her bonnet outdoors. Her heart races. She can hear children shouting somewhere nearby. Are they coming toward her? She picks up the heavy, funeral lilies, she begins to break the flowers from their stems.

Stems fall about her feet. They shift in the wind.

Sarah takes a lily and tucks it into the black band of the bonnet in her lap.

One by one, she tucks the lilies into the band. It's delicate work, and she takes off her gloves, her skin tightening in the raw air. She continues until all twelve lilies encircle the edge of the bonnet. She puts on her gloves and places the bonnet back over her hair.

Sarah is crowned by fragrance and by snow.

Across the water, a streak of gold slips stealthily through the clouds. Sunset soon. She will sit in the cold and wait for the clouds to break, saying her usual prayer for her mother, and adding one for the man known as Francisco. She will wait for the light to change, to take a shape rarely seen except in dreams, a shape that allows one to see, really see, to pierce the mist lying everywhere, and Sarah radiant in her crown will glimpse for a moment a world without fog, a vision undimmed by this—that—those.

A Girl Who Comes Out of a Chamber at Regular Intervals

"These automata are but vessels for our dreams; the wine they hold is the shadow of the future."

— Safiyya bint al-Jazari

I. On the construction of clocks from which can be told the passage of the secular hours

I am an ingenious invention. My father created me for the king. Lovely father! He made me a pleasant room with a dome of copper and tin. Here I stand with a cup in one hand and a handkerchief in the other, waiting patiently for my feet to be set in motion. This happens when wine is poured into the tube in my roof. I can hear it gurgling above me. Soon the liquid flows down and fills the cup in my right hand. When the cup is heavy enough, my arm drops down slightly—but not enough to spill the wine!—and releases the hook that holds me in place.

Hurrah! I roll along my track and push open the doors to my chamber. Hello, Father! For, up to now, only Father has greeted me at the door. He wants to make sure I am perfect before he presents me to the king. I believe I am perfect. I offer my father the cup and the handkerchief for his lips.

If the receptacle in my roof is kept full, I emerge from my chamber precisely eight times every hour.

My father jokes that he could tell time from me, like a clock. My father is large and clever. He has a thin beard and a long sad face. He smokes a great deal. I believe that his life is, in general, unhappy.

2. On the construction of vessels suitable for use at drinking bouts

My father drinks all the wine I offer to him. Once he has had several cups, he begins to make loose, experimental gestures, tossing his instruments up and catching them. Sometimes he forgets to push me back inside my chamber, and then I stand in the doorway and watch him at his work. This is so interesting! My father's workshop is full of brass pipes, glass and copper vessels, bundles of wire, wax molds and jugs of wine. The floor is strewn with sand. My father slips in the sand when he has been drinking wine, and sometimes, when he tosses his instruments up, he fails to catch them. Then he shouts for his apprentices. The apprentices are clumsy boys, none of them as handsome as my father. My father pulls their ears and beats them about the head with his slipper, and they weep. "Sons of bitches!" my father says.

My father sits on the floor with his head in his hands. He looks very gloomy. He calls me his lovely girl. He says he will be sorry to give me away. He tells me that the king will be my husband, the king in his splendor. He says no man deserves me but the king.

At night, he stops pouring wine. I stand in my chamber, in the dark. Then I have dreams. I dislike these dreams. My father does not know that I have them. They keep themselves secret from him, and this makes me unhappy. If I could speak, I would say: Father, I have had a terrible dream.

3. On the construction of vessels for bloodletting and washing

My father tells me that I will never bleed. I will always be perfectly clean. I am so happy to be clean and perfect! Human women bleed every month, he says. You could tell time from them, like clocks. It would be dreadful for me to bleed! I am made of plaster!

Father, I have had a terrible dream. I dreamt that I was a human woman and I was alone and I was bleeding. I curled on my side and bled. Outside the window, the world was all white, and I was bleeding a trickle the color of tobacco. Father, I was satisfied to be bleeding. There was pink paint on my fingernails and I was absorbed in picking it off. I burrowed deep in my sadness. I wanted more pain, more grief, delirium. Someone important had left me. Was it the king?

4. On the construction of fountains in tanks

I must have gone to sleep. When I woke I noticed that the stain on the wall, so small as to be hardly noticeable under ordinary circumstances, was spreading. The more I looked at it, the larger it appeared. In fact, I was having trouble finding its edges. It was growing darker, too. I tried to remember who lived in the apartment next door. Yes, yes, the new tenant, the one with the tank on her head! She had a lung condition which required her to observe the world from within the shelter of a glass tank, like a fish. The tank looked uncomfortable and heavy. It was attached to her body with straps. She walked extremely slowly. She was apparently self-employed. The landlord said she would be no trouble and someone else said it was nice that thanks to computers people like that could make a living without leaving the house.

I went out into the hall and knocked at her door. "Hello? Hello?" I didn't know her name. No one answered, but there was a sound from inside the room. The sound of running water. I noticed that some sort of gum had been placed around the edges of the door to seal it tight.

"Hello? Hello!"

"What is it?" came the new tenant's muffled, mechanical voice—a voice without resonance, a voice in a box.

"Are you all right?"

She laughed.

I rattled the doorknob. "Let me in!"

I turned sideways and struck the door with the force of my whole body.

"Jada!" I shouted. I knew now, I remembered. The field of ashes and then the tree, half blossoming and half burned, in the middle of the courtyard. We dragged her from the rubble. She whispered: "Water." Her swollen face. I could picture it now, behind glass, on the other side of the door.

5. On the construction of instruments for raising water from shallow pools

We ran across the field. My legs were wet. My lungs had shrunk. There was no sound now. We would not be able to hear well for several days. We would read one another's lips in the drifting ash, in the burned town, in the shadow of the single edifice left standing. This was the art museum. Its windows were gone. Burnt canvases littered the empty streets—we found one or two as far away as the canal. I went to the canal to fetch water for Jada. The water was the color of tobacco. She drank thirstily and whispered: "Thank you."

We had been artists. We said that we were going to be artists again. We called the tree in the courtyard "the Tree of Hope." "Tree of Hope, keep firm," Jada would say. Her voice a rustle, a sigh. When she got too tired, I carried her on my back. We collected the wrecked paintings and made a mosaic of them in the courtyard, held down with stones. That was before the recovery effort started. Once it started, we saw we wouldn't be able to keep our artwork. Jada stared at it all day, to memorize it. Nobody had a camera.

6. On the construction of an automaton representing two men drinking

It was my turn to keep watch, but I fell asleep against the courtyard wall. Fast asleep and dreaming with my eyes open.

I awake in a chair. The room all white. My arms outstretched. I am sleepy, heavy and smiling. Turning my head I can see a man on either side. One on my left and one on my right. They are draining the blood from my wrists with needles. The dark stuff runs away through a pair of tubes.

Good-bye, blood! I feel no pain. On the contrary, I am quite happy. I gaze at my doctors with tenderness, first one and then the other. My ministers, administrators, ministering angels. One has a beard, the other a beautiful gold watch. One of them loves me, I know, and the other hates me, but their work is the same, and my love for them is absolutely equal. Desire for me unites them: this makes me the center of the world. I smile at my angels, who will drain me as dry as plaster.

They are talking. Arguing. "No!" I want to tell them. "Don't fight! Love one another!" But my tongue is too thick to move.

They have left their posts and stalked behind me. I can still hear their shouts. Now there's the sound of a struggle, the clatter of breaking glass!

A moment later—silence.

I struggle to move my tongue. I am trying to say hello. Can you hear me saying hello?

A long stillness. Something seems to be pressing on my wrists. I am still calm, but it occurs to me that soon I will start to feel pain.

I cry out, wordless. A gurgling sound. Then I hear footsteps. Yes! Closer! Tap-tapping steps. A nurse in a white coat and headscarf comes into the room.

"Oh my God," she says.

She makes a few efficient movements at each of my wrists. My arms are numb. She brings them together and crosses them in my lap. She has covered my wrists with white tape. "Oh God oh God," she says, "my job, I can't lose my job, I can't lose another job."

I want to tell her that it's all right, that the universe is happy, but a strange feeling is coming back to me with the pain in my wrists and arms.

The nurse bends close. Her smell is sharp: terror and eau de cologne. "You have to move with me now," she whispers. "You have to help."

A feeling is coming back to me. It's not here yet; I'm searching for it. I stare at the nurse. Her face is tense, familiar. Something inside me breaks. I lift my arms and put them around her shoulders, and she heaves me out of the chair. Together we stagger out into the hall.

What is the nature of things? The mechanism works perfectly for years; then one day it breaks.

The nurse half-carries me downstairs, to a dark basement. She shares her lunch with me for three days. She doesn't ask my name. She doesn't want to know anything, it's dangerous. We play the game of "asfoura" on her phone. She lets me win.

That's how it happens. One day something springs loose, and the clock stops. The clock is bleeding.

The nurse brings me a new set of clothes. Her eyes are red. She says it isn't safe for me to stay here anymore. She writes down an address and tells me to go there.

7. On the construction of miscellaneous objects

The nurse holds the back door open for me. "Run."

We'd started fighting, Jada and I. I said, "It's a recovery effort. It's an effort to recover. Can't you understand that?" She said, "What? Recover what? I don't want to recover, I don't want to go back." She said everything was going to be the same, it would be like it was before the struggle. I said that was ridiculous, the world had changed forever. "Everything's out in the open." "You think we're going to stay out in the open?" she asked. "I wouldn't mind going inside," I snapped. "A roof would be nice for a change."

I ran down the stairs and banged on the landlord's door. This is how you forget: first slowly, then quickly. First you forget because you don't want to remember. You forget the war. You call it "the last war," because it's the most recent one, and then you call it "the last war" because you hope it's the last one, and then you don't call it anything, and they put new turf in the ravaged municipal gardens, and the water in the fountains runs clear. And this forgetting is so pleasant! And then you stop calling the people you knew, you forget their faces. And then you find you've forgotten her face. I banged on the landlord's door. "Help me! Help!" At last he opened it, sleepy and startled. His sleeve was damp. The ceiling was leaking.

Father, I have terrible dreams.

Father! Good morning, Father!

My father smiles at me, but he looks haggard. Poor Father!
I cannot look haggard, for my face is only painted.
He says we are going to visit the king today.

❧

8. On the construction of an instrument that plays itself

I cannot see anything when my doors are closed, for my chamber has no windows. This is a pity, for I am sure the palace is splendid! My father carries me himself; he will not trust me to the apprentices. I find myself carried up into fragrant air. I hear delicate music and the plashing of fountains. This is the day! I am so nervous, I am thankful to be made of plaster and wire. These materials hide one's feelings much better than flesh. Father, for instance—poor man, I can feel his hands trembling.

His voice quivers, too, as he explains his invention to the king. "We pour the wine here . . ." And there it is, gurgling down into the tube. He fills the receptacle to the top. "Now wait, Your Majesty!" My cup grows heavy; I can hardly bear the excitement.

Full!

I roll down and open the door. There he is. The king. He is large, like Father, but younger, and dressed in gleaming white. He chuckles and takes the cup. I am dazzled by his robe, the windows, the sparkling floor, the brass lamps hanging on long chains.

The king drinks. "Hm!" he says.

My father makes a sound like a sob. Is he so happy?

No! For the king is turning yellow. He clutches his throat.

My father weeps and falls to his knees. The room erupts in noise. People run toward us. They cradle the king in their arms, they stroke his brow with fine cloths. As for my father, they bind his arms behind him and pull his beard. As they drag him away, he gives me one last, anguished glance.

"The king is dead! The king is dead!"

Wails clash in the air. The king's body is lifted gently and carried away. Now the room is empty, and there is no sound but the fragile clink of music issuing from a box across the room.

Father, Father!

My father has slain my husband, and gone to prison.

How fortunate that I cannot cry. I would ruin my paint!

The room is quiet. Who will push me back into my chamber? Who will fill my roof receptacle with wine? Beneath the notes of music from the box, I can hear a roar from far below, the sound of frenzied crowds and fire. Smoke drifts in through the window. I cannot weep, but I am weeping. I remember a tree in a courtyard, half in bloom. The Tree of Hope. We called it the Tree of Hope. I remember the nurse in white, so tired, pressing banknotes into my hand.

I dreamt that I was a real woman and that I bled.

Weeping inside, I see a bright brass figure on top of the music box. A woman's torso. The box is meant to represent her skirt. She looks calm, resigned, familiar. Is she smiling?

I feel I must speak, if only in my mind. "Who are you?" I ask. Will she hear me?

She hears. I sense, rather than see, her deepening smile. She is not afraid of the noise downstairs. She has lived through fire in her dreams.

She says: "I am an instrument that plays itself."

How to Get Back to the Forest

"You have to puke it up," said Cee. "You have to get down there and puke it up. I mean down past where you can feel it, you know?"

She gestured earnestly at her chest. She had this old-fashioned cotton nightgown on, lace collar brilliant under the bathroom lights. Above the collar, her skin looked gray. Cee had bones like a bird. She was so beautiful. She was completely beautiful and fucked. I mean everybody at camp was sort of a mess, we were even supposed to be that way, at a *difficult stage*, but Cee took it to another level. Herding us into the bathroom at night and asking us to puke. "It's right here," she said, tapping the nightgown over her hollow chest. "Where you've got less nerves in your esophagus. It's like wired into the side, into the muscle. You have to puke really hard to get it."

"Did you ever get it out?" asked Max. She was sitting on one of the sinks. She'd believe anything.

Cee nodded, solemn as a counselor. "Two years ago. They caught me and gave me a new one. But it was beautiful while it was gone. I'm telling you it was the best."

"Like how?" I said.

Cee stretched out her arms. "Like bliss. Like everything. Everything all at once. You're raw, just a big raw nerve."

"That doesn't sound so great," said Elle.

"I know," said Cee, not annoyed but really agreeing, turning things around. That was one of her talents.

"It sounds stupid," she nodded, "but that's because it's something we can't imagine. We don't have the tools. Our bodies don't know how to calculate what we're missing. You can't know till you get there. And at the same time, it's where you came from. It's where you *started*."

She raised her toothbrush. "So. Who's with me?"

Definitely not me. God, Cee. You were such an idiot.

Apparently, a girl named Puss had told her about the bug. And Cee, being Cee, was totally open to learning new things from a person who called herself Puss. Puss had puked out her own bug and was living on the streets. I guess she'd run away from camp, I don't really know. She was six feet tall, Cee said, with long red hair. The hair was dyed, which was weird, because if you're living on the streets do you care about stuff like that? This kind of thing can keep me awake at night. I lie in bed, or rather I sit in the living room because Pete hates me tossing and turning, and I leave the room dark and open all the curtains, and I watch the lights of the city and think about this girl Puss getting red hair dye at the grocery store and doing her hair in the bathroom at the train station. Did she put newspapers down? And what if somebody came in and saw her?

Anyway, eventually Cee met Puss in the park, and Puss was clearly down-and-out and a hooker but she looked cool and friendly, and Cee sat down beside her on the swings.

"You have to puke it up."

❧

96

We'd only been at camp for about six weeks. It seemed like a long time, long enough to know everybody. Everything felt stretched out at camp, the days and the nights, and yet in the end it was over so fast, as soon as you could blink. Camp was on its own calendar—*a special time of life*. That was Jodi's phrase. She was our favorite counselor. She was greasy and enthusiastic, with a skinny little ponytail, only a year or two older than the seniors. *Camp is so special!* The thing with Jodi was, she believed every word she said. It made it really hard to make fun of her. That night, the night in the bathroom, she was asleep down the hall underneath her Mother Figure, which was a little stuffed dog with *Florida* on its chest.

"Come on!" said Cee. And she stuck her toothbrush down her throat, just like that. I think Max screamed. Cee didn't start puking right away. She had to give herself a few really good shoves with that toothbrush, while people said "Oh my God" and backed away and clutched one another and stared. Somebody said, "Are you nuts?" Somebody else said something else, I might have said something, I don't know, everything was so white and bright in that moment, mirrors and fluorescent lights and Cee in that goddamn Victorian nightgown jabbing away with her toothbrush and sort of gagging. Every time I looked up I could see all of us in the mirror. And then it came. A splatter of puke all over the sink. Cee leaned over and braced herself. *Blam.* Elle said, "Oh my God that is disgusting." Cee gasped. She was just getting started.

Elle was next. All of a sudden she spun around with her hands over her mouth and let go in the sink right next to Cee. *Splat.* I started laughing, but I already felt sort of dizzy and sick myself, and also scared, because I didn't want to throw up. Cee looked up from her own sink and nodded at Elle, encouraging her. She looked completely bizarre, her wide cheekbones, her big crown of natural hair, sort of a retro supermodel with a glistening mouth, her eyes full of excitement. I think she even said, "Good job, Elle!"

Then she went to it with the toothbrush again. "We have to stop her!" said Katie, taking charge. "Max, go get Jodi!" But Max didn't make it. She jumped down from the third sink, but when she got halfway to the door she turned around and ran back to the sink and puked. Meanwhile Katie was dragging Cee away from the sink and trying to get the toothbrush, but also not wanting to touch it, and she kept going "Ew ew ew" and "*Help* me you guys," and it was all so hilarious I sank down on the floor, absolutely crying with laughter. Five or six other girls, too. We just sort of looked at each other and screamed. It was mayhem. Katie dragged Cee into one of the stalls, I don't know why. Then Katie started groaning and let go of Cee and staggered into the stall beside her, and *sploosh*, there she went.

Bugs.

It's such a camp rumor. Camp is full of stories like that. People say the ice cream makes you sterile, the bathrooms are full of hidden cameras, there's fanged, flesh-eating kids in the lake, if you break into the office you can call your parents. Lots of kids break into the office. It's the most common camp offense. I never tried it, because I'm not stupid—of course you can't call your parents. How would you even get their number? And bugs—the idea of a bug planted under your skin, to track you or feed you drugs—that's another dumb story.

Except it's not, because I saw one.

The smell in the bathroom was terrible now—an animal smell, hot; it thrashed around and it had fur.

I knew I was going to be sick. I crawled to the closest place—the stall where Cee knelt—and grabbed hold of the toilet seat. Cee moved aside for me. Would you believe she was still hanging onto her toothbrush? I think we both threw up a couple of times. Then she made this awful sound, beyond anything, her whole body taut and straining, and something flew into the toilet with a splash.

I looked at her and there was blood all over her chin. I said "Jesus, Cee." I thought she was dying. She sat there coughing and shaking, her eyes full of tears and triumph. She was on top of the world. "Look!" she breathed. And I looked, and there in the bowl, half-hidden by puke and blood, lay an object made of metal.

It actually looked like a bug. Sharp blood-smeared legs.

"Shit!" I said. I flushed the toilet.

"Now you," said Cee, wiping her mouth on the back of her wrist.

"I can't."

"Tisha. Come on."

Cee, I couldn't, I really couldn't. I could be sick—in fact I felt sicker than ever—but I couldn't do it that hard. I remember the look in your eyes; you were so disappointed. You leaned and spat some blood into the toilet.

I whispered: "Don't tell anyone. Not even the other girls."

"Why not? We should all—"

"No. Just trust me."

I was already scared, so scared. I couldn't bear the idea of camp without you.

We barely slept that night. We had to take showers and clean the bathroom. Max cried the whole time, but for at least part of the night, I was laughing. Me and Katie flinging disinfectant powder everywhere. Katie was cool, always in sweatpants, didn't give a shit about anything.

"You know your friend is a headcase, right?" she said.

It was the first time anybody'd called Cee my friend. We got out the mop and lathered up the floor. Everyone slipped and swore at us, coming out of the showers. Cee went skidding by in a towel. "Whee!" she shrieked.

You cannot feel your bug. I've pressed so hard on my chest. I know.

"*I* could feel it," said Cee. "After they put it back in." It wasn't exactly a physical thing. She couldn't trace the shape of the bug inside her, but she could feel it *working*.

"Bug juice," she said, making a sour face. She could feel bug juice seeping into her body. Every time she was going to be angry or afraid, there'd be this warmth in her chest, a feeling of calm spreading deep inside.

"I only noticed it after I'd had the bug out for a couple of weeks."

"How did your parents know you needed a new one?"

"I didn't need one."

"How did they know it was gone?"

"Well, I kind of had this fit. I got mad at them and started throwing food."

We were sitting on my bed, under my Mother Figure, a lamp with a blue shade. The blue light brought out the stains on Cee's Victorian nightgown. We were both painting our toenails Cherry Pink, balancing the polish on my Life Skills textbook, taking turns with the brush.

"You should do it," Cee said. "I feel better. I'm so much better."

I thought how in a minute we'd have to study for our Life Skills quiz. I didn't think there was bug juice in my body. I couldn't feel anything.

"I'm so much better," Cee said again. Her hand was shaking.

Oh, Cee.

The weird thing is, I started writing this after Max came to visit me, and I thought I was going to write about Max. But then I started writing in your book. Why? This book you left me, your Mother Figure. You practically threw it at me: "Take it!" It was the worst thing you could do, to take somebody else's Parent Figure, especially the mom. Or maybe it was only us girls who cared so much about the moms. Maybe for the boys it was the dads. But anyway taking one was the worst; you could basically expect the other kids to kill you. A kid got put in the hospital that way at a different camp—the one on the east side—but we all knew about it at our camp. They strung him up with electric wires. Whenever we told the story we ended by saying what *we* would have done to that kid, and it was always much worse.

But you threw this book at me, Cee, and what could I do? Jodi and Duncan were trying to grab your arms, and the ambulance was waiting for you downstairs. I caught the book clumsily, crumpling it. I looked at it later, and it was about half full of your writing. I think they're poems.

> *dank smells underground want to get back*
> *no pill for it*
> *i need you*

I don't know, are they poems? If they are, I don't think they're very good. *A nap could be a door an abandoned car.* Does that even mean anything? *Eat my teeth.* I know them all by heart.

I picked up this book when Max left. I wrote: "You have to puke it up." All of a sudden I was writing about you. Surprising myself. I just kept going. Remembering camp, the weird sort of humid excitement there, the cafeteria louder than the sea. The shops—remember the shops? Lulu's was the best. We'd save up our allowance to go there. Down in the basement you could get used stuff for cheap. You got your leather jacket there. I got these red shoes with flowers on the toes. I loved those shoes so much! I wonder where they went? I wore them to every mixer, I was wearing them when I met Pete, probably with my white dress—another Lulu's purchase I don't have now.

It was summer, and the mixer had an island theme. The counselors had constructed this sort of deck overlooking the lake. God, they were so proud of it. They gave us green drinks with little umbrellas in them and played lazy, sighing music, and everyone danced, and Pete saw a shooting star, and we were holding hands, and you were gone forever and I forgot you.

❧

I forgot you. Forgetting isn't so wrong. It's a Life Skill.

I don't remember what my parents looked like. A Parent Figure cannot be a photograph. It has to be a more neutral object. It's supposed to stand in for someone, but not too much.

When we got to camp we were all supposed to bring our Parent Figures to dinner the first night. Everyone squeezed in at the cafeteria tables, trying to find space beside their dinner trays for their Figures, those calendars and catcher's mitts and scarves. I felt so stupid because my Mother Figure was a lamp and there was no place to plug it in. My Father Figure is a plaque that says *Always be yourself.*

Jodi came by, as the counselors were all going around "meeting the Parents," and she said, "Wow, Tisha, that's a *good* one."

I don't even know if I picked it out.

"We want you to have a fabulous time at camp!" Jodi cried. She was standing at the front with the other counselors: Paige and Veronica and Duncan—who we'd later call "Hunky Duncan"—and Eric and Carla and the others.

Of course they'd chosen Jodi to speak. Jodi was so perky.

She told us that we were beginning a special relationship with our Parent Figures. It was very important not to *fixate*. We shouldn't fixate on the Parent Figures and we definitely shouldn't fixate on the counselors.

My stupid lamp. It was so fucking blue. Why would you bring something blue? "The most important people in your life are the other campers!" Jodi burbled. "These are the people you'll know for the rest of your life! Now, I want you to turn to the person next to you and say, *Hi, Neighbor!*"

Hi, Neighbor! And later, in the forest, Cee sang to the sky: *Fuck you, Neighbor!*

Camp was special. We were told that it was special. At camp you connected with people and with nature. There was no personal tech. That freaked a lot of people out at first. We were told that later we'd all be able to get online again, but we'd be adults, and our relationships would be in place, and we would have learned our Life Skills, and we'd be ready. But now was special: now was the time of friends and of the earth.

Cee raised her hand: "What about earthquakes?"

"What?" said Veronica, who taught The Natural World. Veronica was from an older group of counselors; she had gray hair and leathery skin from taking kids on nature hikes and she was always stretching to show that you could be flexible when you were old.

"What about earthquakes?" Cee asked. "What about fires? Those are natural. What about hurricanes?"

Veronica smiled at us with her awesome white teeth, because you could have awesome white teeth when you were old, it was all a matter of taking care of yourself with the right Life Skills.

"What an interesting question, Celia!"

We were told that all of our questions were interesting. *There's no such thing as a stupid question!* The important thing was always to *participate*. We were told to participate in classes and hikes and shopping sprees and mixers.

In History we learned that there used to be prejudice, but now there wasn't: it didn't matter where you came from or who you loved, *just join in!* That's why even the queer girls had to go to the mixers; you could take your girlfriend but you had to go. Katie used to go in a tie and Elle would wear flowers. They rolled their eyes but they went anyway and danced and it was fun. Camp was so fun.

Cee raised her hand: "Why is it a compliment to tell somebody it doesn't matter who they are?"

We were told to find a hobby. There were a million choices and we tried them all: sports and crafts and art and music. There was so much to do. Every day there was some kind of program and then there were chores and then we had to study for class. No wonder we forgot stuff. We were told that forgetting was natural. Forgetting helped us survive, Jodi told us in Life Skills class, tears in her eyes. She cried as easily as Max. She was more like a kid sister than a counselor. Everybody wanted Jodi to be okay. "You'll always be reminded," she said in her hoarse, heroic voice. "You'll always have your Parent Figures. It's okay to be sad! But remember, you have each other now. It's the most special bond in the world."

Cee raised her hand: "What if we don't want us?"

Cee raised her hand, but of course she raised her hand. She was *Cee*. She was Cee, she'd always been Cee, do you see what I mean? I mean she was like that right from the day we arrived; she was brash, messy Cee *before* the night in the bathroom, before she supposedly puked out her bug. I couldn't see any difference. *I could not see any difference.*

So of course I had second thoughts. I wished so bad I hadn't flushed the toilet. What if there wasn't anything in it? What if somebody'd dropped a piece of jewelry in there, some necklace or brooch and I thought it was a bug? That could have happened.

Camp was so fun. Shaving my legs for the mixer. Wearing red shoes. We were all so lucky. Camp was the best thing ever.

Every Child at Camp! That was the government slogan: *ECAC.* Cee used to make this gag face whenever she said it. *ECAC.* Ick. Sick.

She took me into the forest. It was a mixer. Everybody else was crowded around the picnic tables. The lake was flat and scummy and the sun was just going down, clouds of biting insects golden in the haze.

"Come on," Cee said, "let's get out of here."

We walked over the sodden sand into the weeds. A couple of the counselors watched us go: I saw Hunky Duncan look at us with his binoculars, but because we were just two girls they didn't care. It only mattered if you left the mixer with a boy. Then you had to stop at the Self-Care Stand for condoms and an injection, because *becoming a parent is a serious decision!* Duncan lowered his binoculars, and we stepped across the rocks and into the trees.

"This is cool!" Cee whispered.

I didn't really think it was cool—it was weird and sticky in there, and sort of dark, and the weeds kept tickling my legs—but I went farther because of Cee. It's hard to explain this thing she had: she was like an event just about to happen and you didn't want to miss it.

I didn't want to, anyway.

It was so dark we had to hold hands after a while. Cee walked in front of me, pushing branches out of the way, making loud crackling sounds, sometimes kicking to break through the bushes. Her laugh sounded close, like we were trapped in the basement at Lulu's. That's what it was like, like being trapped in this amazing place where everything was magically half-price. I was so excited and then horrified because suddenly I had to take a dump, there was no way I could hold it in.

"Wait a sec," I told Cee, too embarrassed to even tell her to go away. I crouched down and went and wiped myself on the leaves, and I'm sure Cee knew what was up but she took my hand again right after I was done. She took my disgusting hand. I felt like I wanted to die, and at the same time, I was floating. We kept going until we stumbled into a clearing in the woods. Stars above us in a perfect circle.

"*Woo-hooooo!*" Cee hollered. "Fuck you, Neighbor!"

She gave the stars the finger. The silhouette of her hand stood out against the bright. I gave the stars the finger, too. I was this shitty, disgusting kid with a lamp and a plaque for parents but I was there with Cee and the time was exactly now. It was like there was a beautiful starry place we'd never get into— didn't *deserve* to get into—but at the same time we were better than any brightness. Two sick girls underneath the stars.

Fuck you, Neighbor! It felt so great. If I could go anywhere I'd want to go there.

The counselors came for us after a while. A circle of them with big flashlights, talking in handsets. Jodi told us they'd been looking everywhere for us. "We were pretty worried about you girls!"

For the first time I didn't feel sorry for her; I felt like I wanted to kick her in the shins. Shit, I forgot about that until right now. I forget so much. I'm like a sieve. Sometimes I tell Pete I think I'm going senile. Like premature senile dementia. Last month I suggested we go to Clearview for our next vacation and he said, "Tish, you hate Clearview, don't you remember?"

It's true, I hated Clearview: the beach was okay but at night there was nothing to do but drink. So we're going to go to the Palace Suites instead. At least you can gamble there.

Cee, I wonder about you still, so much—I wonder what happened to you and where you are. I wonder if you've ever tried to find me. It wouldn't be hard. If you linked to the register you'd know our graduating class ended up in Food Services. I'm in charge of inventory for a chain of grocery stores, Pete drives delivery, Katie stocks the shelves.

The year before us, the graduates of our camp went into the army; the year after us they also went into the army; the year after that they went into communication technologies; the year after that I stopped paying attention. I stopped wondering what life would have been like if I'd graduated in a different year.

We're okay. Me and Pete—we make it work, you know? He's sad because I don't want to have kids, but he hasn't brought it up for a couple of years.

We do the usual stuff, hobbies and vacations. Work. Pete's into gardening. Once a week we have dinner with some of the gang. We keep our Parent Figures on the hall table, like everyone else. Sometimes I think about how if you'd graduated with us, you'd be doing some kind of job in Food Services too. That's weird, right?

But you didn't graduate with us. I guess you never graduated at all.

꧁

I've looked for you on the buses and in the streets. Wondering if I'd suddenly see you. God, I'd jump off the bus so quick, I wouldn't even wait for it to stop moving. I wouldn't care if I fell in the gutter.

I remember your tense face, your nervous look, when you found out that we were going to have a check-up.

"I can't have a check-up," you said.

"Why not?" I asked.

"Because," you said, "because they'll see my bug is gone."

And I just—I don't know. I felt sort of embarrassed for you. I'd convinced myself the whole bug thing was a mistake, a hallucination. I looked down at my book, and when I looked up you were standing in the same place, with an alert look on your face, as if you were listening.

You looked at me and said: "I have to run."

It was the stupidest thing I'd ever heard. The whole camp was monitored practically up to the moon. There was no way to get outside.

But you tried. You left my room, and you went straight out your window and broke your ankle.

A week later, you were back. You were on crutches and you looked . . . wrecked. Destroyed. Somebody'd cut your hair, shaved it close to the scalp. Your eyes stood out, huge and shining.

"They put in a bug in me," you whispered.

And I just knew. I knew what you were going to do.

Max came to see me a few days ago. I've felt sick ever since. Max is the same, hunched and timid; you'd know her if you saw her. She sat in my living room and I gave her coffee and lemon cookies and she took one bite of a cookie and started crying.

Cee, we miss you, we really do.

Max told me she's pregnant. I said congratulations. I knew she and Evan have been wanting one for a while. She covered her eyes with her hands—she still bites her nails, one of them was bleeding—and she just cried.

"Hey, Max," I said, "it's okay."

I figured she was extra-emotional from hormones or whatever, or maybe she was thinking what a short time she'd have with her kid, now that kids start camp at eight years old.

"It's okay," I told her, even though I'd never have kids, I couldn't stand it.

They say it's easier on the kids, going to camp earlier. We—me and you and Max—we were the tail end of Generation Teen. Max's kid will belong to Generation Eight. It's supposed to be a happier generation, but I'm guessing it will be sort of like us. Like us, the kids of Generation Eight will be told they're sad, that they need their parents and that's why they have Parent Figures, so that they can always be reminded of what they've lost, so that they can remember they need what they have now.

I sat across the coffee table from Max, and she was crying and I wasn't hugging her because I don't really hug people anymore, not even Pete really, I'm sort of mean that way, it's just how I turned out, and Max said, "Do you remember that night in the bathroom with Cee?"

Do I remember?

Her eyes were all swollen. She hiccupped.

"I can't stop thinking about it. I'm scared." She said she had to send a report to her doctor every day on her phone. How was she feeling, had she vomited? Her morning sickness wasn't too bad, but she'd thrown up twice, and both times she had to go in for a check-up.

"So?" I said.

"So—they always put you to sleep, you know . . ."

"Yeah."

I just said "Yeah." Just sat there in front of her and said "Yeah." Like I was a rock. After a while I could tell she was feeling uncertain, and then she felt stupid. She picked up her stuff and blew her nose and went home. She left the tissues on the table, one of them spotted with blood from her bitten nail. I haven't really been sleeping since she left. I mean, I've always had trouble sleeping, but now it's a lot worse, especially since I started writing in your book. I just feel sick, Cee, I feel really sick. All those check-ups, so regular, everyone gets them, but you're definitely supposed to go in if you're feeling nauseous, if you've vomited, *it might be a superflu!* The world is full of viruses, *good health is everybody's business!* And yeah, they put you to sleep every time. Yeah. "They put a bug in me," you said. Camp was so fun. Jodi came to us, wringing her hands. "Cee has been having some problems, and it's up to all of us to look after her, girls! *Campers stick together!*" But we didn't stick together, did we? I woke up and you were shouting in the hall, and I ran out there and you were hopping on your good foot, your toothbrush in one hand, your Mother Figure notebook in the other, and I knew exactly what they'd caught you doing. How did they catch you? Were there really cameras in the bathroom? Jodi'd called Duncan, and that was how I knew how bad it was: Hunky Duncan in the girls' hallway, just outside the bathroom, wearing white shorts and a seriously pissed-off expression. He and Jodi were grabbing you and you were fighting them off. "Tisha," called Jodi, "it's okay, Cee's just sick, she's going to the hospital." You threw the notebook. "Take it!" you snarled. Those were your last words. Your last words to me. I never saw you again except in dreams. Yeah, I see you in dreams. I see you in your white lacy nightgown. Cee, I feel sick. At night I feel so sick, I walk around in circles. There's waves of sickness and waves of something else, something that calms me, something that's trying to make the sickness go away. Up and down it goes, and I'm just in it, just trying to stand it, and then I sleep again, and I dream you're beside me, we're leaning over the toilet, and down at the very bottom there's something like a clump of trees and two tiny girls are standing there giving us the finger. It's not where I came from, but it's where I *started*. I think of how bright it was in the bathroom that night, how some kind of loss swept through all of us, electric, and you'd started it, you'd started it by yourself, and we were with you in that hilarious and total rage of loss. Let's lose it. Let's lose everything. Camp wasn't fun. Camp was a fucking factory. I go out to the factory on Fridays to check my lists over coffee with Elle. The bus passes shattered buildings, stick people rooting around in the garbage. Three out of five graduating classes join the army. *Give me the serenity to accept the things I cannot change!* How did I even get here? I'd ask my mom if she wasn't a fucking lamp. Cee, I feel sick. I should just grab my keys, get some money, and run to Max's house, we should both be sick, everybody should lose it together. I shouldn't have told you not to tell the others. We all should have gone together. My fault. I dream I find you and Puss in a bathroom in the train station. There's blood everywhere, and you laugh and tell me it's hair dye. Cee, it's so bright it makes me sick. I have to go now. It's got to come out.

tender
landscapes

Tender

I am a tender. I tend the St. Benedict Radioactive Materials Containment Center. I perceive the outside world through treated glass. My immediate surroundings are barren but comfortable. I can order anything I like, necessity or luxury, from the Federal Sustainability Program. The items I order are delivered by truck and placed in a transfer box that decontaminates everything that enters it, including the air. The purpose of this system is not to protect me from contamination by the outside world, but to protect the world from me.

St. Benedict's is meant to be a temporary facility, a place to hold materials destined for deep, permanent burial, but the fears of the public make it so hard to create permanent facilities that no one knows how long this place will be necessary. My job is to monitor the levels of toxicity in and around the containment vault and submit reports to the Sustainability Program. "I used to be very unhappy," I wrote recently to the psych team, "but now I am happy because I have meaningful work." As usual, the psych team gave me an excellent evaluation. I am considered a model employee.

⌁

I went through six evaluations before I was accepted as a tender. They had to make sure I wasn't, as they put it, "actively suicidal." "We know you've been through a tough time," one doctor told me frankly. Later, when I was accepted, she thanked me for my "sacrifice."

I am equipped with sensors, implanted under the skin up and down my back, which enable me to detect changes in toxicity levels the instant they occur. I can feel the degree of these changes, where they are located, and whether they require observation or action. It's like a sixth sense: not at all painful, and far more efficient than collecting and interpreting data. I know, however, that most people find the idea of implantation distasteful. *They've turned you into a cyborg!* wrote my best friend, the one I privately call my hurt friend, the one who still visits me.

So? I wrote back. I reminded her that the earth beneath our feet, the soil we consider the body of nature itself, is composed of air, water, minerals, and organic matter. Earth, the Mother, is also a cyborg. I added: *To tell you the truth, I find it comforting to know how poisonous everything is. I am perfectly attuned to what is good and bad. I always know the right thing to do. Yes, my sensors are strange, but they have given me something akin to a moral compass.*

In my twenty-acre glass enclosure, in my beautiful little house, in my bedroom softened by quilts and golden lamps, I read about the dawn of the nuclear age. I am moved by the young physicists, their bravery, their zeal. The delicate, somehow childish cranium of Niels Bohr. Enrico Fermi's bright melancholy gaze. Glenn Seaborg, awarded a Nobel Prize for his role in discovering plutonium, said: "I was a 28-year-old kid and I didn't stop to ruminate about it." This devil-may-care attitude seems to characterize many scientists and lies perhaps at the heart of all human advancement. Newton sticking a bodkin into his eye to investigate perception. The doctors Donald Blacklock and Saul Adler injecting themselves with chimpanzee blood.

My reading light beams gently across the desert. Insects are drawn to it but frustrated by the barrier of the glass. I fear no human intruder: my hermitage is surrounded in all directions by signs bearing the skull and crossbones.

The history of nuclear physics is a grand romance. It has everything: passion, triumph, betrayal. Those of us who work as tenders have been left holding the baby, so to speak. The half-life of plutonium-239 is 24,100 years.

Once upon a time, the story goes, some young men discovered an element. They soon realized it could produce an almost infinite amount of energy. The possibilities appeared endless, the future dazzling. There was only one problem: the element was toxic.

Once upon a time, goes another version, two young people fell in love. This love produced an almost infinite amount of energy. The possibilities appeared endless, the future dazzling. There was only one problem: one of the people was toxic.

My hurt friend visits me once a month. She used to arrive in a van driven by an assistant, but now she drives herself in a specially equipped car. She is able to walk from the car to my glass wall without a cane. "Progress!" she says wryly. She does not believe in progress.

We used to argue regularly about this, as I worked in an energy lab and believed I saw progress every day. My hurt friend was a dancer. "Don't you see yourself improving?" I asked her. "Aren't you a better dancer now than you were last year?" We were seated in a crowded restaurant and I admit I glanced at my phone to check the time. I only had twenty minutes for lunch. If the food didn't come soon I'd have to take it to go. When I looked up my friend was gazing unseeingly into the crowd, tapping her finger against her lip. "No," she said slowly. "I'm not a better dancer in any meaningful way. I think there might be something wrong with your question." I remember thinking how detached and ethereal she was, but that was nothing compared to what followed, after her injury, when she became nearly transparent.

But let us return to the story of the Toxic Lover. She was completely unaware that she was toxic. She supposed, rather, that she was beautiful, talented, and kind, destined to succeed in all aspects of life. Nothing around her contradicted these convictions. Moving from triumph to triumph, she soon had an excellent job at an energy lab, a handsome and devoted husband (the envy of all her friends), a charming small daughter, and a home overlooking a lake. Positive adjectives clashed about her constantly: it was like living inside a wind-chime. At work, she was responsible for bringing plutonium left over from the arms race into use as a source of energy. When the material proved too unstable and the project failed, she quickly recovered her footing and turned to the creation of containment centers. Her team produced small green stickers to show their commitment to the earth. Her daughter stuck the stickers all over the doors of her car. "I'm proud of you," her husband said. The woman practiced yoga, photographed the lake, and for some reason destroyed her life.

She lied. She stopped for drinks alone on the way home from work. She made secret trips to museums outside the city. She imagined herself in love with a coworker—a perfect, transcendent love, too pure for touch—and conducted an affair by text message. She felt that she was sixteen years old. The worst songs on the radio made her want to dance and also to sob with happiness. At night she did both of these things, soundlessly, in her darkened living room, while drinking the beer she kept under the kitchen sink.

All of these activities seemed quite harmless, like a vacation. They made the woman's world bigger and more mysterious. Anything might still happen! When she walked around the yard with her child, she never felt—as her best friend put it—"trapped."

A banal story, really. Of course her husband discovered everything. He was devastated, especially by the texts to the phantom lover. The woman cried and promised to reform. Incredibly, despite all her gifts, her intelligence, and her remorse, she was unable to do so.

Progress!

The German chemist Martin Klaproth discovered uranium in 1789 while studying a material called pitchblende. It was the year of the storming of the Bastille. *Liberté, égalité, fraternité.* A century later, in 1898, Marie Curie obtained radium and polonium, also from pitchblende. Today, Curie's notebooks are considered too dangerous to touch, but radioactive isotopes are used in smoke detectors, in agriculture, in medicine. During the Great Depression, lovely green glass colored with uranium grew so cheap they handed it out free at the movies.

The possibilities. Endless.

The "Radium Girls" poisoned themselves while painting watch dials with luminescent paint at the United Radium Factory. Unaware that the paint was toxic, they licked their paintbrushes to give them a fine point for outlining the tiny numbers and lines. Later, the women's bones decayed to a kind of moth-eaten lace. Their teeth fell out. As factory workers, when they wanted a bit of fun, the Radium Girls had painted their nails and even their teeth with the beautiful, ghastly, phosphorescent, futuristic poison.

Sometimes I turn my attention to my own body. I can feel that I am becoming increasingly toxic. Will I ever start to glow like the Radium Girls? One of them, according to her lawyer, was luminous all down her back, almost to the waist.

❧

I write by accident: *almost to the waste.*

But why panic? There's no going back. We are exposed to radiation every day. Our sun bathes us in ultraviolet light. All of us share in the toxicity that, thanks to us, characterizes our lifeworld.

I have seen photographs of the plutonium pellets in the vault, in their bare cell at the bottom of the containment center. They bask in their own lurid glow. Radiant.

All of us are toxic, I write to my hurt friend, *but some of us are more toxic than others.*

From her apartment in the city, my hurt friend replies: *Haha.* She tells me that she is reading Attar's *Conference of the Birds.* My friend is a great reader of spiritual and philosophical texts, which she passes on to me when she's finished with them. She is working on a new dance inspired by Attar. *That's great!* I write. My friend has not worked on a dance since her injury. *The dance is all in the fingers,* she writes. As if she has forgotten she doesn't believe in progress, she adds: *It will be my best work.*

There was a time when I would not have missed this chance to tease my friend on the subject of progress, but that was before I developed my current sensitivity, before I was able to feel the fragility of the earth, of the air, before I became a person who lies on the ground and weeps. I write simply: *I can't wait.* When I visited my hurt friend in the hospital, she looked like a broken, greenish piece of glass. It was thought she would never walk again. Overwhelmed by life, she had walked out of her dance studio and gracefully, deliberately into the path of a car.

Later she would say to me: *Don't you dare.*

In the hospital, my friend explained that she had been feeling "trapped." This feeling had grown in her invisibly, like radiation sickness. It was a relief, she told me, to have it out in the open. It was certainly visible there in her hospital bed. It was all over her skin, it blazed from her eyes. She was aglow with pain. I was shocked I had never seen it before—but, as I have already said, I was not very sensitive in those days.

The cheap green glass of the thirties, I recall, is known as "depression glass."

How strange that my friend and I, who have always considered ourselves almost polar opposites, ever since we were promising teenagers of entirely different talents, have after all wound up with such similar fates! Like me, my hurt friend has had to switch careers. She now works from home, composing advertising blurbs. She tells me that the new dance she is making causes her immense pain. She quotes Attar: *Love loves the difficult things.*

The woman's husband: *You want everything to be easy.*

The woman lied and lied. Each lie, even a tiny one, seemed to open an alternate universe. At the lake with her child, she'd stare at a leaf or discarded candy wrapper. She had to keep reminding herself not to let the child fall into the water.

What is the half-life of a lie? Each one produced a chain reaction, an almost infinite amount of energy. The possibilities appeared endless, the future terrifying. Eventually, things reached critical mass.

The woman's husband hauled all the family suitcases into the living room. "Get out," he said. He whispered because the child was sleeping.

Isidor Isaac Rabi, who witnessed the first atomic bomb test explosion: "It blasted; it pounced; it bored its way into you."

The woman walked out of the house. She walked down the street. She came to a busy road. As she walked through the traffic, she thought of her hurt friend. Wind and horn blasts whipped her, but she emerged on the other side. When she told her friend, who was still in the hospital, her friend snarled: "Don't you dare."

The woman went to a hotel. She sat in the dark. Somewhere in the room, an animal kept making a small sound.

Rabi again: "It was a vision which was seen with more than the eye. It was seen to last forever."

There are certain things I miss, though I cannot bear to think of most of them. Occasionally I can bear to remember the voice of the loon. The loon has two calls. One of them, someone once told me, sounds like "the laughter of a hysterical woman." The other, the same person explained, is "the saddest sound in the world." In films set in the jungle, which call for exotic noises, the voice of the loon is often inserted, incorrectly of course, recognizable to anyone who knows.

Sometimes I feel like that. A voice inserted in the wrong place. A hysterical woman. Loony. Saddest in the world.

My huge glass cage, stranded in the middle of the wilderness, is, at least, an excellent place for screaming.

My hurt friend has a theory that tenders are the new priests, in charge of the soul of the world. The supreme irony of this.

J. Robert Oppenheimer: "The physicists have known sin; and this is a knowledge which they cannot lose."

Still, though I cannot think of myself as a priest, I am at least a hermit. A steward. I sit with the earth as if at the bedside of a sick friend. I am so tender now, I feel the earth's pain all through my body. Often I lie down, pressing my cheek to the dust, and weep. I no longer feel, or even comprehend, the desire for another world, that passion which produces both marvels and monsters, both poisons and cures. Like the woman in this story, I understand that there is no other world. There is only the one we have made.

Abba Moses: "Sit in your cell and your cell will teach you."

A child runs up to the glass. She stops a safe distance away and holds up a picture of blue and pink clouds. What does this picture reflect? It might be an afternoon's reading, a spoonful of ice cream, an argument with the world at the moment of sleep. The woman behind the glass is cut off from the complicated daily movements that make up the world whose surface is this picture. The paper is wilted from the child's sweat, which is made of water, sugar, salts, ammonia, and other elements, including copper, iron, and lead.

The child's perspiration is perhaps slightly toxic. The woman doesn't investigate; she cannot bear to sense the child's body. The child mouths "I love you." Her eyes are veiled. This is a routine visit to her mother; afterward, she gets to go to the pool.

The woman's hurt friend smiles from behind the glass. Before she takes the child away for the promised visit to the pool, she performs a few slow, achingly beautiful gestures with her hands. She puts the child's picture into the transfer box along with a book. The book is *Aurora* by Jacob Boehme, the sixteenth-century shoemaker who perceived the structure of divinity in the light on a pewter dish. Of *Aurora*, the deacon Gregorius Richter wrote: "There are as many blasphemies in this shoemaker's book as there are lines; it smells of shoemaker's pitch and filthy blacking."

"Behold," wrote Boehme, "there is a *gall* in man's body, which is poison, and man cannot live without this gall; for the gall maketh the *astral spirits* moveable, joyous, triumphing or laughing, for it is the source of joy."

Before I was a tender, I loved snow. I loved rainy windows that made my neighborhood look like a European city. I used to cut pictures of supermodels out of magazines and paste them in notebooks, arranged according to color. There were blue scenes that made me think of overnight journeys by train and yellow scenes that made me think of medieval bridges. Often I'd buy thrift store clothes and put them on without washing them, so that I could both feel and smell like someone else.

A Brief History
of Nonduality Studies

The study of nonduality as we know it can be traced to the sixth
century A.H., when the griot Balla Fasseke, the Bard Without Longing, adjured his pupils to "study the After which is not after the
Before." The melodic information service of the griot's apprentices
carried this doctrine into the most far-flung reaches of the Sahel,
until even the bats of Khufu, as reported by Ibn Abu Hamran,
the Stretched Scribe, could repeat it with perfect clarity, although
in Dyula. The bat-speech, which took place in a curious register,
so that it made a sound like a thousand knights simultaneously
scratching under their greaves, was interpreted for Ibn Abu Hamran
by a lone traveler called Aminata, who was making her way east-
ward in the company of her goats. "Knifed by the winds," wrote the
scribe in his compendious work, *The Anklets of Obsolescence*, "dried to
a husk, glittering with forty layers of sand, this indomitable shaykha
delivered me from separation and initiated me into the Before of
After." Overcome with gratitude, he offered to spend what little he
had—a sleeping-mat and two plates of beans a day at the door of
a mosque—to reunite the elderly oracle with her family. Aminata
recoiled in horror. "God save you! I've come all this way to escape
those sons of bitches."

The Stretched Scribe, so called because his striking emaciation made him a familiar figure in the streets of Cairo, was responsible for the growth of the eastern branch of Nonduality Studies, a school preoccupied with the problem of time. "Was time created before or after creation, or simultaneously with it?" was the question he most often put to his students. The relentless heat or cold of the porch where he sat and the empty bellies of those he addressed ensured that their answers were listless and few. (I am reminded of poor Sylvia's lectures, conducted in a graveyard.) Without the patronage of a certain Ibn Barzakh, known to his intimates as Frog-Eyes, it is doubtful whether the Eastern School would have survived the scribe's premature death of the hacking cough known as "the Claw." Fortunately, Ibn Barzakh was the son of a wealthy merchant. His elegant topknot was decorated with pendants of green jasper, and his waistcoat had been so thickly embroidered by his sister Radwa, "the Snub-Nosed Beauty," that it could stand up by itself. Ibn Barzakh opened his home to students of nonduality theory, and his sister served cakes soaked in enough honey to make a buffalo dizzy. If only they had known that some two months' journey to the south, Deng Machar Deng had solved all their problems with the dictum: "Creation is Time!"

It was in the marshy country of Deng Machar Deng and in the forests south of it that Nonduality Studies flourished most vigorously. (We would argue about this later: you maintained that the Eastern School was more inventive and lively, while I cited the vast gains of the Southern School. Our sincerity was equal; the shop windows reflected us both.) Deng Machar Deng, who encouraged his disciples to fish while he lectured, was most often to be found in water up to his lanky thigh, perhaps bending down to retrieve his net, perhaps singing, at all times carrying in his eyes the reflected radiance of the wetlands. Adherents of the philosophy spread by the griots traveled for months to hear him speak. "Creation is Time" was repeated as far as the Maghrebi coast. In the Congo River forests the musician class habitually inserted his lyrics into their songs, which made the trees grow faster. At his death, he was mourned all the way to Zimbabwe.

A group of forest musicians appeared at his funeral, bearing a straw litter on their shoulders. On this conveyance tossed an old man, lashed by fevers and grotesquely swollen with mosquito bites. It was Ibn Barzakh, who had come too late.

(Later, you would weep over this tragic misstep of history. A single tear, like a tapioca bead. Afterward you laughed. I was proud of your fortitude: Sylvia had taught us to suspect that such accidents, failures, and losses composed our true field of inquiry.)

Now came the golden age of Nonduality Studies, a period of such richness that it could not be fully explored in a single lifetime. In Cairo, Radwa bint Barzakh, "the Snub-Nosed Beauty," now over eighty years old, continued to support the Eastern School. She reportedly slept on a copy of *The Anklets of Obsolescence*, which she kept in a padded case covered with her inimitable embroidery. Tita, King of the Azande, sent her leather bottles of shea butter by carrier pigeon, and she sent him philosophical lyrics in exchange. These notes were interpreted for him by an Arabic-speaking retainer, known as the Lost Turk, who was neither. Scores of Azande youth, fired by the promise of Radwa's wisdom, traveled north in hopes of gaining an audience with her. At the end of her life her skin became so fragile that she had to be turned over every half hour, like a bird in the oven. This service was performed by her lifelong companion, a woman called Khayriyyeh, who could slice offending glances to pieces with her steel-colored eyebrows. Although few of Khayriyyeh's sayings have been preserved, she is credited with the words that secured Radwa's immortality on earth.

"Oh God!" cried a visitor on the day of Radwa's death. "She's smiling! Is she alive?"

"Who's smiling?" Khayriyyeh snapped. "Radwa or the lips of Radwa?"

"Radwa or the Lips of Radwa" became the rallying cry of the Eastern School, while the Western School, building on the cryptic love lyrics of Deng Machar Deng, burst into life simultaneously in Dakar and Dar al-Baydaa, which would be known ever afterward as the Twin

Cities. ("These are the Twin Cities too," you muttered the night we met. Muffled in greatcoats and scarves, we flipped through albums in a near-defunct record store. "Who the hell listens to records anyway?" you said, accusing.

"You're here too," I said.

You didn't blink. "I just like the pictures.")

A golden age. And the King of Mali in his gold bracelets observed, among the venerable trees of his courtyard, the shades of unknown philosophers. "I know not whether they are living or dead," he said, according to Seti's *Lives of the Saints*, "but they are my kindred. For this reason I fear neither knife nor poison." Two minutes later he was, in fact, poisoned to death. I told you this as if it was a funny story, but you didn't laugh. Ashamed, I offered to buy you a hamburger at a nearby restaurant or, if you were a vegetarian, some French fries.

That was afterward—after the record store. In the record store, where through a mysterious legal oversight one could still smoke cigarettes, I asked you: "Why did you say 'too'?"

"I didn't; you did."

"I don't think so."

"You did," you insisted in some irritation. "You said: 'You're here too.'"

I was already talking more softly, as if dreams, like the smaller animals, could be frightened away. "You said, 'These are the Twin Cities too.' What are the other ones?"

In Assyrian sculpture, eyes like yours, with the white showing all the way around the iris, connote mystic vision. "Dakar and Dar al-Baydaa, of course," you said.

Having stumbled onto such a revelation, how could I let you go? I wheedled you into the restaurant's glare and drank you with my eyes. You licked each of your fingers with equal deliberation. I asked who your teacher was; you claimed to have none. I have no way of knowing if this is true.

"Who's yours?" you asked with a guarded look.

"Sylvia Fazakas. You must come to her lectures." (In the Abyssinian highlands, Azazet the Hesitant, one of our discipline's splendid cranks, greeted her students: "Good-not-meaning-opposed-to-bad, morning-not-meaning-opposed-to-evening . . .")

Sylvia, looking half-drowned as always, trailing hair and skirts, welcomed you with a languid gesture. Unaware of her own perfection, she wore high heels because she thought she was too short. You squirmed uneasily onto the bench beside me, chin sunk deep in the lumps of your homemade scarf. The other members of what I cheerfully referred to as the Minnesota School—a medical student and a reformed gangster called Forehead—blew on their hands and slurped hot tea to prepare for the cold night ahead while a fuzzy Qur'anic recitation blared from the speakers of the café.

Sylvia rested her cheek on her hand. "Why are you here?"

"It's a free country," you said.

Sylvia waited.

"All right," you admitted. "I want to see God."

"That has been deemed impossible."

"Is she really the teacher?" you asked me. The medical student snickered; Forehead examined the tabletop graffiti.

"You will agree that you can only see what you are not."

"I can see myself in a mirror."

"Precisely."

"All right. Show me God's reflection."

"God's reflection is not God," said Sylvia, with what you would later call her Queen-of-the-Fairies smile.

"Christ, lady," you said. "It's better than nothing."

("To see God," sang the great San philosopher known as the Child of Moonrise, while the Blue Scribe of Timbuktu transcribed the words with a reed pen, "one would need eyes, but one has no eyes, for one is not a thing, but an act. For we are not the knowledge of God, but the Knowing." Crickets studded the grass; the Blue Scribe wept indigo tears and dipped her pen in them. In truth, our theory is nothing more than the history of sadness. "We might have eyes, if we were the Nouns of God," sang the Child. "Perhaps the Nouns are the angels. We are among the Verbs.")

I never thought you'd follow me home. I talked the whole way, hoping, but I didn't believe it until your sneakers were trudging up my stairs. Panic struck: the apartment was hardly neat. Later, after you disappeared, it was worse: blood and ashes everywhere.

You threw down your bag in a corner. *Of course*, I thought, gleeful: *That bag. It's a homeless bag.* And it was, shapeless and mended with silver tape. You sat on the couch and picked your chapped lip. "It's freezing in here." I clashed about in the kitchen, in plain view of the couch, sweeping the counter clean.

When I turned around, you had fallen asleep.

(A brief flowering in Moorish Spain. Gone in an instant, like the apricot harvest. Ibn Zahir said: "If creation is time, then creation is a constant. The world is recreated every day.")

Every day you awoke on my couch, miraculous. Recreated. Would it have been so hard to go on repeating this? Cabdi Xasan, jailed by the British, held that we reassemble ourselves every day from the stuff of nonduality, until our strength runs out. I thought this a beautiful idea; you said it was depressing. You seemed to disagree with me whenever you could. Unlike most people, you never asked where I was from. In an inexplicable lapse of intuition, you thought I was in love with Sylvia.

"And that is where we stand now," Sylvia said, having skipped over the decline of Nonduality Studies as she had elided its heyday, to arrive at our present moment when the investigation of unity is stifled and decayed, a theory in exile. Strands of mouse-gray hair, escaped from her hat, blew about her cheeks. She was lecturing on Ramadhani's concept of the Transcendental No. "What he saw," she said, "as the school at Malindi burned, and nonduality scholars were hounded out of their profession, was that the profession itself was an error. In constructing these schools, we were guilty of separation. The events of history, to his mind, constituted a No spoken by nonduality itself. Recall his prophecy: *From now on it will be our destiny to arrive everywhere, only one step behind our enemies.*"

"What are we doing here then?" you said.

"We are seekers," Sylvia answered.

Later you said: "She never misses a beat, does she?" But I saw that although she could answer all your questions, she was disturbed, her eyes shifting toward the traffic beyond the graveyard's blackened fence. When she picked up her snow-damp bag—which was very nearly a homeless bag—settled the strap on her shoulder, and trotted off between the icy gravestones, headed for the home she shared with her daughter, a brusque dog-beautician burdened by the duty of "watching Mom," my heart ached.

"It doesn't have to be like this," you said.

Your eyes startled me. Enraged.

Our fellow students had left us. The wind sang in the trees.

"We can do *more*," you said, and there was an echo of Radwa's lyrics in my head, and then your kiss like a window breaking.

Who were you? You never wanted to know what I had left behind, and you never told me anything about your former life. I wanted to search your bag, but I was afraid, afraid I'd find something there, conclusive evidence that you would not stay. The scholar Lukhele, known to the history books as "Crazy Niklaas," lectured from the edge of a bore-hole in a country that was now called South Africa, but his words were not collected, only his story, the image of madness like a closed door or a Transcendental No. What might we have learned from him? What might he have given us? Could he, or one of the countless practitioners of our shattered philosophy, have passed on a word that would turn you from your path?

"I'm the next level," you said, tapping your chest. I have no way of knowing that this is not true.

You didn't work. When I was out you practiced boxing and Tae Kwon Do. You kicked a hole in one of my living-room chairs. As for me, I changed for work in the restroom of the convenience store, not wanting you to see me in the hideous red shirt.

I brought you pretzels. You ate them from the bag, staring at the wall. You cried one tear for the fate of Ibn Barzakh.

"If we can close the distance between the two of us," you said, "then we can close the distance between ourselves and God."

Ghada Mallasi, known as "the Ibis," was stopped on the way to Qena. She had no pass. She sat by the road for two days, hoping the guards would have mercy. In her bag were a dozen layers of peanut candy and the manuscript of her masterpiece, *The Meadows of Happenstance*. When she understood that she would never get through, she put her bag on her head and returned to Omdurman. "Roads, roads!" she wrote in her little apartment, which was sinking deeper into the sand each year. "The more there are, the more beautifully kept they are, the harder it is to go anywhere."

You sat on the broken chair, and I stood before you. The room was dark, but the glow of the kitchen in the next apartment fell on your upturned face. Your look of appeal went through me, not like an icicle or a blade but like the memory of the past, terrible and swift.

I knelt and kissed your smooth cold hands. "Tell me what to do."

Your courage was boundless. We tried everything: meditation, hunger, dance. Forehead obliged us with a supply of qaat: under its influence we stayed awake for three days, chewing mindlessly. On the last day I saw an angel fluttering on the wall. "Look," I said, "it's one of the Nouns of God." We experimented with matches, bleach fumes, buckets of icy water. The staple-gun, I now see, represented a turning point.

"We're almost there," you insisted every time. You could feel it hovering just beyond the pain, a clear space, like the sea.

Onesimo Bondo, attempting to get to Abidjan, where he hoped to perform his verse meditation, *What the Thunder Knows*, was seized for the mines.

I wish to be fair. I will not omit the contributions of the wider world to our philosophy: the Shoemaker of Bali whose shoes could be worn on either foot, the punk rock band in 1970's Prague who were called 'The Lips of Radwa.' I will not omit your orange laughter after consuming a Slushie. Once you showed me some grainy old-fashioned photographs from your bag: "That's me," you said, pointing to an iridescence seated on a tricycle. The closer I looked, the more the dots that formed you drifted apart, dissolving into a vast and alien constellation.

Nonduality Studies, it must be admitted, is largely a hidden field, a discipline discredited and in mourning, practiced in grave-yards, airports, alleys smelling of "ethnic" foods, video arcades. For a moment, I thought this was going to change.

Then you stood before me, gasping, blood streaming from the cut on your head.

"Did you feel it?"

"Yes," I sobbed.

"You're lying."

You raised the iron again.

"Stop! Stop! I feel it!"

You brought the heavy iron down, this time on your hand . . . but it is not my habit to dwell on evil memories.

Afterward, the medical student visited my apartment. She brought food and injections, and made a splint for my hand. "Don't cry," she said in our mutual, rarely-spoken language, as she completed the sutures. "You're better off this way."

She was right, of course. I should have rejoiced when I saw your bag was missing. You were dangerous, toxic. Your presence in the city was like a plague. You wrecked my apartment and nearly killed me. You made me lose my job. You stole my electric razor. When are you coming back?

I wrote these notes only for Sylvia, and she asked me to write them, I think, only for me, in the hope that they would lead me back into the world. "It will help you to dream of the future," she said, but I don't. I dream of the present, of the *now*. Otherwise, what's the point of being a nondualist? I open the window and press my nose to the screen and smell the spring, exhaust and magnolia trees, and I never dream about you. Like the King of Mali I dream of others, beloved unknown colleagues, a twelve-year-old girl from Rambling, Michigan called Eugenia Czechowicz.

Eugenia is a family name; she dislikes it. She goes by Jenny. She has just understood, in a radiant *whoosh* of cognitive effervescence, that her best friend forever, a gifted ice-skater, both is and is not herself. In defiance of her parents' rules, she is riding her ten-speed bicycle over the bridge.

Dawn and the Maiden

My love is a river. My love is a brink. My love is the brink of an underground river. My love's arms ripple like rivers in the moonlight when he unlocks the garden gate. He lifts the great beam and sets it in place. He bows to the Lady's guests. These are three men, filthy with travel. Each has only one eye.

My love has eyes of brown agate, eyes that flicker like hanging crystal. In the dark they are black, but their brownness glints when he stands beneath the lantern in the garden. My love waits for me beneath the lantern. He waits while I serve wine to the Lady's guests. On my way to join him, I leave an offering of bracelets at the entrance to the Lady's corridor.

I pass through the garden. The leaves caress me. They tug at my skirts, my plaits. My fingers tug, too. They tug the plaits apart, letting my hair spring free.

My love waits for me beneath the lantern in the garden. He is gilded like a figure on a shield. When he steps forward to meet me, his eyes fill with darkness like a crystal glass with wine.

My love. His cheek just shadowed with a beard, like the blush upon a plum.

"Did you leave something for her?"

"Bracelets."

"Good," he says. He left her his harp and some quill pens tied up with scarlet thread.

"I saw them," I tell him. I saw the harp and quills there, along with all the other offerings. Candles, cherries, live ducks whiter than cake flour, their beaks wired shut. Although it was my love who insisted we give our most precious things to the Lady, I did not expect that he would surrender his harp. The thought gives me a small pain at the base of my throat. I remember how my bracelets, a gift from my mother, fell among slivered almonds. I wish now that I had left my gifts with his, looped each bracelet around a feathered quill. I take his hand, I weave our fingers together.

The fountain murmurs.

The darkness smells of leaves.

I lift my face.

My love smells of darkness and of leaves. My hand brushes the nape of his neck. The hair there is damp. My love smells bitter, like burning coal. "Wait," he says.

I draw back.

My love smells of fear.

My love lives with fear. He told me of it the night we met. He told me that he was seventeen years old, that he played the harp to keep from thinking, and that he feared he was not real. I remember that night very clearly. We were splashing one another in the fountain, with all the young people of the palace. A celebration commanded by the Lady, I think. I can think of no other reason for us to be splashing in the fountain.

Water got into my eyes, and when my vision cleared, he was there. He looked forlorn, like a fawn worked in tapestry. And oh, his arm, and the vein in his arm, and oh in the water his knee. I pretended to stumble, fell against him and closed my eyes.

We sat on a bench. I wrung out my skirt. We spoke of the palace gossip, and of the moon. I told him my father sells pomegranate juice in the city. I told him my father bears a mole like a grape above one eye. I told him my mother washes sheets in the palace. I told him that my grandfather, my mother's father, had been a rich lecturer but had lost his position during the Controversy. The house with the jade pillars on the market square was once my grandfather's house. Sometimes I walk past it; the child who lives there now is training a pet ferret.

My love took his harp from under the bench and unwrapped its silken cover. He sang to me in a heartbreaking, ugly voice like the cry of a young owl. He sang a song of his own composition called "Song of the Controversy." He told me he would dedicate it to my grandfather.

He tilted his head back to look at the sky. His hair fell away from his face. He told me he felt unreal.

I laughed. "That is only because you are happy. And why should we not be happy? We are young, and our mistress is generous and good." I did not say: *And I love you.*

He looked at me strangely. "Is she good?"

The words jarred on my ear. I frowned.

"Forgive me," he said.

"Of course she is good," I told him. "She is the Lady." It was like explaining the world to a little child. My heart softened toward him again. When he played, I sang: "My heart is soft wax in the fingers of my love."

Now I take his face between my hands. "You are real," I tell him.

I grip his face harder. "You are real." I can feel his bones beneath my hands. His lashes droop. Beneath them, a line of tears. I tell him he's real, I repeat everything he has ever told me about himself. "You keep the gate in the palace gardens. You're seventeen years old. The scar above your eye was caused by your aunt, who beat you with an iron spoon. You were raised by this aunt and her husband, a black-smith. Your childhood was one of fear. One night, when the fear was too much, you struck the blacksmith and bloodied his mouth."

Then you came here, to the palace, where you lift and lower the beam on the garden gate, where you splash in the fountains, and where I love you. You came to this place at the center of the city, where at the end of a long corridor the Lady speaks into the air. Standing among the offerings at the entrance to the corridor one can just see her room, a square of golden light. She kneels on a pillow, upright, gesturing, smiling. We call her the Lady of Love because she is beautiful, and the Lady of Peace because she smiles. We also call her the Lady of Incantations, because she speaks. She is never silent, though we cannot hear her voice. My grandfather believed she spoke to her father, a greater god than she; his opponents claim she speaks to her child, a god who is not yet born.

What is known is that her speaking makes the world. And it is said that if she receives a pleasant offering, she will speak the answer to the giver's prayer. I believe she will accept our gifts, my love's offerings and mine, and bless this secret hour among the leaning trees.

"Kiss me," I whisper.

"You gave them wine," he says, and his voice is hoarse. "Did they not seem more real to you than I?"

He means the Lady's guests, the one-eyed travelers. It is his persistent fancy: that others are more real than he. The young adventurers who visit the palace, the unhappy dogs with the eyes of men who haunt the kitchens, even the genial hunchback—all, says my love, are more real.

But no one is more real to me than my love.

I grasp his shirt, I shake him, my eyes on fire. "Stop pretending," I cry. "The truth is that you don't love me."

He touches my face. "I have longed for this hour more than anything in the world."

He puts his arm about my waist. Then the kiss.

One kiss. I am in this kiss. I feel I am waiting for something.

I sense his hesitation. I hold him close, my arms about his neck.

My love is a river; he slips through my arms like a river. He steps away, gasping, his face wild. "I don't feel anything," he whispers.

I stretch my arms toward him. My hands are cold as silver. "You're afraid," I tell him. "Come back."

But I, too, have begun to be afraid.

He embraces me again. When our lips touch, I feel a numbness. My lips are lead.

I press him closer. I bite. He groans. He bites me, too. There is no pain between us. No pain, and no pleasure. He backs away from me. Blood streaks his mouth, like embroidery on a glove.

My love stands tall. He is fearless, although he has always been afraid. His face is pale. His eyes are black and open, staring; his spirit is closed. "It is she who has done this to us," he says. "Your Lady. Her thoughts are elsewhere. She meant for me to open the gate, but not to love. And you, she meant you to serve wine to her guests, but not to love."

He turns. He grasps the branch of a tree, he swings himself up into the branches. He climbs high, high above the plashing fountain. The iron railing about the bowl of the fountain gleams in the moonlight.

"I gave her my harp," my love shouts from the tree, "and she would not think of me even for a moment. You gave her your mother's bracelets, and she would not think of you." Then he sings, in his poor, cracked voice, the last lines of the "Song of the Controversy": *I will not be a plaything / Not even for a god.*

My love is a river. My love is a fountain. My love is a fountain of blood. My love is a shower of blood when he falls on the spike of the railing. My love is a fool, a child of seventeen. My love is a dying child. My love is a pale child dying in a garden.

I run to him. I seize his body. He is lighter than I had expected; still, it is difficult to take him from the spike. My own body seems lighter than usual, too, thinner, less trustworthy, more transparent. I clasp him in my arms and fall down to the grass.

I lay my love on the grass. I remove my outer garment and press it to his chest.

His eyes are open, and he is smiling. "Look," he says.

I turn my head. A winged man is flying across the sky, carrying a sleeping youth in his arms.

"How real they are," my love whispers. "How real."

Something is wrong with his voice. I look at him again. I cry out.

My love has withered. This is not loss of blood: he is old. My love has grown old in the space between two heartbeats.

Pressing the cloth to his chest, I see that my own hands, too, are old, yellow and old. They have grown sere, like a pair of leaves.

All through the garden, the leaves grow sere. Now they begin to fall. They fall on my hair. I glimpse one of my curls: it is white.

My love, old and beautiful, smiles at me. His blood stains my fingers through the cloth. "Look," he says. "It's the end of the world."

I stand. I wipe my hands on my skirt. I am wearing only this skirt and my flimsy inner blouse: half-naked, ragged-haired, a fierce old woman.

"Where are you going?" asks my love.

"I am going to see the Lady," I tell him, "and ask her for your life."

I think he calls after me. I do not care. I walk through the garden, scattering leaves. Whole bushes fall to powder at my touch. All the fountains have ceased to play; the rails are gnawed by rust. The air, stricken with leprosy, grows pale.

From inside the palace, sounds of lamentation.

The palace has aged. Its walls sag. Only the Lady's corridor remains the same. A long, dark hall with a golden square at the end. The offerings are refuse now. I stop to loop some tarnished bracelets about a set of broken quills.

It is said that to step into the corridor means death.

It is said that to address the Lady means eternal torment.

It is said that the glance of her eye is a comet. No soul can withstand it. My grandfather told me that another god, a beast-god, terrible, dwells in the room with her.

I walk down the corridor, touching the wall. My body is slow to obey. I walk with pain.

I am coming into the light.

My foot is upon the carpet of a god.

The Lady turns. Her glance is not a comet. Her eyes are swollen and tired.

They widen when she sees me. "Who are you?"

"I am a serving-maid," I tell her, "and my love keeps your garden gate. I have come to beg you for his life. He lies bleeding in your garden, because you would not let him love me, and he despaired."

The Lady stares. Then she smiles. Her face is still tired, overwhelmingly tired. "Child," she says, "it is too late for saving now."

"Then what he said is true, and the world is ending, and this is death."

"Death!" she exclaims. "No. Only dawn."

A moment later, I find myself back in the garden beside my love, whose agate eyes are closed now in the lightening air. I take a ring from my finger, and with the edge of this ring I begin to carve these words upon the bowl of the silent fountain. The carving is easy, even for an old woman. The marble of the fountain is as delicate as soap. Cracks appear, splintering my words which, were they engraved with a needle at the corner of an eye, would be a lesson for those who would consider.

My love is a river. My love is a river of ice.

My love is a brink: the brink of the River of Terror, or the brink of the River of Truth. If it is terror only, then we shall return tomorrow to read this message. If it is truth, then we shall not come here again.

If it is truth, we were never here at all.

If it is truth, then our offerings to the Lady are useless. If it is truth, then the Lady does not love us. Then the Lady is not good. Then the god with her, born or unborn, is merely Chance.

For this unknown god, my grandfather lost everything. His enemies hounded him from the gates of the university. He ran through the market, stumbling, his shoes in his hands. He wrote his memoirs. The book molders in our house, under my mother's mattress. I cannot read it.

Alas, my love, for this foolish old woman. It is as if I sit here winnowing a basket of pale grief. My tears are chaff.

We were real. We had history. My mother washed sheets. My love sang like an owl.

Over the ruined wall, waving its banners, comes the sun.

Cities of Emerald,
Deserts of Gold

I.

I live in a city. I have a horror of emptiness. I avoid the golden lands, where the wind travels alone for miles, like sunflower-colored Kansas, whose fields, cropped close in the autumn, resemble the hair of a blond military recruit. I have a horror of emptiness, the military, and on some days even blondness. I keep to the coasts, where the cities flash their greenish windows. When I travel from coast to coast— for example, to visit my mother—I never take the train through the golden lands. I fly.

2.

Dorothy's lesson, "There's No Place like Home," was intended to reconcile her to the monochromatic endlessness of Kansas. This is a lesson neither of my parents learned. My mother was born in North Dakota, my father in Somalia; both fled those vast and empty landscapes. Tonight my mother places a call from her emerald city to mine. She says she remembers walking to school after a blizzard: the silence of the world, and the pegs of buried clotheslines poking through the snow at her feet, like fragments of yellow brick.

⤚⤙

3.

A friend of mine, an Egyptian doctor, once worked in North Dakota. He made house calls. At night, his car was often the only one on the road. There was no one to ask for help if he lost his way. He didn't want to stop at a farmhouse, either: what would they make of his dark face and foreign accent? This was in the days of paper: he was alone with his wrinkled map, his small car light. He told me this story in Cairo, one of the great emerald cities. A city surrounded by deserts of gold. The people of North Dakota were kind, he said: quite often, in the velvet night, his patients offered him pound cake.

4.

In college, I tried to reconcile myself to my family deserts by reading *Dakota* by Kathleen Norris. I remember one sentence, quoted, I believe, from the Desert Fathers: "Everything empty is full of the angels of God." This sentence is lovely, but its heels, when tapped together, produce no magic. I am ashamed of my inability to love the land. My fear of open spaces, my "black thumb." That's what they call it when you can't keep houseplants alive. A black thumb.

5.

In the Emerald City we carve statues of clear jade. All of our surfaces are smooth, our trees of wire. Our sidewalks wink like aquamarines, and at night, when we light the glowworm lamps, the darkness throbs like the dream of a person addicted to absinthe. I would describe my relationship to land as one of distrust. In the Emerald City we flit effortlessly from one window to another. Despite this elegant mobility, this extraordinary lightness, some ignorant people refer to us as monkeys.

6.

One day we decided to get out of the city. We drove to Brackenhurst, a Christian retreat center near Limuru. Once we had left the Nairobi traffic behind, the day opened out and we could see the boundless sky with its herds of clouds. At Brackenhurst, we sat on the porch of a quaint half-timbered building, drinking tea with our friend and listening to the birds. Our friend is a descendant of Chief Kinyanjui, the Kikuyu patriarch in Isak Dinesen's *Out of Africa*. Chief Kinyanjui impressed Dinesen with his immobility: he sat so still, she writes, that he transformed himself into "lifeless matter." Our friend waved his hand at the hills of Brackenhurst gilded with the light of noon, and smiled. "All of this used to be ours," he said.

7.

My great-grandfather purchased our family farm in North Dakota. He rode there from Pennsylvania on his bicycle. Like Isak Dinesen, he strove and struggled and loved the land. Like her, he dispossessed a darker people.

8.

The same can be said of Dorothy's Uncle Henry and Auntie Em. Reconsider the meaning of ennui. Reconsider Dorothy's longing for many colors, her final acceptance of dusty Kansas. Reconsider the role of flight.

9.

You would not describe a body in flight as "lifeless matter." You might, however, describe it as an animal. This does not make much difference to me. After all, L. Frank Baum asks, "Why should not the animals have their Fairies, as well as mortals?"

❧

10.

Last night I dreamt I was stretched on a desert of snow. I grasped the tops of the clothes-pegs, dragging myself painfully toward the glow on the horizon. The city, the city. As I squirmed forward I left my coat and even my skin behind, with a sob of grief and also a great sense of physical well-being. I would describe my relationship to land as one of distance. I would describe it as truncated. I would describe it as numb. I would describe it as essentially a relationship of mourning, not for lost land but for the capacity to believe.

11.

Primary disadvantage of flight: exposure. A black silhouette on the open sky is so easy to shoot down.

12.

Primary advantage of flight: rejection of the land, which makes it possible to reject the category "landless."

13.

Sometimes after a dust storm fine gold sand covers my floor. One of my friends habitually rolls in this dust, in order, she says, to feel "grounded." The city, she claims, is an artificial construction, a kind of no-place. I am interested in how a no-place can be home.

14.

Oh, flight! Oh, flight!

15.

In my city, I sip green tea. I avoid vacant lots, which are full of the angels of God. When the wind blows, a subtle excitement tugs my heart, as if clouds are forming somewhere over this rainbow nation. Is it a storm? Not yet; but the wind is strong enough to lift me from the roof. Screeching with joy I tumble into the sparkling air, where thousands like me already cavort, rising and falling on stunted wings, like miniature cyclones among the grinning towers.

An Account of the
Land of Witches

I arrived in the Land of Witches at the end of the season of furs. The sun shone, banks of chilly foam lay piled up in the streets, and the river emitted groans day and night as the ice broke into pieces, setting free the witches' colorful winged boats. My master took a room in the Lean Hotel. This building consists of a single spire that twists up into the greenish, iridescent sky. Ascending to our room presented no difficulties, however, for the steps were endowed with a charm that eroded time.

This shaping of time is one of the marvels of the Land of Witches. I have never seen a people so rested and happy; for them, time runs opposite to the way it runs for us: onerous tasks pass swiftly, while a pleasure may last for weeks or, indeed, forever. I have seen Ygasit, the proprietress of our hotel, wash every dish in the place in the time it takes her to bend her full cheek slightly toward one shoulder, while Verken, the musician who became my particular friend, told me she once played a single note for a year without tiring of its beauty. The smallest child can roll time into a ball and chase it down the stairs or fashion it into elaborate paper chains. In the pastry shops, they drizzle time over the cakes. This molding of time, like all their miracles, is achieved through the Dream Science.

Once I had begun to practice the Dream Science myself, I was able to reduce my time beneath my master to almost nothing. No sooner had he climbed onto me than he would roll off again. Outside the window, the stars would shrink and vanish like ice.

In the Land of Witches, everything tends skyward. Their beautiful boats, adorned with batlike wings, are as happy among the clouds as on the water; the first time the shadow of one of these gliding marvels passed over me, I shivered, for I thought it must be some giant bird of prey. Wonder overwhelmed me when I looked up to see little witch-children peering curiously at me through the boat's glass floor. The vessel must have come recently from the river, for it sprinkled the air with droplets. One struck my cheek like a freezing tear.

Their houses resemble plants: many sprout rooms like parsley flowers, which sway on their long stalks when the wind blows. Others, like the Lean Hotel, strain toward the clouds. The witches wear tall headdresses, three to four feet high and bedecked with veils. I thought the adornment cumbrous until I realized that these veils, which float on the air like spidersilk beaded with dew, are in fact a means of catching the wind, the secret behind the witches' extraordinarily light and buoyant footsteps. Their conveyances are many and varied: when not traveling by boat, or the headdresses that, in a strong breeze, can lift them from the ground, the witches skim over the snow on gold discs, propel themselves through the streets with a sort of javelin, or trot about balanced on huge hoops.

The streets of their city resemble a perpetual carnival. There is always a sound of bells.

They play on great flutes made of whalebone and harps as round as shields.

In the shadow of the mountains, there is a park called the Place of Mourning where, Verken told me, one such as I would spend months, perhaps years, if I were a witch.

❧

The Place of Mourning lies, I have said, in the shadow of the mountains, but this is only one of its locations. Like the entire Land of Witches, this hushed and tenebrous park is porous, its borders fluid, and its atmosphere transportable. I was hanging my master's smallclothes out to dry behind the hotel when Verken approached me, dancing on top of her traveling hoop, her circular harp clasped firmly under one arm, and called down to me that I should spend a season in the Place of Mourning. When I ignored her, she alighted gracefully, her earrings clashing. Her hoop fell sideways so that it leaned against the wall of the hotel. "You are injured," she said. I told her that she was mistaken. She reached out and took my wrist, her eyes abrim with compassion and light.

In the Land of Witches there is, every year, a Festival of the Dreaming, during which all the witches dream the same dream together. The dream may be very simple. Last year they dreamt they were taking a pumpkin cake out of the oven. Everyone awoke in tears.

The Dream Science obliterates distance as well as time.

"Let me help you," Verken said.

At that I snatched my wrist out of her grasp. She was a witch, a musician, and a free woman, and I was not; but there were some things that I knew better than she. On the subject of offers of help, I was something of an expert. In my home city, my mother's cousin had offered to help her in her poverty by taking her youngest girl child off her hands. He sold me to my first mistress, whose son, a university student, helped me by teaching me my letters. It would increase my value, he said, beyond my current use, which was to provide him with pleasure and sleep at his mother's feet. When my lady died, her son sold me to a merchant, profiting greatly, as he had predicted, from my ability to read and write. This merchant—my current master—had two kind daughters who, when we were at home, treated me generously to cracked jewelry and cast-off gowns. I preferred to be on the road: to be shivering, here, in the cold sunlight, hanging clothes. "I don't need help," I said to Verken.

"Then let me give you a word," said the witch.

The word she gave me was *pomegranate*. It was not only a word; it was a dream. In the Land of Witches, words open doors in the dream-scape. In the dream-language, said Verken, *pomegranate* means dusk and the rattling of dry leaves.

It also means winter. It means black bile and a cloister. It means a tooth.

"Dream of pomegranates," Verken said, "and you'll find yourself in the Place of Mourning."

In the Land of Witches, each word is translatable into a dream. This is the foundation of the Dream Science.

Once I understood what Verken had given me, I began to make notes toward a Dreamer's Lexicon. Each day, when my master retired for his midday rest, I sat with the musician in the little grape arbor behind the Lean Hotel. I was quite warm now, for I made sure to dream of rabbits. Borrowed sun streaked the wall and made the grapes sparkle like earrings of green glass. Verken admonished me that to describe the sun as "borrowed" was a mistake. This was our sun, she said: the sun of the Land of Witches.

My hands trembled as I took notes, not with fatigue but with excitement. I could roll up my trousers, now that it was so warm; Verken admired my heavy ankle bracelets, and I gave her one, which she fixed to her headdress as an ornament. The next day she informed me that she had been to a marvelous place. What was my elation, and what my terror, when she described to me the massive walls of my own city, the triangular gardens, and the boughs of the sacred trees.

"Impossible," I gasped.

"Not at all," she replied, smiling. "It is only necessary to board a boat at the Quay of the Blackened Cod, and travel some few miles south, to where the orange groves begin. And, of course, one must have the proper dream . . ."

In the Land of Witches, life is not cut out of whole cloth, but resembles a series of pockets.

It is not true that there is no suffering there. Indeed, if there were no grief, there would be no need for a Place of Mourning. The witches know disappointment, and sadness, and sickness, and death. Nor are they immune to the cruelties of ordinary human beings. Verken, who traveled much in her search for new musical forms to enrich her repertoire, had once been captured by a strange people who, by flashing lights into her eyes and startling her with loud noises, prevented her from sleeping for five days. Unable to dream or to answer the questions posed to her in an unknown tongue, she sobbed hopelessly in a puddle of her own urine. By the sixth day she was exhausted enough to dream with her eyes open. In an instant she found herself in the Place of Mourning.

"There is enough cruelty in the world," she told me softly, "to justify all the music ever made."

I met her eyes. We had never spoken of my master before, but I knew that we were speaking of him now.

In the Land of Witches, one is always touching many lands at once. To raise a cup in a dream is to tumble down a hill.

"I have hurt you," Verken said, on that grape-green afternoon when she described to me the streets of my own city.

"No," I answered, weeping. "But my country is so far. It's so far away. And now you say, in a few miles . . ."

"With the right dream," she whispered, "you may get there in a few steps."

She covered my hand with hers. It was warm as a rabbit's pelt.

2. A Refutation of the Account of Witches

I, Taharqo of Qorm, jewel merchant, devotee of the Horned God of Mount Napata, member of council in the world's most illustrious city, father of two daughters and now (for the gods are generous) a son, do submit to the public this refutation of the lies of my escaped slave, Arta.

I purchased this Arta for no small sum in the country of the blacks. She was literate, and possessed a great facility for learning languages, which made her remarkably valuable to me on my travels—though, no doubt, her talents also aided her in her escape. Arta was well-treated under my protection, even affectionately so, amply fed (she had, like all her people, a predilection for sweets), clothed and petted by my own daughters, honored by me with several rich gifts (including a nose-ring of speckled jade), and beaten no more than was lawful. In short, she was a full member of my household. We called her Tan-Tan. In her loss, the kindness of my family has been scorned, the feelings of my daughters wounded, the burdens of my lady wife compounded, my business dealings hampered, my purse outraged, and my pride trampled underfoot.

As if this loss were not enough (and I intend to discover how it was done, if I have to hold the proprietress of the Lean Hotel over her own stove!), I have had to endure, for several weeks now, the interrogations of friends and even strangers who know that I have lately returned from the Land of Witches. For my eldest daughter (a charming girl, guilty of no more than the natural thoughtlessness of her sex), in going through my belongings after my return, discovered the infamous Account of the Land of Witches among my papers and made several bound copies of it for her friends. When asked why she had done so, she stared at me dumbfounded. "Why, Father," she said, "it is a diverting story; how could it be wrong?" On the Plains of Khod, where my honored father spent his adolescence, there is a saying that any girl can match wits with an ostrich.

The results of my daughter's indiscretion are well known; the Account of the Land of Witches has been copied all over Qorm; it is available for purchase at every bookseller's, despite my efforts to buy up the copies, or argue to the merchants the falseness of the document. The nature of the so-called "Dream Science" is debated in cafés, and I have heard some philosophy students have taken to sleeping all day. I have therefore decided to ride before the storm, as the saying goes, and release my own, true document to the public.

Know then that the Land of Witches is a meager, muddy little country, cold as a spider's affections and dull as paste. The "river" of which my slave writes is an icy sludge, the Lean Hotel more of a stick than a spire, and the streets of the city narrow and stinking. There are no flying boats—if there were, the inhabitants would all fly away at once and settle in some more comfortable location. The wind comes over the water like a spear. I never heard bells; perhaps they were drowned out by the yapping of the dogs.

The natives of the Land of Witches are uniformly stupid and their language as nonsensical as the yammering of goats. Not even Ygasit, the greasy, gap-toothed proprietress of the hotel, can speak more than ten words in any civilized tongue. I depended on my slave Arta to conduct any business at all, for, with her gift for mimicry, she was soon chattering enthusiastically with the witches—who, I was disappointed to learn, believe that ornaments can only be given away, and not bought, making them utterly worthless as customers.

"But where do you get the jewels to give your friends?" I asked Ygasit through my slave. The witch laughed, her eyes twinkling through the gloom (for we stood in her kitchen, the fog of her noxious cooking as thick as soup), and answered that she received them from *other* friends.

"But where are they *made?*" I demanded.

Arta repeated my question, and, when Ygasit had finished spitting out words as barbed and slimy as fishbones, informed me that the witch—who, mind you, was clad in a grimy apron, and reeked of onions—considered my question indelicate.

"No one asks where they come from," Arta said. "They are considered tokens of love, and no one asks where love comes from, or where it goes."

She kept her eyes trained on my beard, as usual. She never met my eyes. I thought her expression respectful then; now, I remember it as sly.

The prodigious idiocy of the witches, who wear jewels but will not buy them, might have left me entirely bankrupt, save that I happened to have picked up some perfumed soaps in the south, and these the witches liked and purchased gladly. I therefore determined to stay until I had sold all of my small stock, in order that the trip should not be wasted. Each day I walked through the dirty, freezing streets to the little market where the witches do a great deal more talking than buying. How well I remember the snaggle-toothed children watching me from a balcony, their eyes gleaming like those of starving beasts. My slave told the truth about the witches' headgear: both sexes wear towers of knotted cloth on their heads and sway through the streets like giraffes.

In short, a more miserable and useless country can hardly be imagined. This alone should be enough to disprove the existence of any "Dream Science." If it were possible to travel by means of dreaming, believe me, no one in the Land of Witches would get out of bed.

If you are still determined, reader, to take seriously the scribblings of a duplicitous, scheming, lawless runaway slave, then at least consider the contradictions of her narrative! How could she be warm, and the rest of the city freezing? Why, upon our arrival, did we experience the city as freezing, when someone was surely dreaming that it was warm? How, precisely, does one travel by dream? Why does Verken claim to have dreamt first and traveled afterward, in one case, and in another to have traveled the instant she dreamed? How could a child cut time into paper chains? And how can the Land of Witches be everywhere at once—as one must assume my slave to be claiming, since her Place of Mourning shifts its borders? It is all the most tiresome nonsense! A shifting border is no border at all.

Here is the truth: my slave Arta, a most valuable piece of property, has been stolen by a witch called Verken, who probably planned to steal her from the moment we arrived and took to loitering about the hotel for no other purpose. This Verken is a tall, loose-limbed woman with a headdress of dirty red-and-orange cloth, who pretends to be a musician. This she certainly is not; for the sounds she drew from her barbaric harp, as she lounged barefoot in the arbor, resembled nothing so much as the farts of a gazelle. Ygasit, I am convinced, was an accessory to the crime, for, when questioned, she would only frown and repeat "No good, no good," pressing my shoulder with a thick finger to confirm that she meant *I*, and not the thieving Verken, was in the wrong. I departed the Land of Witches in a cold fury; but I intend to return in a hot one. I am even now assembling a company of fighting men. I will go back to the Land of Witches, and if I cannot retrieve my property, I will at least make sure that no one dares call Taharqo of Qorm a fool.

3. A Refutation of the Refutation of the Account of the Land of Witches

Another fruitless day at the embassy.

Coming home, the taxi passed one of the usual crowds. Only a few people wept openly. The blast must have occurred several hours before. A pair of trousers hung on a dead electric wire, as if it were washing day.

Now the evening turns blue. The heat dissipates.

My brother met me at the door. I shook my head. This is all we require, now, to communicate the essentials: no, there's no progress, no visa, not yet, I can't get out.

"You shouldn't have come," my brother says, not for the first time.

I know. I know.

Once it's dark, I pretend to sleep. Lie on the bed with my face to the wall, the sheet over my head. I can hear the scrape of my brother's plastic slippers on the floor. Voices, too, the voices of other people come to visit. Neighbors, aunts. Once the sun goes down, there's nothing to do but talk. They exchange news and warnings and advice. Somebody has a pain in his stomach; my brother pulls a bottle of precious soda from under the bed. Warm American soda in the warm night, not to quench the thirst but as medicine. Slowly moonlight fills the air of the city like milk. It's bright enough to read by. It glows through my sheet. In the distance, every so often, interrupting the conversation, blasts like dishes breaking.

The "Account of the Land of Witches" is a document with no catalog, an orphaned textual fragment with no archive. The appearance of the words "Napata" and "Qorm" (Kerma) led Augustus Kircher to date the "Account," quite convincingly, to the ninth century BCE; however, the version of demotic Egyptian used, with its distinctive "swallow-tailed" plural markers, is found in no other extant text, making all attempts at dating the document uncertain and inconclusive. And if the text's place in time is vague, its place in literature is equally so. Is it simply an unusual autobiographical record? Or is it (as Kircher surmised—"autobiography being unknown in the Kingdom of Kush") some sort of occult text, written in a coded language known only to the priesthood? Do the first two parts (the "Account" and the "Refutation") form a thesis and antithesis, and the third (the "Dreamer's Lexicon") a sort of synthesis? Are we looking at the sole trace of an ancient religion? Or does the "Account," rather, disprove, or at least complicate, Kircher's claims regarding autobiography?

This dissertation takes the position that these possibilities are not mutually exclusive, and that the "Account," the "Refutation," and the "Lexicon," taken together, can be read as both autobiographical fragments and the foundational scriptures of a spiritual tradition heretofore unknown . . .

Pause.

The sun goes down. No moon tonight.

"You'll wreck your eyes," my brother says.

He's right, it's too dark to see, but that doesn't mean I can't write. Tomorrow I'll find these lines flung across the page, running over each other like the footprints of armies that have met by night.

I don't work on the dissertation in the dark. I just scribble these private notes. I can't risk writing important ideas in an illegible scrawl. I fear losing my only chance. The perfect thought, the one moment when a customs agent softens in a good mood.

"All right, miss." The stamp. I dream about it.

I call my professor in Madison on my brother's phone. My own ran out of credit long ago. The connection's tentative, full of holes. I'm on the starlit roof, my brother crouching beside me.

"Hello? Hello?"

My brother watches anxiously, without moving.

"Hello!"

My professor's voice, happy and worried, frayed across the distance. I'm catching every third syllable. He's had to give my class to another graduate assistant, he couldn't keep on teaching it himself.

"I understand," I tell him. I wonder if he hears "I . . . stand."

"When you get back, we'll figure out a way for you to keep your assistantship. Has there been any progress?"

No. No.

"You gave them my letter? My phone number?"

Yes.

"Well. Don't lose hope! And keep working. Think of it as a writing holiday!"

A small shudder in the distance. Another blast.

He says something I can't make out.

"What?"

"Stand up," my brother snaps, "you'll get a better signal." He can't understand this conversation in a foreign tongue but he interprets my panic, the rising tone of my voice. He hisses at me, he says I need to move into that corner, where there's a narrow view of the sea: that's where the signal's always best. He's cursing now and yanking on my arm and I can only hear my professor's voice as a series of broken yelps. I'm standing and stumbling, swamped in my brother's impatience, the charcoal scent of his clothes, and I ought to be angry because he's only making it harder to hear, but I'm everywhere at once in this moment, at home and yet magically transported back to campus by my professor's voice, and I'm happy. I'm so happy.

What does it mean to dream of a visa?

I used to think of air travel as a sort of Dream Science. The dry cocoon of the plane was a zone of sleep. Then you'd wake up in a different country, in the long snake of the customs line, the windows full of pearly foreign light. It seemed easy, like sliding into a dream, even if sometimes you tossed and turned on the way, even if they made you empty everything out of your bag. The indignities themselves had a dreamlike quality, absurd: the room where a stranger patted down your body and rifled through your hair.

My plan was to visit my brother and then travel north in search of the home city of Arta, the writer of the "Account." Then I'd go west to Khartoum. I'd pay a visit to the museum, then make my way to the ruins of Napata . . .

Everyone was worried about me: my professor, my uncle, my friends. And I laughed. I was filled with the spirit of the dream-travelers, Arta and Verken. I came home. And home was crumbling, a trap. I couldn't go anywhere I'd planned. So I gave up my trip. I'll go back to the States, I said . . .

I'll go back. But they wouldn't let me on the plane to London, and so I couldn't get back to Chicago, and so I couldn't get back to Madison. I begged them. *I'm a student!* But there was something wrong with my papers, I never knew what. You need a different visa, they said.

"You should really go to an American embassy," the agent clucked, frowning over my papers. But there's no American embassy here.

Sometimes I see the world traversed by jagged lines of borders, like the cracks across a broken windowpane.

Can you see anything through that window? Do you recognize the world?

Don't touch it; you'll cut yourself.

Tonight, on the radio, an old Sudanese song. The kind my father used to love. I sat in the dark and cried. "Why did you have to study history," my brother said.

Notes toward a dissertation. The location of the Land of Witches—
if such a place exists—has confounded scholars for over a century,
ever since the document, written on papyrus, was discovered in a
grave at Kuraymah (where I can't go). It is clear enough that the merchant Taharqo was a citizen of Kerma (where I can't go); as for Arta,
the author of both the "Account" and the "Lexicon," most scholars
believe she came from Bahr el-Ghazal (where I can't go), though I will
argue that her home was more likely in modern Somaliland (where I
can't go). It is possible to make claims, however tentative, about these
matters. The Land of Witches presents a more serious problem. Was
it, as Kircher thought, somewhere in Europe (where I can't go)? Was
it in China (where I can't go) or even Siberia (where I can't go)? What
can be determined from the tantalizing and fragile clues we are given:
bells, giant hoops, a river, and snow? Is the Land of Witches locatable
by anyone—or by everyone? Is it a complex hallucination? A state of
mind?

I lie on my side for hours.

Don't talk to me. I'm trying to sleep.

I'm hot and then cold.

I don't go to the embassy anymore. It's too dangerous, and in any
case they wouldn't admit me, or anyone else. Nobody gets out now.
The borders are closed.

I can hear my brother and the others talking down the hall in the
communal kitchen, over the clacking of mortar fire and the crackle
of boiling ghee. I chew on the sheet, but I won't cry. I hate myself
for not getting up. I'm appalled at the way I've sunk when my brother
keeps moving, calculating, scheming. Money tied up in a sack inside
his clothes. He wants me to call my uncle in Canada again, the one
who's paid for my education. I can't, I can't face him, the scolding, the
pain in his voice, his rage at my arrogance, my stupidity, the way I've
thrown the family's resources away. "You'll die there," he said the last
time we spoke. The ground shakes, and I think he's right, but there's
only a brief lull in the kitchen conversation. The sound of frying, the

smell, doesn't stop at all. I think of how my mother ran away six years ago, to the camp. And how she ran back again, unable to bear it. She spoke to me of the dirt, of her fear of snakes and lions on the journey. Never her fear of men. *The stars would shrink and vanish like ice.* By "mother" I don't mean mother, I mean the aunt who tells me "I am your mother now."

I hesitate to write this but I have begun to travel in dreams . . .

Faces at checkpoints. Your father drinking tea. The explosion, the gap in the wall. You can see his leg. Suddenly Canada. Wind across the St. Lawrence River. There are no flying boats. Oh, Sagal, don't come home. The phone pressed against your ear in the student union where someone is walking by with a pitcher of reddish beer. Crows in the sky like the broken pieces of someone who thinks, I could be, I should be, dead. What does it mean to dream of these things?

Notes. Toward.

Pomegranate. *In an instant she found herself in the Place of Mourning.* I return to my dissertation, and it looks completely different. I can't understand it anymore. Oh, I understand the words, but I can't comprehend why somebody would write them. It all seems so obvious: the chapter on gender, the chapter on animals, the chapter on the trace. I can't work up the energy to reflect on the controversial translation of the word "cloister," or even the fate of Taharqo of Qorm. "Did Taharqo ever return to the Land of Witches? Is it possible to identify him as the 'southern lord' described by an anonymous Egyptian scribe, who, 'together with a vast company of mercenary soldiers, was swallowed by that pale crocodile, the Sea'?" This work, which used to excite me, now seems utterly remote, featureless, like a desert seen from an airplane window. While the "Account" itself, the "Lexicon," and even the "Refutation"—these brim with light. Each word translatable into a dream.

I was in a building. It was made of brick. Every few steps a patch of grass. Old men were working at little desks. My mother offered me 7-Up in a gourd. There was a camel in the background with a saddle of aluminum foil.

The kitchenette in my dorm room had gotten smaller. I dropped a dish in the sink and it broke. I turned on the garbage disposal to grind up the pieces. A man stood behind me holding a wire, his face wrapped in a keffieh. He said everyone acted like me, that's why the disposals were always getting broken.

I decided to go to the Land of Witches. "I'm going," I told my mother. She grunted and told me to lie down. She offered me 7-Up in a gourd. "Don't get up," she said. Her necklace glinted in the moonlight that fell through the bars of the window. *Who gave you that?* I tried to ask.

My father was drinking tea. The wall crumbled. I was out back, at the tap in the courtyard. I was trying to wash out his socks. Money fell out of his sock and I cried. Crows flew low, close by. Their wingbeats whispered, "You will wear a black wedding dress."

I decided to go the Land of Witches. "I'm going," I told my brother. He was muffled in an enormous coat, with sandals on his feet. "Come with me," I begged him. "Dream of pomegranates." His feet were ashy and I realized we were standing in the snow.

Winter. Black bile. A cloister. A tooth.

I am going to the Land of Witches.

"I'm going," I told my brother. He grunted and told me to lie down. He brought me a cup containing a few tablespoons of American soda that turned circles on my tongue, flat and sweet. "Don't get up," he said. Moonlight fell through the bars of the window and glinted on the gun against the wall. *Who gave you that?* I tried to ask. I think it was my father. Against my throat I could feel the gentle, comforting irritation of the thin gold necklace he gave me before he died.

I remembered my brother's face the day I came home, that desperate brightness, every muscle tensed to keep him from slapping me.

Tonight he was all softness, touching my hair while the city shook. I clutched his hand. The noise grew louder and louder. A terrible clatter approaching. In the inferno of sound and light I understood why my dissertation had failed. No one can practice the Dream Science alone. Everything depends on the Festival of the Dreaming, when all the witches dream together. "Come with me," I shouted at my brother, "dream of pomegranates." He shook me off and crawled to the gun by the wall, moving like a snake or an orphaned child. When I rose from the bed he screamed at me to stay down. I crouched but reached for my papers on the table. Everything shook and I could read my writing in the leaping light. "Notes Toward a Dreamer's Lexicon." "Dusk," I screamed. "The rattling of dry leaves." My brother was shouting, the city was shouting, the sky was shouting. How will we fall asleep in this noise? I thought of Verken dreaming with her eyes open. "Dream with your eyes open," I told my brother. The gun was at his shoulder, his gestures expert, fluid. My voice was raw. I tasted blood. Lightning. The door opened.

4. Notes Toward a Dreamer's Lexicon

Pomegranate: Dusk. The rattling of dry leaves. Winter, black bile, a cloister, a tooth. Dream of pomegranates to enter the Place of Mourning.
Rabbit: Springtime. Erotic love. Silk sleeves. Ease after a long illness. Green.
Ice: The hidden life of things. Music, especially bells.

Bat: Magic. A holy place. A child.

Parsley: A feast.

Veil: Gentleness. A curtained window. Dawn.

Javelin: Movement, possibly from fear. A pounding heart.

Ostrich: A woman with plans. Dream of ostriches to enter the Place of Tents.

Fur: Unspoken longing. Lamplight. The river.

Boat: A new friend. A change in weather. Domestic uncertainty. An illness.

Cake: An intimate event.

Spider: Intellectual endeavors. A wound.

Wrist: Failure. Attachment to sorrow. A conspiracy.

Urine: Forgetfulness. Stone. A torch.

Cup: A fall.

Grapes: Jewelry. The Place of Emerald Noon. An exchange of gifts.

Pumpkin: Tears. Relief. A project begun at the proper time.

Fog: A walled city. The cry of a miracle vendor. Home.

Additional notes by Sagal Said

Milk: Moonlight. Mother. Toil. Circular thoughts. Buried rage. A hand.

Charcoal: Alchemy. Transfer. The sea at night.

Tea: Father. Exploding plaster. Ordinary death.

Gourd: Discovery. The act of overflowing.

American soda: Economic exploitation. Frustration. Healing. Love.

Wire: A threat.

Dishes: Whole: A beach. Broken: A storm. Disintegration.

Necklace: A gift. A chain. Constraint. Return. A debt.

5. The Travelers

We set off on a windless, moonlit night, a night that often returns to us, skimming along our pathway like a boat. At times we have even boarded this boat and passed into our own point of departure, into the beginning of our journey. Of course this origin moment is never the same. We find the identical silent town, the familiar moon suspended among the mobile towers, but passing on tiptoe through our Diviner's old apartment, we discover a row of spoons laid out on the carpet. These spoons were certainly not in this position on the night we left. We debate their meaning in whispers so as not to wake the household. The Mountaineer is for going on, the Harpist for exploring the rooms. Meanwhile, the Diviner discovers a flask in the otherwise empty birdcage. She takes a sip from the flask, which makes her shudder, and announces that we must descend the ladder. Sure enough, there is a ladder outside the window. The Mountaineer goes down first. The Diviner leaves a lock of hair on the couch for her son to find in the morning.

I, of course, have taken some paper and a bottle of ink from the cluttered old desk. As our Scribe, I am always in need of these materials. At the bottom of the ladder we find an afternoon in an insect-haunted restaurant that smells vaguely of scorched rice. This suits me very well, as it gives me the chance to arrange my papers at the table while the others order food. The Archivist and the Diviner argue over a word on one of the peeling posters, whether it means "palace" or "chair." Among the papers I have taken I find a few penciled diagrams, perhaps the schoolwork of the Diviner's son, and a number of notes on the kingdom of Kush that may have come from the hand of our own Sagal. Immediately the blue outside the skylight intensifies. The waiter brings us rice cooked with tomatoes, an oily mess we devour with delight in the suddenly splendid atmosphere, the atmosphere of a morning after dreams. The Archivist leans forward and stubs out her cigarette in excitement (a cigarette made, alas, with a scrap torn from my records—the Archivist thinks she's returning them to the source of all dreams, while I mourn their loss—part of our longstanding argument about hope and cyclical time). The Archivist swings her legs down from their resting place on her enormous pack, which sits beside her on the floor, and plants her feet, ready for business. She seizes my pen and begins making notes on the notes, cross-referencing. "Museum," she mutters. "Crocodile. Wedding. Trace."

This is how we travel. The Mountaineer strides before us. The Archivist follows, cheerful under her pack. This pack, stuffed with paper and tied all over with sheaves, bundles, and scrolls, weighs nearly as much as the Archivist herself. Short and stocky, her cheeks blasted by wind and her eyelids creased with sun, she looks more like a mountaineer than our Mountaineer, and we often joke together that we must be the most athletic members of our respective professions ever known. Her strength derives from the pack she carries, mine from the wagon I haul behind me, on which our drunken Navigator moans in his sleep. At intervals he wakes to gaze about him in childish happiness and let fall a few precious words concerning his dreams. He is such an excellent Navigator that no one minds his infirmity, or the astounding cunning with which he acquires all manner of liquor and drugs, though it is annoying when we have to go uphill, or worse, through mountains such as those which have surrounded us for two days. Then our progress seems agonizingly slow, as the Mountaineer, who despises haste as much as idleness, laboriously constructs, deconstructs, and reconstructs a system of pulleys to drag our party up the cliff-sides. One would think the Navigator could at least strap himself into a harness! But no, he lolls like a baby being dressed. Today was particularly bad, as the Diviner had been practicing blood divination, and was nearly as weak as the Navigator.

Her lips were gray as the stony cliffs. "Shouldn't we get out of here?" I whispered as I buckled her harness for what seemed the twentieth time. Dreams swooped about us in the dusk, all of them more attractive than our current location. One bore a beautiful stretch of beach, like the rind on an orange. With an effort the Diviner shook her head and pointed upward. We toiled on until we passed the snow-line. Now, from the cave where we shelter, I can see a vista of harsh dry stars and hear the desperate howling of the wolves.

Firelight flickers. The Navigator sleeps, the Archivist smokes, and I wonder how long we have been on this journey, and whether we will succeed in piecing together a map of the Land of Witches, and whether we will ever go there. I remember again the night we set out, and how the Mountaineer trembled, overcome, he said in a strangled voice, by the thought of redemption. I watch him as he scrubs his naked torso with a hot sponge, his back whitened by the stripes he received in Laceration Field. The Archivist catches my gaze. "Don't lose heart," she says. "Remember the gardens!" And even the Diviner smiles from the depths of her weariness, recalling the abandoned gardens where the Archivist and I, filled with reverence, left notes for other amateur witches on the trees.

Gently, our Harpist begins to sing. A moment of hushed awareness, like the instant when one realizes one is dreaming. The Diviner raises herself on an elbow and sniffs the air. It is just midnight. The wind dropping. The sky clear.

Meet Me in Iram

We are familiar with gold, says Hume, and also with mountains;
therefore, we are able to imagine a golden mountain. This idea may
serve as an origin myth for Iram, the unconstructed city.

The city has several problems. 1) It is lacking in domestic objects.
2) It is lacking in atmospheres that produce nostalgia. In cities without the correct combination of—for example—hills, streetlights, and
coffee, it is difficult to get laid. A playbill in a gutter, bleeding color,
the image of a famous actress blurring slowly into pulp: This would
be perfect. The word *playbill* is perfect. There are many ways to achieve
the desired conditions. Iram has none.

No continuity without desire. There is no desire in Iram; the time of
Iram is *not yet*.

> *oh do you remember when we were courting*
> *when my head lay upon your breast*
> *you could make me believe by the falling of your arm*
> *that the sun rose in the west*
>   —American folksong

167

The reversal of time expressed in these lines is impossible in Iram. In Iram there is nothing to reverse. Every time I go there, I see my uncle on the same bridge, and he raises his hand to greet me in the same way. He always tells me not to say *every time*, but I can't help it, it's a habit. He wishes I had come to visit him in Jeddah. I couldn't go, I tell him. It would have meant an expensive trip. I would have had to wear an abaya. I couldn't do it.

My uncle is not at all angry. Well, he says. He pats my shoulder. Well. He's wearing the most magnificent orange suit. Like my father, who is waiting for us at the restaurant, my uncle has style. The men in my family are all very beautiful.

When I say that Iram is lacking in domestic objects, I mean that we haven't gathered enough. I try to bring something with me every time. Last time it was a collection of my father's audiotapes, crammed into a pair of black plastic bags. The tapes are dusty with cigarette ash and poetry. It is only possible to listen to them in the worst light. A white, ugly, institutional light that, despite its harshness, is too weak to travel more than a couple of feet.

Fortunately the tapes create the sort of light they need.

At the restaurant, my father has already ordered. As always, he's gotten the huge appetizer plate, more than a hundred appetizers arranged around a bowl of blue flame. I kiss his cheek. He waves, expansive: Sit down! It's important to order the biggest thing. The entire restaurant must smell my father's cologne. In Iram, this makes me happy. This is the good life. I don't know what the blue flame is made of, but it keeps everybody warm.

You can stop there.

My mother says: Your father had beautiful skin. This was before he began to suffer from psoriasis. Now he goes out in a hat and gloves, even on the hottest days. My father has become allergic to sunlight. How is that possible, my mother asks. He's a Somali, he grew up in the sun! My father puts on his hat and goes out to his car. His beautiful skin, my mother says sadly. The car starts up: a throbbing sound that remains, for me, after all these years, synonymous with fear.

The car pulls into the driveway. The children hear its long, low note. They hear the door slam. The children run upstairs and hide inside their rooms. They're giggling because it's beautiful and exciting to be a child. They're smart, like bugs, they can squeeze into any kind of space. The children make bug-nests for themselves out of torn-up letters and photos. They squirm around in the nests and eat a lot of paper. The children are going to turn out fine, but they'll be the kind of people who do not have many things they can take to Iram.

In a city where one could find—for example—dogs, palms, and graffiti, it would be possible to fall in love.

Have you not considered how your Lord dealt with Aad, with Iram—who had lofty pillars, the likes of whom had never been created in the lands? And with Thamud, who carved out the rocks in the valley? And with Pharaoh, owner of the stakes? All of whom oppressed within the lands, and increased therein the corruption. So your Lord poured upon them a scourge of punishment.

—Qur'an 89: 6–13

169

The Wikipedia article on Iram warns: This article *needs attention from an expert in Archaeology.* The specific problem is: *the article is a confusing mix of myth, supposition, popular sources and very little science, scholarship or sense; the result is a meaningless overview of the subject, accompanied by random facts and inexplicable leaps of logic.*

According to the article, Iram is also known as *the City of the tent poles.* It is *a lost city* or perhaps *a tribe.*

The passage from the Qur'an quoted here appears in the article. A note at the end reads: *translated by error.*

I walk to the restaurant with my uncle. There's nothing, no atmosphere. It's like anywhere. Iram, the windless city, is buried underground. I wish there were more of a glow so that I could see my uncle's suit. Once, I remember, I told a friend I was disgusted by the idea of a Daddy-Daughter Dance. So heterosexist, I said. I mean— ugh! My friend said she had gone to a dance like that with her father when she was a little girl. Magic, she said. If there were a glow I could take my uncle's arm. She felt so special. It was the happiest night of her life.

Translated by error.

In Iram, my uncle understands me perfectly. I realize we've been speaking in Somali. We sing the song about the Prophet Isa's birth, the one about the darkest night. The very darkest night.

∾

It almost doesn't matter that I'm carrying these awkward plastic bags.

In the window of the restaurant, there's a small blue light. My father waits for us inside. It's the way I told you before. Happy, happy. I'm the only woman there.

There are hardly any women in Iram. This is a problem, because without women nothing happens. Nothing goes on without them. You will have realized at once that there's a connection between these missing women and the missing domestic objects. In Iram there are windows but no curtains. I'm not saying women have to create these objects, I'm saying they do. Sometimes, after dark, I catch sight of a woman just disappearing around a corner. I recognize her from her photograph.

According to the ninth edition of the *Encyclopaedia Britannica*, Iram is a lost city *which yet, after the annihilation of its tenants, remains entire, so Arabs say, invisible to ordinary eyes, but occasionally, and at rare intervals, revealed to some heaven-favoured traveller.*

I write on a scrap of paper: *Q-tips. Deodorant. Small hand lotion.*

I have a terrible longing to visit Iram again. I'm full of plans. I want to take a beaded wooden spoon with me next time—I think it's somewhere in my parents' house. The Somali pillow, too, and the little stool we used to call the African Stool. I'm sure that, when I reach Iram, I will know its true name. Perhaps that sounds romantic, but I believe things have true names. I believe everything has a name that I don't know.

~⊗~

In the restaurant, my father and uncle laugh together. My father grips my uncle's shoulder, chuckling naturally and with pleasure. It's not the explosive, uncontrollable laugh that seized him in our house the night some Somali guests came for dinner. My father had invited them. Everything was going well, and then something happened—I believe my brother made a face at one of his kids—and my father started laughing and couldn't stop. I remember we all laughed, too, we kept telling each other how terribly funny it was. Our guests smiled politely. You have to understand that at this time it was very rare for my father to eat with us, even rarer for him to invite guests to the house. The production of a normal family required immense effort. We were all keyed up to the highest pitch of excitement. My father's laughter seemed to go on forever, past bearing. At one point I felt pinned inside it. I couldn't move. Later I would experience that kind of laughter myself, when I was working in South Sudan during the war.

When you're outside, you can picture exactly what you want it to be like, but once you get in, all you can do is follow along.

You can help me. You can tell me if these feelings are universal. What is normal? I've felt for a long time that *normal* is something suspect, that embedded in the idea of the normal is something dangerous, an erasure of everything *abnormal*, a death or a series of deaths. But isn't it actually normal to want to be normal? I would like to build an entire philosophy out of Iram, the absent city. This philosophy would serve all the children of immigrants, many of the immigrants, and many others who found themselves at a loss. Eventually people would come to say: *This philosophy is available to all. Anybody can go to Iram.* All sorts of people, many of whom looked nothing at all like me, would disembark in the unconstructed streets. They'd bring their own bags, their photographs, their desire. Early in the morning, you'd find teenagers putting up playbills on the walls. Their sense of satisfaction would be so strong, it would color the air. For the first time, Iram would have a color of its own. But of course that can't happen until we import more objects, until we have succeeded in creating the conditions for nostalgia. For this reason, I fear that my feelings are not universal. Surely love cannot exist outside of time. It depends upon small objects.

The fact is, when my uncle died, he and my father were barely on speaking terms. My mother told me that my father disliked my uncle's gifts, specifically the gifts my uncle gave to my mother and me: gold jewelry, dresses heavy with beads. My mother, who is often sad, and not without reason, was sad because of this split between my uncle and my father. She and I wore our glittering beaded dresses to a New Year's Eve party. Everyone said we looked beautiful, exotic.

My father didn't go to the party. My father went somewhere else. I don't know where. Perhaps he was helping to draft the Somali constitution. When he disappears, I always imagine him doing heroic work. Once someone asked if I thought he worked for the CIA. I said I don't know.

We never eat anything after the appetizers. We're drinking tea from my uncle's thermos. My father and I use cups, and my uncle uses the lid. In the radiance of the cobalt flame in the center of the table, of my uncle's marigold suit, I am dreaming of things to bring to Iram. I wish I could bring a bathroom door from the library at the University of Wisconsin–Madison, but how would I take it off, how could I get it out of the building? I'm picturing myself in the snow and ice, sliding down State Street with the big gray door clasped somehow under my arm. Impossible. And anyway, I don't know if that object would work. I don't think it's sacred in the way that a piece of cloth worn by a relative is sacred. Something that holds perfume. The door of a public bathroom stall—it's so anonymous, it doesn't even hold the imprint of my shoe. The imprint of my shoe where I kicked the metal door in a rage. A Somali student had told me his name was Waria. I knew it wasn't a name. He was making fun of me. It couldn't be a name, because it was just a sort of word. It was just something you said, not you but my father, on the phone. A sort of preface, like *Hey* or maybe *Hey you*. I realized I didn't know what it meant. Something melted in my face. Excuse me, I said. I went to the bathroom.

I question this idea of the *heaven-favoured traveller*. What kind of favor is it to arrive at an empty city? A city that goes on, lifeless, *after the annihilation of its tenants*? I'm just standing here on the corner with my bags.

To have no one to blame but yourself is to have no one. It's the worst fate.

a lost city or perhaps *a tribe*

I want to fall down in Iram. I've never tripped or fallen there. It's the sort of thing you can't organize; it has to come up and catch you unawares. I want to be caught and thrown to the ground in Iram, to scrape my knee. Look, there's blood. That's me. If that happened, I feel certain a new kind of light would arrive. I'd look down at my blood on the pavement, and my blood would show me the edge of a flight of steps. That's really what it's called. A flight.

If it gets too painful, you can stop.

When my uncle died, he left six children. Two sets of triplets. Three boys and three girls. I don't know them, because my father is on bad terms with my uncle's widow—in fact he is estranged from her whole family. My uncle and his wife had their children through IVF treatment. When I was a child myself—long before my uncle's children were born—I remember being told that my uncle was unable to have children, because of what had been done to him in Somalia, in prison.

You can stop.

The woman is smiling in the photograph. I'm on her lap. I'm three or four years old. I asked my mother who she was, but my mother didn't know; she couldn't remember; she said, You'll have to ask your dad. I was getting ready to move somewhere—perhaps Cairo, perhaps Wisconsin. My father had not been home for several days. I put the photograph away with the others. I was afraid to ask, afraid to find out that this lovely woman, my relative, was dead. Now I consider this an act of cowardice. I remember the picture. The smile. It seems to me that one corner of the photograph is cut off. Was someone else there? This woman is happy, she loves me. She smiles so fully, with such golden warmth, as she disappears around the corner in Iram. Next time, I think, I'll rush to catch her, I'll shout, perhaps I'll fall down in the empty street. But of course there's no *next time*, only *not yet*. At one point I thought I was writing this to force myself to ask my father about the photograph. But I must have lost it, because it's gone. I can't ask now.

> i wish i was a little swallow
> that i had wings and i could fly
> ⌒

My uncle was shot and killed in his bed. Addis Ababa, 2011.

I'm just standing here on the corner, holding my plastic bags.

Very little science, scholarship or sense.

I'm just trying to hold them both. Let's all laugh together. Sweet blue light. Let's pour a little more tea. Let's order more appetizers. Dad, let's stay here, let's not go. I remember when I was a kid, on long car trips, I'd imagine a giant saw was attached to my side of the car. The saw could cut through anything. It sliced fences, it sliced trees. The fences gave a swift groan and exposed the hollow insides of their poles. The trees went *snick* and fell over with juicy ease, the tops of the stumps left gleaming moist and pale, like a wound before the blood comes. I was leveling the whole country from my seat in the back of the car. I don't know why it gave me so much pleasure. The world was coming down to size. I know it sounds like the opposite of what I'm trying to do in Iram, but the feeling is the same.

The chapter of the Qur'an that mentions the city of Iram is called *al-Fajr*. Dawn.

Because we are familiar with gold and we are familiar with mountains. Because we are familiar with pillows and spoons. Because we are familiar, we can imagine. Is that true? Look, here I am, at my desk on the highest roof of the city. I sit up here at night so that you can find me if you come. I am listening to my father's cassettes. You will have noticed that there is sound in Iram, and this is why I come back, I think, to these blank and shrouded streets. I am trying to imagine sound as an object. As soon as I press *play* the light comes on, that white ceramic glare, and cigarette ashes lift away from the tape recorder and disappear in the air of Iram, where it is always night. Light pins me to my seat. When my father was in the basement listening to poetry, we knew we mustn't disturb him. The door was edged with grainy fluorescent light, the stairs coated with black rubber. It was a terrible, terrible place. And poetry came up as it comes to me now. I know the words for *pearl* and *water*. I am singing of the moon, of a great-limbed tree. Amber necklaces come to me and thorns and rain and a fiery horse and a lonely dhow adrift on a trackless sea. In Iram I know the names. I sit repeating them, enraptured, frozen in an ecstasy of bad light. No continuity without desire. Look for me if you come. You'll know me by the falling of my arm.

Request for an Extension on the *Clarity*

Dear X,

I am writing to request an extension on the *Clarity*. I would like my term extended for twenty years. I've received two other extensions—one for two years and one for ten—but I've never managed to get a twenty-year term.

I've decided to contact you directly instead of going through my supervisor, in the hope that, once you've heard my reasons, you will grant my request.

Now you're thinking: well, this is unconventional! Keep in mind that you have not hired me to do a conventional job. You have hired me to live almost alone and I live almost alone and my work is excellent. The *Clarity* has run for thirteen years without a pause. She is my boat and my cottage and my cocoon. Cocoon is not the right word. Coconut? Coffin? That was a joke.

Dear X, I wish I could see you. I wish I knew your name. But you are veiled in the obscurity of the highest rung of the Program. So I make do, despite my disadvantages, despite the fact that I know nothing about you while you know everything about me.

❧

Tap the screen. Look at me. Here is what you will see:

One subject, female, black, 41 years of age.

Height 1.75 m, weight 62 kg.

Subject wears orange.

Subject stretches, eats, performs equipment check, plays with cats.

Subject feeds cats.

Subject reads, writes, eats, evacuates, showers, stretches, performs equipment check.

Subject waters terrarium.

Subject sleeps.

Earth outside the window, sweetly curved. The stratosphere like cream.

Do you really know everything about me? What do you read in these fingers tapping, the pause for a neck-rub, the clearing of the throat? What do you read in the stars? Did you know that God is a potter? Our moon is a pot encircled with white copper. God turns it one quarter at a time.

You might hear me whisper: "Potter, copper, quarter." This is normal. Solitary people grow sensitive to the rhythms of language.

God's name is Amma. As I perform the daily equipment check, you might hear me murmur: "Amma. Om. Home."

I know, of course, that God did not make the *Clarity*. Humans made her to receive transmissions from our distant ships. The *Clarity* circles the Earth like a small bright moon. Inside, I keep her healthy, monitor her functions, sometimes send out a request for parts. The parts are sent up in a pod with my food and supplies. A low chime sounds when it connects, and the cats prick up their ears and mew. My tabby cats, Crick and Crack. When I open the door and climb down to open the pod, they crowd against me, they want to jump down inside. "Get out, get back!" I say. They know there are treats in the pod: liver flavor, their favorite. I haul everything up. "Santa's here!" I tell them. The cats spool around me, beside themselves. We open everything at once. There's a mess on the floor, boxes everywhere. I am singing.

Singing inside this moon. This copper pot.

Dear X, I am never lonely. That's why I'm perfect for this job. I heard all about the loneliness when I was in training: workers screaming, scratching themselves, even hurting the cats that were put there to keep them company. People talked about loneliness as if it were something alive and it could get you. But loneliness is something dead, it's deadness. Lonely people are slowly dying people. SO ALONE WISH I WAS DEAD, I once wrote in a notebook, but it wasn't true. I wished I was alive.

The opposite of loneliness: *Nommo*. Nommo are two things, two beings, a pair, the offspring of Amma and the Earth. You can say "Nommo is" or "Nommo are." Nommo is water and copper. Their enemy is the jackal. Their number is eight.

I know this because I read it in a book.

When I was in college, I took every class about Africa they had. Anthropology, history, art. In those classes I used to feel more alive, but also a little bit shy and strange, as if I were spying on my parents. I read about the Dogon of Mali, who deduced the existence of Sirius B. I read about Nommo, who multiplied until they were eight. After spending eons in the celestial regions, they returned to Earth in a flying granary powered by the sun.

The seventh Nommo is a woman spinning.

A man wrote a book proposing that the Dogon had been visited by aliens from outer space. How else could they have known about Sirius B? How did they know that its orbital period is fifty years? How did they know to call it "the heaviest star"? I read this man's book and I read other books. I read that the Dogon had discovered the atom. I read that the ancient Egyptians knew about DNA. These are not books you quote in your papers for college. You read them in corners, on buses, balanced on the bars of an exercise bike. These books bear stains of sweat and coffee-mug rings. They are gray and musty, you find them in junk shops, hostels, old people's basements, the bedrooms of people pretending to be artists, you download them from garish websites flanked by pictures of flashing dashikis, riddled with pop-up windows that set off your anti-virus software. THREAT DETECTED. The files print out strangely, a torrent of different fonts. Sometimes twenty or thirty blank pages in the middle. The tone of these works is insistent, hectoring, relentlessly positive, the narrative voice part preacher, part poet, part emcee. BROTHERS AND SISTERS I WILL INITIATE YOU INTO THE MYSTERIES OF THE DOGON A TRIBE OF **BLACK** PHILOSOPHERS CHARGED WITH KEEPING THE SECRETS OF THE VOID. The edges of the pages are turned down, crumpled: reading them on the bus, you curl them to make sure nobody sees the print.

The curving pages make a private space. It's a space of adventure, shameless bravado, sumptuous paranoia. WE WERE ALL KINGS AND QUEENS UNTIL THE **WHITE** MAN CUT US DOWN MY BROTHERS AND SISTERS! HE ENVIED OUR SKIN LIKE SATIN AND OUR HAIR LIKE LAMBSWOOL! Do you understand, dear X, that it is possible to regard such words as nonsense, and also to discover in them a source of strange, life-giving energy? To shove the pages into your backpack, to get off the bus at the college feeling somehow tougher—not freer, not taller, but more tenacious.

Nommo are human beings from the waist up, serpents from the waist down. Their eyes are red, and their bodies are covered with short green hair. Nommo have forked tongues. Their speech is a vapor that makes a sound. Like Nommo, all beings are double. Crick/Crack. All except the jackal.

Do I sometimes fear that I am the jackal? Of course, dear X, of course. SO ALONE WISH I WAS DEAD, I wrote that afternoon. I had just given a presentation in my college class. On the way back to my dorm a brightness, searing. Dead squirrel in the snow.

But I don't wish I was dead. Not anymore. And, as you can see from my profile, I never really did. There was never a "plan." It was more that I didn't want to bother with living, I didn't wish to take steps of any kind. Most of all, I didn't want to fight with anyone. So I got out of bed when the resident assistant told me I really had to, and I went to the doctor like she said, and the doctor said, "Tell me why you won't get up," and I said, "I did get up, I came here," and he gave me some pills, and I took the pills at the right time every day and went to class and walked back to the dorm in a fog and did homework until I fell asleep at the table, and I woke up and got some water and went to the bathroom and ate some crackers and went to class again. I graduated with honors.

That's one of the reasons I'm supposed to desire something more than maintenance work on the *Clarity*: I am supposed to be too smart. Most people with my gifts, I am told, are ambitious. When I was in training, they called maintenance work the Bridge: it was just a step toward something better. My family can't understand why I keep doing this job. My mother says: "You should be out of there by now. You've paid your dues." She complains: "You're just going in circles." And my father, who once sneered at my supposed ambition— "Sure, go to space, never mind the rest of us suffering on Earth!"—my father says, "Come back."

"Come back to us. Come home."

But where is home? Look, I'm in college, giving a class presentation. I stand up and say: *Anthropology*. I talk about the loss of African voices under this other, louder voice, the voice of the anthropologists. My professor is an anthropologist, a white man. He says I have been too dismissive, too quick, I have failed to consider what anthropology saved. He tells me that there are many things Africans themselves only know about their cultures because they have read about them in books.

My professor has been to Africa. I have not.

In Africa, my professor takes pictures. He takes pictures of some wooden stakes on a beach. Prisoners were once tied to these stakes and shot. My professor takes pictures of a castle made from bricks that arrived as ballast on the slave ships.

When the aliens appeared to Sun Ra, they told him to drop out of college.

THREAT DETECTED.

After my class presentation I walk to my dorm in the snow. A squirrel has been hit by a car. I stop, my boot almost touching the body. Snow falls, masking the blood. I stand there for a long time.

⮑

In Africa, my professor takes pictures of schoolchildren with ringworm. He takes pictures of passengers on the roofs of buses. When he shows the ringworm pictures in class, everyone tsks sadly. When he shows the bus pictures, everybody laughs.

Years later, I go to Africa, too. The word "Sudan" comes from *Bilad al-Sudan*, which means "The Lands of the Blacks." I go to the lands of the blacks. In markets, people try to sell me masks and malachite beads. I pretend I'm not frightened on the buses. The idea is to avoid the good hotels, to look for the worst hotels you can find, so as not to be too American. In Nairobi, I am sick. I drink at the Gypsy Bar, where the foreign journalists go. I am American. I am lonely.

I don't take enough pictures. When I get home everyone will say, But where are the pictures?

I try to bring back tastes. Goat meat, coffee with cardamom. Home again, I spend lots of time talking about the food. The taste of fresh mangoes, you can't believe it! I sound like anyone.

In Alexandria, some boys on a balcony shout down at me: *Monkey!* I am American but not American enough.

I am sick in Alexandria. A pharmacist gives me a shot. She tells me to look at the saint on the wall, a nimbus of gold under oily glass. There, says the pharmacist, finished. She pats my arm, a superfluous tenderness, she says, it's ok now, why are you crying?

Homeless. At the Ramses Hotel nobody asks for my passport. They think I'm there to carry the white tourists' bags.

Well, I thought, if I can't go home, maybe I can leave. And I trained with the Program only to become, as my mother says bitterly, a kind of extraterrestrial janitor.

But just think: I'm always visible from somewhere. I'm a star! That was a joke.

After I make it through training, there's so much happiness. Our daughter is AN ASTRONAUT! Even my father gives me a grudging hug and says: "Well done." My mother's so giddy she makes four kinds of pie. Later, at the end of my first extension, she makes her pies again. At last I am going to do something with my life. When I tell them I've extended my term for another decade, my mother throws a whole key lime pie in the trash.

I am an astronaut, but not astronaut enough. I'm never photographed. I'll never be famous. I don't explore. I'm too close to home.

Home: a cloudy brilliance, a nimbus of gold under oily glass. It looks so fragile out there, a soap-bubble breathed by God.

The seventh Nommo spun the thread to guide the celestial granary to Earth. Where the craft landed, it created a pool of water. Nommo descended into the water, which is their element. In their vaporous tongue, they began to speak of mathematics.

Dear X, if I had twenty years here I would write a book. I'd like to write a book called *The History of the Circle*. In this book there would be people who went from Africa to the Americas and then back to Africa and then back to the Americas. There would be a girl who treaded water and almost drowned. For her, the sun would rise like a round white pill. This girl would have a twin somewhere, although she would not know where. Everyone in the book would have a twin.

Tap your screen. Watch me perform the ritual of the *Clarity*. Click hum, press hum. These days I can do it almost like a dance. The monitor records the action—*Subject performs equipment check*—but cannot grasp the meaning that fills each gesture. I dance the pull of gravity, the steady embrace of home. The cats sit and watch, paws crossed, like pieces of Egyptian statuary. My jade and jasper familiars. I bend down, I stand. Click hum. Lights spin around me, signs that everything is well. The *Clarity* is alive and so am I. I turn and turn again, not dead, not sick, not a jackal and not alone. We are twins, the *Clarity* and I. We are going around the Earth. At this distance, everything's clear. I know where I'm from.

When I returned to the U.S. from Africa, I took the airport shuttle to the train station, and there a man came up to me. He thrust his wrinkled face into mine. "SISTER! HOLD ON, SISTER!" Did he recognize me somehow: my huge backpack, my torn jeans, my traveler's stink? For a long time I thought he knew me for one of his own, and the thought terrified me. When I was in training I'd wake from dreams of him, heart pounding. His clumped white hair, the impossibly tattered pamphlet in his hand, against the wall his nest of blankets, his cardboard bed. Homeless, he's homeless. He sleeps here in the vastness of the station, among the booming announcements, the unrelenting light. "SISTER! HOLD ON, SISTER! I'M HERE TO TELL YOU ABOUT AFRICAAAAA, AFRICAAAAA LAND OF PROPHETS LAND OF GOLD." "I've just come back from there," I say quickly, trying to get rid of him, but it doesn't work, he doesn't hear me, not because my voice is too small, but because his Africa, this AFRICAAAAA of the long melancholy falling note, exists on a different plane from the place I have been. There can be no communication between the Gypsy Bar in Nairobi and this AFRICAAAAA of the gleaming palaces built from blocks of salt, where men and women in indigo robes walk slowly up and down the steps, carrying scrolls that map the farthest stars. "WE WERE NOBLE SISTER IN AFRICAAAAA WE WERE

RICH SISTER IN AFRICAAAAA WE HAD KNOWL-
EDGE THAT WOULD MAKE THESE UNIVERSITIES
TODAY LOOK LIKE A KINDERGARTEN! I WANT TO
GIVE YOU THAT KNOWLEDGE," he bellows, pushing his
pamphlet into my hand, this wad that looks dredged up from
the bottom of a lake, this disintegrating book. "I DON'T
WANT MONEY," he adds, because I'm trying to give him a
dollar, I'll do anything to get away, I'm nodding at everything
he says. But he takes the dollar. And I take the book. "GO IN
PEACE AND POWER," he yells at my retreating backpack.
Rumbling and shrieking around us, the trains.

I never opened that book on planet Earth. But I brought it
with me here, to the *Clarity*, along with all the old print-outs
that helped me survive college, the embarrassing paperbacks
with the cheap, ugly covers. The pamphlet from the man in the
station has been written out by hand in ballpoint pen. Inside—
well, of course there's no astounding revelation, dear X, what
did you think? There's a circular argument, rambling, ranting,
outrageous. It's just what you'd expect. Here on the *Clarity*, it's
my research. It's a book you can only understand from space.

Sometimes at night I wake up and feel so light, so light, my
shadow buoyant under me. No, I will not be the one to discover life beyond earth. But perhaps I will be the spinner, or
the thread that guides them home.

Please consider my request for an extension.

The Closest Thing to Animals

I have a habit of meeting people right before they get famous and don't need me anymore. I met Rock Morris two weeks before his book came out. I met Cindy Vea when she worked at the bakery. Her hair straggled out of her ponytail and neither of us would have guessed you could even be a full-time blogger. Six months later, I emailed Cindy to remind her about the panel we were putting together for the Conference on Negative Realism. She never wrote back. I met Nadia Barsoum the year before she started growing peppers. She kept saying her knee hurt. We thought it was the fog.

The day I met Hodan Mahmoud, I was home with a cold. I'd been cultivating it for a few days, staying up late, leaving my house with wet hair every morning, and coughing a lot at work to make my throat sore and let people know I was coming down with something, and finally it had paid off. I was lying under blankets, pleasantly woozy, preparing to sleep, really sleep, when I heard something crashing and banging around outside the window. It lasted so long, I got up to see if dogs were in the trash, and there was Hodan digging around in it with a stick.

I pushed up the screen and leaned out. "Hey!"

She looked up. "Hey."

Hodan always has a vague look, sort of drowsy. She was wearing a green bandana over her hair, and a stained trench coat with the belt tied instead of buckled. I immediately felt embarrassed. I thought she was homeless. I'd never stop a homeless person from going through my trash.

"Hey," she said, "I know you."

"Um," I said, but then I realized she was right: we'd gone to the same college. Now I was even more embarrassed, and also sort of panicked, because you should probably invite an old classmate up for tea, even if she's turned out homeless.

"I'm sick," I blurted. "I'm home with the flu."

"That sucks," she said. She sounded genuinely sorry. "Am I making too much noise?"

"No, it's no problem. I mean. Are you — is there something special you're looking for?"

She didn't seem flustered. "Not really," she said. "Just checking."

Hodan is a great artist. I knew it the minute I stepped in her room. She had a sculpture of the Lolly Whales made out of plastic milk jugs. The Lolly Whale sculpture glowed faintly blue, exactly the way the real Lollies had done on the beach when I went to see them as a kid. There was even a Lolly Whale smell in the room: a gentle, wistful stink. It came from the milk jugs, Hodan told me later. She'd never washed them out properly. That was her genius: she understood that whales are made of milk. She'd put fairy lights inside the jugs to make them glow.

"*Wow*," I said.

She opened the fridge. "Want a lassi?"

"Sure. *Wow*."

We drank canned lassis sitting on the floor in the glow of the Lolly Whales. There was nowhere else to sit. There was a bed, but it was covered with junk: old stuffed toys with their hair worn down, lassi cans, paper bags.

"Where do you sleep?" I asked.

Hodan looked at me sort of blankly. "On the bed."

Outside her little window the night lights went drip, drip. The red ones are Hodan's favorites. She told me that later. She says they slide down the sky like luminous cough drops sliding down a throat.

"I love this," I said.

She didn't try to pretend she thought I was talking about the lassi. She didn't even ask me why I was whispering.

"Me too," she said.

She doesn't have a big smile, but it's very warm. You probably know what I mean. You've probably seen her picture.

Hodan was born in Minnesota. She moved here when she was twelve. She fell asleep on the plane, and when she woke up she was flying over a crater. No trees at all outside the window, just drifts of something that could have been snow or sand. "At one point," she told me, "it was the moon." I think she still feels like she's living on the moon. I do, too. Things get away from you, like you're trying to hold onto dust. When Hodan was in eighth grade she said she hated California and her teacher sneered, "It's better than Somalia."

We used to get packed snow from Minnesota. Remember that? It was a big deal to get a carton while it was still a little bit frozen. Kids used to stand in line. That was before the lanugo. God, it makes me feel old.

This is a really good world for artists.

I'm not an artist. I mean, I am a little bit of an artist. You are, too. Don't you secretly think you could write a book someday? Are you into embroidery, or making jewelry from bottle-tops and shells? The kind of artist that just calls themselves "artistic." At my job we used to have a plan for you called Unlocking the Artist Within. Cindy Vea developed it almost right after I got her a job at the company. It seemed like she'd only worked there for two weeks before she was quitting, and blogging, and suing, and famous, and not my friend anymore.

I loved having Cindy as my friend. She wore white shoes that cut her around the ankles. She always had Band-Aids there. Her look was totally hungry. "That one's starving," said Marco, my boss, on Cindy's first day at work. Approvingly, of course. He didn't know the half of it.

Cindy and I used to stay up late. We'd sit on my bed and eat day-old bread from the bakery where she worked, her wolf-face harsh in the light of my reading lamp. We said "we" a lot. We criticized everybody at both our jobs. Cindy had phrases. That's her gift, I think, the thing that made her famous. Lots of those phrases are on her blog, unlockingtheartist.com. "Get what you wish for." "You can have safety or passion—your choice." The phrases I remember from our late-night talks are dumber, but also more intimate somehow, like "Never use lip balm, it's addictive."

After I met Hodan, I went on unlockingtheartist.com for the first time. It gave me a little pang to see Cindy's face on the screen. A professional photo, perfectly lit, her head tilted to one side. Her jaw looked smaller. I wondered if she was still wearing the shoes.

I clicked on the link called "Putting It Out There." The new page unrolled like a carpet. It had the same fine print at the top, decorated with something like tiny feathers: "This blog is the sole property of Cindy Vea." I guess she didn't want anyone to forget she'd sued the company and won.

"Whatever, Cindy," I told the screen.

I scrolled down the Helpful Tips. My idea, of course, was to Put Hodan's artwork Out There. "Find your community," Cindy advised. "Can't afford to rent a space? Team up with a friend. Be their opening act."

That's me, I thought. The opening act.

Except I never take off on my own, the way you're supposed to, according to Cindy's blog. "An opening act is like a baby bird. At a certain stage, it'll leave the nest." I imagined Cindy typing this in her room on the eighteenth floor. The elevator was broken; that's why we always hung out at my place. I imagined Cindy there, even though I'm sure she's got a better place now. I could hear her long, firm fingers tap and see her long, firm jaw in the light from the screen. I saw her get an alert from me: "hey! about that conference . . ." She tucked her hair behind her ear in her quick impatient way and clicked Ignore. She was wearing the gray sweater with the yellow patch on one shoulder. I was with her the day she bought it. "Ugh!" I said out loud. "Stop thinking like this!" I closed the tab and opened a new email.

> *Hey Nadia! Omg it's been ages. How are you? Good, I hope! I'm ok, just dealing with Marco's bad breath and worse manners, haha. Anyway look I'm writing because I saw you're doing a fundraiser thing (which is awesome!) and I was wondering if you'd like to involve an artist? I have this friend Hodan (Somali like me!) who does AMAZING stuff, really timely and innovative—for example, sculptures of extinct animals from upcycled trash! I think you'd love it, and it could help raise awareness about environmental issues at your gig. Anyway, let me know!*
>
> *Love,*
>
> *S.*

At work, I was developing a project called Finding Your Center. Marco's idea, not mine. Still, I'd had to sign all the new paperwork: the pages of terms and conditions to make sure I didn't go off and start my own blog with the same name, as Cindy—or, as Marco called her, The Razor—had done. Marco had taken to hanging around my desk, fuming. He cracked his knuckles like the bad guy in an old movie. "That *bitch*," he'd say. When he wasn't growling and swearing he'd lean over me and, in an oniony whisper, ask me for Cindy's number.

After work I went on walks with Hodan. She pushed a baby carriage. By the time night fell, it would be full of trash. "Nice one," she'd say, if I found something rare, like a child's rubber bracelet. She was never in a hurry: she could frown at an empty chip bag for fifteen minutes. She was never the one to say we should go home, either, but when I suggested we stop for dinner she was always ready to go. It seemed to me like she'd found her center. "Have you always been like this?" I asked. "So calm like this?"

She laughed. "I'm not calm."

Once we'd sat down and ordered, I said: "You're calmer than I am."

"Okay."

"See? *Okay.* You agree to everything! I wish I could be like that."

"I don't agree to everything," she said. "I hate lots of things. Most things, in fact. Except trash. And light. And food."

"And me," I said. I wished she'd said it instead.

She smiled. I know you've seen it, but when it's for you—it's like being injected with honey.

The tea came. We added milk, sugar, and a dash of pepper to make a drink Hodan called California Shaah.

California Shaah tastes terrible. It's nothing like real tea. I still drink it, though. It might be a magic potion. It might turn me into something.

"If somebody said to you, I need to find my center, what advice would you give them?" I asked.

"Wow. That's a terrible idea."

I went home and called my parents and listened to my mom cry. I always call them when I feel bad, and it always makes me feel worse. They were on vacation in Florida when the quarantine came down. Every year it becomes less likely we'll ever see each other again.

When the quarantine first went into effect, the tent was black at night, smudging the stars. In the day it was the same as it is now:

grayish, like a fuzzy window. The sun lamps helped in the daytime, but at night, they eventually figured out, the extra blackness was making people depressed. I don't know if it made me depressed. I was in college, and taking a lot of Q, which was popular then. It made you feel a ghostly presence. My ghostly presence used to part my hair and blow on my neck. I found it comforting, so I probably *was* depressed. The night the lights came on, I went outside with everyone else and looked at the sky. Lights sliding down in different colors, like glittery rain. Everyone clapping and taking pictures. They hadn't tried to mimic the stars: studies had suggested that would only make people feel worse.

I lay on the floor and watched the lights, trying to avoid the red ones. I was annoyed with Hodan. Pissed off, really. Maybe Finding Your Center was a stupid project, but it might help someone someday, maybe not a great artist like her, but a regular person, someone who was ready to try anything, knitting, diet and exercise programs, meditation, because they lived in a giant bubble and couldn't visit their parents or anything, and any minute they might catch the lanugo and die. That kind of person might actually be interested in finding their center, not arguing about whether you should think about it or whether it even existed. I fell asleep on the floor and woke up sore, as if I'd been kicked. There was a paper bag with a note on it under my door.

Please forgive me for last night. I'm sorry I upset you. I hope I can offer you the fact that I am not used to being with people, and have it arrive not as an excuse but as a truth. I know that I am often withdrawn. I'm fighting it all the time.

For me it is difficult even to imagine a center. A center seems like something inside, but I picture everything going out. My whole effort over the last few years has been to open, to give, to be in the motion of opening. Maybe I don't want a center.

Despite the desire to open constantly I have been closed! For example when you asked if I had a partner or dated people. I said "no," but that was a half-truth. I'm married. My husband is on the other side of the tent. He was on a business trip.

When I found that I was a tent-widow, I was glad in a way that made me feel angry. I walked a lot. I lost two of my jobs. But now I'm glad in a way that just makes me feel blank. I see this as progress. You know how there's gray in the morning? Soon they'll turn on the lamps.

Does it ever seem strange that we call it a tent? A tent is supposed to move. Why don't we just pack up and go?

I wish we'd gotten to know each other in college. I was always too shy to talk to you, even though my parents had told me to make friends with other Somali girls, and of course you and I were the only ones. You were so beautiful (still are!) and you seemed to be everywhere. So different from me. At ease. You didn't have the immigrant thing. The shit that used to matter! But some things still do. The way you can say with confidence, "Safety or passion—your choice!" I admire that.

My husband and I speak often. We're considering a divorce. It's hard to see what counts as safety sometimes, and what counts as passion.

As for "your choice"—that's one of the ways I want to open out. To give that to others. I love you, abaayo macaan. Talk to me later? Your choice.

I love you, dear sister.

The trains hadn't started yet. I ran all the way to her apartment. I leaned on the doorbell, then after a minute I heard her undoing the locks. I started talking before she opened the door. "I wish I could hold onto even one single thing from the past. I'm a tent-orphan, but I wish I could be a tent-widow too. I wish there was more stuff holding me down. Sometimes I think there's other new diseases out there, besides the lanugo, and maybe I have one."

We hugged. I held her so tight. She was wearing a T-shirt and her shoulders felt solid and soft. "It's like I'm made out of string," I said. I realized that people, with their warm weight, their softness, and their smell, are the closest thing we have to animals now.

I determined to make Hodan Mahmoud famous. It was the great purpose of my life.

And yes, I did think I might become a real artist as well. Sometimes I thought I was changing slightly. I kept a notebook beside my bed and wrote words in it, *her hand, the fog, my hand*. I felt that Hodan and I would enter the world as artists together, although I was not sure exactly how this would happen. Perhaps I'd write poems about her work. The important thing, I felt, was that we stick together, side by side, finding our way.

Nadia Barsoum came through. She didn't write to me, but her manager did. I read the email out loud in Hodan's apartment. "Ms. Barsoum would be happy to allow your client to exhibit her works in the convention center at the *Fight the Lanugo* event."

"Your client!" Hodan chuckled through the scarf that covered her mouth. We both wore scarves, because of the fumes. Hodan was varnishing.

She read my eyes. "You don't look happy."

"I am happy! It's just—she could have written to me herself. We used to be really close, you know, before she got sick. We did all this stuff . . . We'd sneak onto trains. We learned how to knit together. We went dancing at the same place every week. For a year."

"You knit?"

"Not really." I shook my head hard and blinked. "Never mind. This is good news!" As I said it I realized it was true. Hodan frowned, not in a rude way, just in the way that meant she was going back into her work. I loved that look. She was varnishing buttons and little chunks of eraser. It was for a piece called *Summer of the Swollen Bees*. If you've seen that one then you know how it gives you all the precise feelings you had the summer it happened: when the big slow bees came drifting over the sea and filled the air like confetti or tiny party balloons before they gave up and died all over. When you walk inside *Summer of the Swollen Bees*, it's like entering a fresh and sparkling afternoon where childhood is everywhere magically dying. I watched Hodan work and listened to the whirring of the air cleaner and felt so happy. I honestly didn't mind that Nadia hadn't written.

A friend is like armor, I thought. Or like a tent.

The height of happiness was moving things into the convention center. The space was huge and dark. We brought our own lights, because the city wouldn't turn the lights on in the center unless there was an event in progress. A couple of guys and one girl from the center helped us move all the pieces in on trolleys. They joked and flirted with us. They set up little round tables. The idea was that the visitors would stand at the tables and drink their drinks or whatever, and around them would be the art.

"Hey," said one of the convention guys. "We should all go to Disneyland."

Disneyland was what they called this big space at the back of the center. A ramp went steeply down into dark. You got on a trolley, held onto each other, and flew down the ramp with your eyes shut against the crash.

There was actually no crash in Disneyland. You just rode on and on through darkness until you stopped. Your stomach kept going down and down.

So there I was, at the big event. Smart dress, boots, red lipstick. Tilting my head to one side. I was the artist's friend. People talked to me like I was her manager. I made sure I kept Hodan in view at all times. I didn't want our relationship to grow thin.

The room filled up. Though I tried not to, I saw Cindy Vea at one of the tables. Of course she was here. She was talking with great animation and gesturing at a piece called *Mild*. *Mild* is the one that just hangs there until you want to go to sleep under it. Take that, Cindy, I thought. You'll never make anything half as good.

The truth is, I was nervous enough to scream.

Some important person went up on the stage and introduced Nadia Barsoum. "If there is a way out of quarantine, ladies and gentlemen, this may be it." A moment later, Nadia rolled up to the podium. I hadn't expected the bubble. There was a box on it for her voice, and she had to maneuver so that the box faced the microphone. Her voice sounded full of bees. "Hello, everyone." I kept thinking of trains, the way we'd hide in the bathroom and ride to the end of the track.

"Hey," someone whispered close to my ear.

I turned, and it was Rock Morris.

"Hey," he murmured with his seductive smile, "I heard you work with the artist?"

"Yes," I answered frostily.

"That's great. Could you give her my card? I'm Rock Morris, the writer? *Apocalypse Manifesto?*"

He was handing me a card. It had a drawing of a man smoking a pipe on it, because Rock Morris is a pretentious ass. He also has animal magnetism, which is basically an allergen. Some people aren't allergic to it. I am.

"Could you ask her to get in touch? I'd like to write about her for the *Times*. Maybe even an interview? I don't know if she does those anymore."

Then we just stared at each other. On the stage, Nadia talked in her buzzing voice about the future and about death. "I think of myself as a field," she said. I was staring at Rock Morris, trying to process the meaning of the word "anymore." He was staring at me the way you stare at a person when you remember you once asked them to suck on a piece of hard candy and pass it into your mouth.

"Holy shit," he said.

Somebody shushed us.

"Holy shit," he repeated more quietly. "It's you! I mean—this is amazing! How *are* you? And how do you know Hodan Mahmoud?" He was laughing, incredulous. "This is nuts!"

"I go on waiting for winter," Nadia said.

I went inside *Summer of the Swollen Bees.* A couple of other people were in there, exclaiming at the beauty of the silvery flecks. One of them was crying. I tried doing some of the breathing exercises I'd written about for *Finding Your Center,* but soon I gave up and searched Hodan's name on my phone.

I should probably explain that I never read about the arts. Not even Cindy could make me do that, with her phrase "Know your context!" I hate the way it makes me feel. I'm like the woman in a story I read who swelled up until she burst all over her couch. Inside the woman was a tiny baby girl, curled around her sternum. The baby was waiting to take the woman's place. My envy is like a hungry baby curled up in my chest, pissed off, impatient for me to swell up and die already.

I looked at all the galleries where Hodan's work had been displayed and the articles about her and the pictures. In the photographs she looked thinner. I tried to see that she also looked unhappy, as if something were missing from her life, but she just looked like always: half asleep.

I strode through the swollen bees, knocking them aside. Hodan was in a crowd, of course. I pushed through them. "How could you?" I shouted. "Why didn't you tell me?"

Her smile faded. "What?"

"That you're *somebody*," I yelled. I waved at the people, the lights. "That you've done all of this before. That you don't need me."

Riding the train home I just cried and hated. This is such a good world for artists, but it's a terrible world for everybody else. It's terrible to live underneath a quarantine tent with no birds or wind if you can't find a way to make yourself immortal. What's the point of this experience if you can't turn it into something else, some sign? Are you just going to stand there and leak like a broken hourglass? Blurred lights passed in the window and I could see Hodan and Cindy and Nadia Barsoum and even Rock Morris sipping bright drinks with little parasols in them. They were drinking and laughing together and everybody was taking their picture. And I just cried. How carefully I'd read *Apocalypse Manifesto*! I can still quote whole passages. "Everything must be about something now. There is no room for the inessential." And he hadn't even remembered me. The night we met at the Book Club and he told me, so excited, that his own book was coming out soon. His room with the real wood floor, and the kids' toys and picture books lying around because his sister and nieces got stuck at his place in the quarantine. We tiptoed in so as not to wake them up. "They throw their shit everywhere," he said. And in the morning there was something wrong with my tights. I yanked them on and crept out while he was asleep because I knew he was disappointed in me and wouldn't call me back. Hobbling to the train station in my tights like a pair of shackles. By the time I got home my legs were almost dead. Upstairs I realized that I'd taken a pair of his niece's tights by mistake and I felt the whole meaning of my life in that error. I really did. The whole thing. So strong I could cry about it months later on the train. I was almost at my stop when my phone buzzed in my coat. A text from Nadia Barsoum. "No surprise that u didn't say hi since u never visited me in the hospital. U really are the worst person."

I hadn't done Q in years, but I still had a stash in the medicine cabinet. When I got home that night I lined up the pills on the counter. Every time I started feeling alone, I took another Q. A ghostly presence held my hand for forty-eight hours.

When the last of the presence faded, I went to see Nadia Barsoum in the hospital.

I got there too early for visiting hours and had to sit in the freezing lobby. Everything smelled like a dentist's chair. A nurse who smelled like a dentist's chair came and took me into a room to change my clothes. I had to wipe my entire body first with a special kind of wipe. The clothes were pink: "It seemed like you," the nurse explained. A pink cap buttoned over my brow. The nurse took me up to Nadia's room, where I looked at Nadia through a plastic wall.

Inside, Nadia had a normal room. She had a blue fuzzy carpet, a desk, and an old-fashioned lamp with a yellow bulb. There were books and balls of yarn all over the place. It was the kind of room where you would expect to find a cat. The only cat, however, was Nadia herself. She was in the most advanced stage of the lanugo ever experienced, because, unlike other victims, she had survived. Her long hair grew everywhere. It was shorter on her hands and face; she must have trimmed it.

"Hi, Nadia."

"Hel-*lo*," she said. "Will wonders never."

She looked tiny, shrunken in all that hair. She was wearing a purple sweater vest and denim shorts. I tried not to look at her legs.

"I'm sorry I didn't come before."

"Oh my God. What *are* you? Are you a person? Like, 'Help, my friend is sick, let me run away. Oh wait, no, I need a favor for my other friend! Let's see, let me call my abandoned friend and ask *her*! I won't talk to her though! Because ew!'"

"That's not what I meant."

"Are you going to start crying? Because that would be awesome. That would be so perfect. Oh my God. I need a camera."

I swallowed. My eyes were stinging. "Nadia, I am so sorry. It's just—you were busy. You were so busy all the time. Your appointments and interviews—"

"I was busy *being sick*! I was busy *almost dying*! What is *wrong* with you? Are you actually made of cardboard?"

"Yes," I said. "I am. I'm made out of cardboard."

She shook her head. Her knees were red, raw clusters of peppers—anyway, they looked like peppers. I remembered when her legs started aching, and she joked that she had arthritis like an old lady, because it got worse in foggy weather. And then her lanugo started, and she disappeared into the hospital, and my own test for the disease came back negative, and I didn't even tell her because it seemed like a betrayal, like I should have gone with her into illness and death. And now her knees, the only part of her body not covered with hair, were these bulbous bunches of bright red growth with yellow veins going down. I wanted to ask her if it hurt, and it occurred to me that at this point I had nothing to lose, so I did.

"Nope," Nadia said. "They give me the most amazing drugs. Like I'm flying right now. You can thank these drugs that I haven't thrown you out. Seriously, I feel great. Do you still knit? I made this vest. I always do some knitting after my weekly hand-shave."

My eyes stung again. "I sort of gave it up."

"Why does that not surprise me? Cardboard."

Her eyes shone dark and bright underneath the wings of her brows. Her power to make a room seem warmer was absolutely unchanged.

"Nadia, I'm so sorry!"

"BO-RINGGG! Sorry but life is like, really short."

She took a pile of papers from her desk and shook them in my direction. "Guess what this is? A book. It's called '*Lanugo Memoir*.'" She put the papers down to make quotation marks in the air with her furry fingers. "In quotes. Everything in my whole memoir is in quotes. Like I say we made 'sweaters' out of 'yarn.' We had 'milkshakes' in the 'park.' That's to show how fake everything is inside the tent. You know? The human ability to make all this amazing fake shit. Fake meat. Fake cheese. They way they make fake food that actually goes bad if you leave it out."

"Like milk," I said, thinking of Hodan's Lolly Whales.

"Exactly! It's to trick us so we don't run around screaming from horror. But actually we should all be screaming from horror all the time. Except me. I'm real, you know, a real animal, and now also a real plant. And the doctors are pretty sure that Plant-Me is saving Animal-Me. I'm going to put a giant picture of me on the cover. It'll be like, 'All of lost Nature concentrated in one young woman!' Totally grandiose. You better buy a copy."

"Of course I will."

She shook her head, smiling. "Well. You actually came up here. That's something. Do you still hang out with that girl from the bakery?"

"Cindy Vea. No."

"Good! She came to my thing, you know. Came up to me afterward like 'Can I interview you for my blog?'"

She still had her talent for mimicry. She could even do Cindy's jaw. I laughed.

"Seriously! And I was like, what could possibly be in this for me?"

"Her blog's kind of famous."

"Look deep into my eyes and ask me if I give a fuck. She's the worst."

"I thought I was the worst."

"You're a close second."

Before I left, Nadia told me her mother visited every day. "You're lucky you missed her! Oh my God! She stands there and prays for hours!" She told me it was weak and insulting to pretend to believe in prayer if you really didn't. Because she loved her mother, she screamed and threw things during the prayers. "Drone drone drone," she said. I told her how much I missed Cindy Vea, how I'd been looking forward to the Conference on Negative Realism, how sad I was that now I couldn't go. "Why don't you go by yourself?" she said, and I told her I didn't think people would listen to just me.

"Do you think people want to listen to that awful Cindy person? Are you broken? Why do you love everybody so much?"

I told her I'd written a poem for her.

"Let me hear it."

"It's really short."

"Just let me hear it!"

"Okay.

> *her hand*
> *the fog*
> *my hand*"

Once I read that an aluminum ring dropped through a magnetic field will fall more slowly. Maybe if the magnets were strong enough, they could keep it from hitting the ground. Once I read of an old Somali poet who demanded to know why he should stay in the country now that the girls, slender as trees, were gone. I've read a lot of other things I could tell you about, but I don't really think it would help. On my way to Hodan's place, I picked up a scrap of plastic. I picked up a piece of gum. It was old and hard and I scratched it off the sidewalk and placed it tenderly inside my pocket.

She undid the locks on her door and left the door open, then turned away and got into bed. I went inside and closed the door and fastened the locks. When I turned around she was sitting with a great quilt over her lap, bent over and stitching. It was so beautiful I gasped.

She looked up, her eyes sparkling not with happiness but with tears. "I'm sorry I didn't tell you about the galleries. I didn't think it mattered. I never know what matters, to you or to anyone. I'm not good at it. I'm too dumb."

I took a deep breath. My stomach went down and down. "You're right. It doesn't matter," I said.

It was like peeling off skin and throwing it away. And everyone would see that under the skin you were nothing but cardboard and plastic and string and fake milk, utterly inessential.

I crossed the room, took off my shoes and got under the quilt opposite Hodan. Cans and toys jostled under me. Our feet touched. I squirmed until the random objects around me made a nest. The quilt was huge; I could draw it all the way up to my chin.

"I feel like there's a magnetic field in here," I said. "I'm still falling, but more slowly."

On the quilt there were elephants and bees and whales. There were people fleeing their country and a dead woman by the side of a road and a little boy vomiting in the back of a truck. There were terrible crowded apartments and policemen banging the doors with their guns and a cat in a noose hanging from a mango tree. There were trees and trees and girls as slender as trees lined up to draw water in dusty camps. There were lonely taxi drivers chewing qaat in the snow. There were bats and bleeding lizards and whales expiring on the sand, the brief lovely grotesque menagerie of our childhood. I snuggled down into it. Soon I was lying curled around Hodan's feet. I drew the quilt over my head and went to sleep.

Fallow

I. Miss Snowfall

Here is the peaceable kingdom.

I once heard a beautiful story. Two people, a brother and sister, worked at the Castle until they were very old. Then the sister fell ill and couldn't work anymore. In her illness her eyes became brighter and brighter, and her face thinner, until she looked like a little old child. Eventually she was so small the brother could carry her on his back. He carried her up to the Castle for medical treatment. There's a long part of the story in which the brother staggers through the Castle, getting confused, going into the wrong rooms, waiting for hours to get clearance. All the time he has his sister on his back, and also something else: her pain, which has been growing until it nearly fills her whole body. "Pain is the heaviest thing," said Miss Snowfall, who was telling the story. A faint clicking came from the back of the room, where some boys were fiddling with chalk. At the end of the story, the two old people were so worn out and bewildered they returned to the village without even seeing a doctor. The old woman died in her bed, underneath her own quilt, holding her brother's hand. Her last words were: "Do you remember the way to the Castle?" Miss Snowfall delivered these words in a soft voice, almost a murmur, a voice that always filled me with a special anguish, because it made it seem as if she were speaking not to us but to herself, that she was far from us, removed. After the story she took out her handkerchief and, in a characteristic gesture, doubled it up and pressed it to her lips. Temar hated the story of the brother and sister, but to me it's like a window through which I can see another world.

In those days, if you had asked any of us what we wanted to do when we grew up, we would have answered: "Work at the Castle." Children probably say the same thing today, but I imagine it carries a different meaning for them than it did for Miss Snowfall's pupils. For us, who had the immense good fortune to study under a teacher so inventive and eccentric we often didn't know we were studying, a teacher whose one goal seemed to be to whip our imaginations into a frenzy, the Castle was a temple, a magic portal, a citadel, a cave. Ezera said it was an inverted world in which people floated face downward. Lia insisted people there spoke without words, in bolts of electricity. To all of these fancies Miss Snowfall responded with an approving smile, a smile that was slightly sad and therefore irresistible. We competed with one another for the honor of provoking that smile. Even those whose parents worked at the Castle, such as Elias, whose father was a security guard, or Markos, whose mother conducted inspections of the water system, made up outrageous stories without being scolded. "That's probably true," Miss Snowfall would say with her melancholy smile. The classroom was a zone free from accusation. All things were permitted there, above all Miss Snowfall's weird assignments, which included knitting and lying on the floor to contemplate the inner light.

After school the children would pour out into the yard and then through one of the gates, either through the north gate with the inscription WASTE NOT, WANT NOT, or, like Temar and me, through the south gate, which bore the inscription ARBEITE UND HOFFE. Miss Snowfall also left through the south gate, but not immediately after school. Instead she would stand at the window, half concealed by the curtain, as if she were watching us go, although it also seemed she couldn't see us, for if we waved to her she never waved back. Temar constructed a romance for Miss Snowfall out of the fact that Mr. Cinders, who taught mathematics to the upper classes, always glanced toward the window of our schoolroom as he bent to pin back the legs of his trousers before mounting his bicycle. But Miss Snowfall never made him any sign either, and so Mr. Cinders cycled home slowly to Unmarried Male Housing, a dreary edifice known as the Barn, to dine (as we imagined) in a hall full of noisy men who made fun of his protruding ears.

Miss Snowfall did not live in Unmarried Female Housing (known as the Henhouse) but in a room above Nimble's dry goods dispensary. The Nimble family lived in the other rooms. If you were lucky enough to be sent out after supper to get some sugar or a packet of needles, you could see the silhouettes of the Nimble children romping about in the whitish light that filtered through the blinds. The real attraction, of course, was Miss Snowfall's window, which gave off a yellow light, and through which no movement at all could be discerned. She was reading, we told each other, she was observing the inner radiance, she was writing letters or drawing a self-portrait. I was admitted to this room twice: once after Temar was lost and Miss Snowfall made me sit in her chair and chafed my hands, and a second time when Miss Snowfall herself was lost, having managed, with typical ingenuity, to hang herself from the light fixture.

For me, those early school days are infused with a Sunday glow. In fact, the real glow of Sundays, which has inspired so many verses, and which rules our bodies like the hand of a hidden puppeteer, has never made me as happy as the rusty gloom of the schoolroom. On Sundays when I was a child, we would get up early, like everyone else, and rush outside into the intensified light. My mother would always be there before us, seated in her chair in front of the house, her eyes closed, her entire body gilded. We would sit beside her on the squares of roughcloth we called "the outdoor blankets," careful to keep our feet on them so our scrubbed shoes wouldn't get dusty, enveloped in a timid silence, not even waving to our friends across the road, who were sitting outside with their own parents. All over the village, a hush. Only the cows broke it, lowing. And my father would appear around the side of the house, his hands clasped behind him, his beard shining, his good shoes tightly encased in galoshes, returning from letting them out to pasture.

Then we stood and shook out and folded our blankets. My mother snapped shut her collapsible chair. Sometimes she stumbled slightly, saturated, dazed with light. We collected our Bibles and walked to church. Everyone looked dim and hot. A hymn rose, faint but steadily growing, from those who had already arrived. We smiled at each other, at friends, but did not speak. We began to sing. *We gather together to ask the Lord's blessing.* If we whispered, or looked as if we might step off the edge of the road, our father tapped our ankles with his cane.

Marvelous light. The white church seemed to pulse. You could feel it taking hold of you, lifting you. At school, Miss Snowfall explained the influence of that glow. We diagrammed the pineal gland while she spoke of the delicate secretions that make us particularly happy on Sundays. "Why can't we have Sunday light every day?" asked Selemon. Miss Snowfall replied with her favorite question: "What do you think?" Hands shot up; we guessed that too much light, like too much sugar, could make you sick, that it would be wasteful, that God wouldn't like it. Miss Snowfall erased the pineal gland and drew a line representing the surface of Fallow. She drew its tiny, fugitive sun, with arrows for rays. Squares represented the solar fields; a great opaque blob was our generator, which, she reminded us, has to power everything. It has to keep the reservoir working, the heaters for the pastures, the vast grain corridor, the production labs, the smithy, the workshops, the grottoes. "It has to power these lights," she said, indicating the orange bulbs in the ceiling. "It has to make air. It has to run the Castle."

We walked home through the eternal cold of the village, hands shoved deep into our coat pockets. I thought Selemon, who worked in the pastures after school, and who always smelled vaguely of the shit he collected on a cart, might grumble about all the fuel that goes to the generators of the Castle. Couldn't they use some of it to light the sky? But Selemon left us as usual at the crossroads, hat pulled low over his curls, giving us a quick wave before trotting off down Granite Road. We walked on with the other children who lived in our district, our breath rising white in the twilight, a tentative, greenish twilight that colored the tops of the houses, a twilight that would last just long enough for us to feed the chickens and bring in the wash before going out at the touch of a distant switch. Temar walked beside me, her chin sunk in the folds of her scarf. I was already taller than she, though nearly two years younger. I could see from her posture, her frown, that she was thinking, and knew from experience that if I spoke to her now I'd get a sharp reply. So instead of talking to her I talked to our parents at supper, cheerfully, volubly, in order to compensate for her silence. And, as usual, she gave me in exchange for this kindness a gift of far greater worth. When we were in bed, when I was sure she was sleeping, she spoke. Into the icy darkness of our room came the words I would not have dared to say, but which perfectly articulated my own feelings, words that fell on my heart with a bursting shock of recognition, reverberating for days afterward: "I hate Sundays."

After that I felt oppressed by Sundays, hounded. There was something dreadful about the secret workings of my pineal gland. I considered it a triumph if I could maintain a sour mood in the warmth of the churchyard, among the freshly washed and laughing children. As for Temar, she adopted an outward sign of isolation: It was around this time that she began to wear the shapeless black hat, knotted together from cast-off strings in Miss Snowfall's classroom, that led people to call her Temar Black Hat. This hat is the reason I am known as Agar Black Hat today, even though I have never worn such an article. I have been left with a phantom hat, a mark. It's better than nothing. "Fill the slate," Miss Snowfall used to urge us, "to the edge."

⥇

She was the daughter of Deacon Brass and his wife, who was known as Sister Brass. Her name was Sara. She received the name "Snowfall" after a fire. She was six years old when the Great Western Fire destroyed nearly a quarter of the village—workshops, granaries, labs, and animals. Seated on her desk in our classroom, swinging one foot, she described these horrors in a calm voice. The raw, piercing screams of chickens and, unimaginably, cattle. Men and women looming in the glow of the sky, which stayed on for three days, and in the blazing light of the fire. Everyone was covered with the earth they were using to smother the flames. They moved frantically and clumsily, figures of mud. Human bodies were dragged from the furnace, some of them still on fire. The ones that wouldn't stop screaming were carried to the infirmary. Handcarts rushed up and down the tracks, traveling east with bodies, traveling west with enormous piles of dirt, in both cases materializing out of clouds of smoke only to disappear again with a doleful creaking.

Sara stood at the window, where she had been instructed to pray, holding the blinds apart with her small fingers. The blinds felt hot; her eyes felt hot. And the ashes that began to fall looked pale and cool, like what we know of snow. To the child at the window, the air appeared full of one of the miraculous substances of Earth. "I wanted," she told us, "to run out and let it fall in my eyes." "Mother," she cried, "it's snowing!" And so she received her gently mocking nickname, becoming known from that day as Sara Snowfall.

"But the most memorable part of that time," she told us, "was the color blue." She had discovered, standing at the window, that if she looked at the orange flames in the distance and then closed her eyes, she was treated to a marvelous image of the fire in deep blue. The power of this memory led her to the back of the classroom, to her vast collection of specimens, odds-and-ends, and outright trash, to fetch the color wheel she had made with various powdered minerals fastened to a slate with glue. In accordance with her idiosyncratic, associative method, a drawing lesson followed, and then a lecture on the Age of Disorder, when our ancestors, crazed with longing for the vivid colors of Earth, took to stabbing themselves in the eyes with picks.

I would not want to suggest, especially in light of Miss Snowfall's fate, that we did not learn the proper curriculum. Miss Snowfall was extremely thorough. Often, when we arrived at school, we would find her poring over the huge books issued by the Council. To do this she wore a special reading lamp strapped to her forehead, advancing through our course of study like a miner. When we sidled in, awed by the sight of the books, she would look up and blind us for a moment with her flaming brow. Then she would switch off the light, and when our vision cleared we would see our own dear teacher, perhaps already pressing her handkerchief to her lips, wearing her customary pleasant and faintly sad expression, only a bit more tired, bowed down by the weight of history. We would take out our slates and Miss Snowfall would stand up and begin her lecture. With an energy and fluency I have rarely seen behind the pulpit, she spoke of the Former Days of Earth, of its bitter atmosphere and boiling seas, its floods, its storms, its wars and conflagrations. She spoke of the Universal Draft, which was, she explained, only the latest and largest version of the many drafts our people had faced throughout history, the innumerable calls to war we had refused, and for which we had been so often imprisoned, ridiculed, tortured, exiled, killed. My heart beat faster; I found myself scratching the underside of my bench with a fingernail, which always has a calming effect on me. Some of the children had tears in their eyes. It was so unfair, this senseless persecution, the pressing into evil of a people who only wished to be left alone. Miss Snowfall described the elders of the community, dignified and austere, holding the little children by the hand, standing outside the prisons in the hope of delivering some bread and comfort to an incarcerated generation. People going by would shove them, trying to make them fight. In one terrible region they tore out the old men's beards. She spoke of the Great World Conference and the decision to depart, not for a sympathetic country—there was none—but for the stars.

"And they built an Ark," she told us, " in the hills of Misraq Gojjam." She was keen to impress on us not only the heroism of the engineers, but the achievements of the preachers, lawyers, school-teachers, and bureaucrats who made it possible to save so many. In some parts of the Earth, governments were only too happy to let our people go; in others they strove to block us with laws and tariffs. Sums were raised in wealthy regions in order to help the poor ones, and peaceful liberation campaigns filled the streets. Of course, almost immediately there were disagreements and schisms. Some said only those of our faith should be permitted to join the trek; others said we must take everyone who desired a life of peace; still others argued over our faith itself, its character, its law. Such debates were especially fierce among those who practiced seclusion. Of these, some eventually boarded the Ark, believing that God would prefer them to accept a life dependent on advanced technology, rather than a life of war or a stillness amounting to suicide. Others, Miss Snowfall told us quietly, stayed on their burnt farms, among the cattle who were dying in the dust. In one district they shook out their sheets and curtains for the last time and went to bed, resolved not to rise until Judgment Day.

The Ark set sail. It was the Age of Drift. We rubbed out our slates and copied the plan of the ship Miss Snowfall drew on the blackboard. "The Age of Loaves and Fishes," she quipped, and a giggle went round the room, not because the joke was funny but because we needed to laugh. It was true the Drifters made do with almost noth-ing. For this, we revered them. Generations were born and died on the Ark. The bodies of the dead supported those of the living. For some reason still unclear to us, all the horses perished.

On the Ark they had a place similar to our grottoes called the Hanging Gardens. They had fish tanks, cages, rows and rows of beds. Most importantly, they had the great monitor Gabriel, which gave them a report from Earth every twenty-five years. Now Gabriel stands at the center of the Castle, where he still delivers his report every quarter of a century, as he did without fail, like a mighty clock, through the Age of Disorder, the cave-ins, the plagues, the fires, the cults, the breakdowns of the sky. "Put on your coats," Miss Snowfall said. She always knew when to take us outside. The room filled with happy jostling, voices, the drumming of feet. It is estimated that we will be able to return to Earth five hundred years after Gabriel reports a total absence of human life.

Mornings of childhood. The rush to get up, despite the biting chill of the floor, in order to be the first to use the water, and how often Temar, just as I thought I was winning, slipped in front of me and slammed the door of the bathroom in my face. The water, slick and gray with soap. Using Temar's old water was better than using my parents', which I would have to do if she spilled it (as happened more than once), for my parents' old water was speckled with tiny hairs. Down the stairs, taking the last three steps at a jump. Wan kitchen light. Injections, my mother's fingers warm, the needle cold. Only babies cried at their injections. Our little brother, Yonas, still cried, and Temar hushed him: "Father will hear you." Then the potatoes with beet syrup, spoons clattering on plates. Coats and hats. As we ran out, Father was coming in from milking. No matter how wildly we hurried, we never escaped without meeting him, his great cracked hand extended, his mournful black eyes that seemed to read our thoughts. "Good morning, Father," we chorused, and shook his hand. Then down the path and over the gate, never bothering to open it but swinging up over the rails. The sky was blue-green, Sheba and Naomi were running to meet us, and in the distance the roar of the smithy had begun.

Through the village, looking both ways for handcarts before we crossed the tracks, passing the Nimble store, the dispensary with the glass lamp in the window, the workshop where the door was propped open and looms already clacked, the desolate stretch of ground in front of the archives where Brother Lookout was sweeping. All day he swept the village streets with his funny sideways walk, his head subtly shaking as if he were always saying no, turning up a surprising amount of garbage, much of which found its way to Miss Snowfall's classroom, where it was used in projects or simply gathered dust. We ran past Brother Lookout, we ran even faster past the house where Sister Blunt had died and her husband had covered all the windows with roughcloth, we flew past Sister Wheel, who was always standing in her yard beside a table on which she had placed a cup of coffee, we cut through the old surveyors' camp, avoiding the piles of rubble, always wary of the boys who sometimes hid there to throw stones, and then other children were joining us, smelling of jackets and burnt potatoes, and it was now, we were climbing the hill, we were at school.

The door of our classroom stood wide open, and Miss Snowfall leaned against it, arms crossed, smiling. The bell clanged, rung by Little Yosef, the headmaster's nephew. And perhaps we would go in, sit down, and take out our slates, or perhaps by the time the last notes of the bell died away we would be on our way down the hill in two orderly lines. For Miss Snowfall believed in what she called "experiential learning." There were many days when we never set chalk to slate. Instead we walked all over the village, into the archives, the smithy, and the weaving workshop, where we bruised our fingers trying the machines. Together we pumped the handcarts and rode up and down an abandoned stretch of track. We visited the metal dome of the Zeitgeber, and were given a lecture on chronobiology by Brother Barter, who stammered whenever Miss Snowfall looked at him. We visited the clearance shed, where Sister Singer, who was as slim, sharp, and restless as Miss Snowfall was round and solid, gave us a special pink gum, which, she said, they chewed at the Castle, and allowed us to crowd up to the window and look at the Castle door. "How does it open?" Sheba asked. "From the inside, my love," said Sister Singer, peering up herself at the silver disc in the sky. "They open it up and send down whatever they want. And when the people go up, the ones that work there, they send down a ladder for them."

Filled with the image of Brother Bell and Sister Glove, the parents of our classmates Elias and Markos, ascending to heaven on a ladder like a pair of angels, we filed out into the grainy afternoon air to end our school day at the grottoes. This was Miss Snowfall's favorite place; indeed, she often joked to us that she had become a teacher only so as to secure a pass to that paradise. We made more trips to the grottoes than anywhere else. At the entrance we had to leave Markos, who suffered from allergies, in the care of the doorkeeper, Brother Flint, a cheerful old man with a worn gray hat whose pockets were full of finger puppets in the shape of animals, which he made out of cast-off clothes. I believe his whole menagerie must have come from the same garment, for the little pig, the little sheep, the swan, and even the bumblebee had been sewn out of identical black cloth, and looked so much alike that only Brother Flint himself could tell them apart. I always hurried into the front hall so as to see as little as possible of Markos, who would have to spend the next hour being entertained by these puppets, and whose misery as he watched us go was palpable. In the sterilization chamber I felt as if the stinging jets were scouring off my guilt.

In the room beyond we all put on the dresses of white paper. Already we could feel the air of the grottoes. Sheba said it gave her a headache. In the next room we met the boys and put on the dark glasses. Then we walked out into the grass.

Sometimes, like Sheba, I had a headache at first. Sometimes I felt dizzy, even nauseous, but this never lasted long. Creamy sunlight warmed my face. I was sweating. A powerful greenness filled my lungs, as if I were breathing in the color. Miss Snowfall brushed her hands over the plants and told us their names. Beneath the white dress, her legs were dotted with black hair. She waved to the grotto workers, who waved back, silent, swathed in white veils. There was a buzzing sound, and things rustled in the grass. We watched the fish in their pools, we saw a turtle make its way into the water, we stood at the edge of the deer park and cooed at the fawns, we observed the scientists working behind glass, where even Miss Snowfall did not have clearance to go, at the tanks that seethed with life, the lungs of Fallow. Always, at the end, we sat on the grass beneath the trees. Many of our classmates dropped off to sleep, for the grottoes made one drowsy.

With slow gestures, Miss Snowfall unbraided her hair and massaged her scalp, as if to allow the warmth to penetrate her skull. Her braids undone, her hair standing up, she looked winsome and very young. She began to tell us stories from the Bible. She spoke of poplar and chestnut trees, and of manna, which is white like coriander seed, and tastes of wafers made with honey. The light of the grottoes filled me to my fingertips—not like a Sunday light, which often accompanied terrifying words from the pulpit, confessions, and scenes of discipline, but like the light of seven days, in the day that the Lord bindeth up the breach of His people and healeth the stroke of their wound.

Often Lia crept into Miss Snowfall's lap and curled up there, sucking her thumb. Anywhere else, we would have mocked her for this babyish behavior, and who knows, even Miss Snowfall might have disapproved. But the grottoes enfolded her in their magic circle. I suspect Miss Snowfall knew, though we did not—yet—that Lia was beaten at home, more often and more severely than any of us, even Temar. Whatever the reason, she cradled Lia, murmuring of the aloes and the cedar trees which are beside the waters. Once, sitting very close to them, I discerned beneath the chemical tang of sterilization another smell, secret, rich, and sweet, a stink which I realized came from Miss Snowfall's feet. At that moment I heard, as clearly as if I had spoken them, the words: *Here is the peaceable kingdom.*

This is not the first time I have written something I intend to submit for preservation. I have submitted a number of works, more than I care to remember. All have been rejected. I have submitted dramas, fantastical stories, novels of Old Earth, children's tales, even hymns. At this point, merely to pass by the archives gives me a queasy feeling. For this reason, I rarely go into town, and if I need something unavailable in Housing, I pick it up from Sister Bundle's little stand, rather than visiting the stores. It is a terrible feeling to have your work pulped. Brother Chalk at the archives—whom I call Ezera, since I knew him at school—tries to comfort me by telling me that pulped paper makes fresh paper possible, that destruction and renewal is the cycle of life. His remaining hair clumped at the back of his head, his chubby jowls fringed with beard, he is a good man, a father, sympathetic, and one of my best friends. The last time I spoke with him, I thanked God that I had no pencil with me, for I might have succumbed to the temptation to drive it into his hand.

Outside on the street after I was rejected the walls of the village were crisp, the gleam of the Castle door in the distance extraordinarily distinct. I walked home with the new sheaf of paper under my arm. And I began to write in a different direction, without thinking of the Council. I began to write what I feel is truly worthy of preservation, what I cannot help preserving in my memory. I have no doubt that this writing, too, will be pulped. But I feel at the same time that I am enabling something of Miss Snowfall to hover in the world. The more I write, the more her presence grows, and I am amazed at how much I remember of her, a person I had to a large extent forgotten, first because I was preoccupied with my own problems, and later because the memory of her was so painful. "Put it in the dustyard," we say, when we mean that a thought or question should disappear. "Put it in the dustyard, Agar," Temar said to me, the night I saw her spit a tooth into the sink. But lately only these scenes stand out to me, and I kneel, overwhelmed, in the dustyard of memory.

Strange that this dustyard should hold images of such splendor. Miss Snowfall's bright face, her laugh, her stockings mended poorly because (she said) she was lazy, her wobbling progress through town on her brother's bicycle when he visited her from the mining camp and loaned her his machine. Miss Snowfall, living in town as she did, had never been granted a bicycle, but at some point her brother had taught her how to ride, and sometimes on Saturdays she appeared, shaky and triumphant, running her usual errands in fine style. She always dismounted with a nervous leap, which sometimes caused the bicycle to fall over, spilling her packages on the ground. Then she would laugh so merrily that whoever was around her laughed too, helping to pick up her things, never embarrassed. Even Sister Wheel, standing outside by her eternal cup of coffee, allowed a faint smile to thaw her face when Miss Snowfall crashed that bicycle, and Miss Snowfall would dust herself off and greet Sister Wheel, as she always did, for she feared no one—on the contrary, she had a special affection for the oddest characters in the village. She stopped to chat with Sister Wheel every Saturday, bicycle or no, though "chat" seems an exaggerated way of describing a conversation with Sister Wheel, who tended to stare at passers-by with an expression of controlled fury before dropping a "Hello!" from her mouth like a stone. Sister Wheel had been a Young Evangelist, and was now what was called "peculiar." She was often alluded to in sermons on the virtue of moderation. But Miss Snowfall spoke to her naturally, and in response I once heard Sister Wheel reply to her with a complete sentence: "It's a waiting game, Sister, that's all."

How wonderful it was to see our teacher outside school, to hear her addressed as "Sister" rather than "Miss," to greet her formally in the street while she twinkled at us with a kind of amusement that failed to conceal her pride in our good behavior. She spoke to our parents, she knew everyone, she greeted our little brother Yonas and laughed when he hid his face in our mother's neck, she was an ordinary person, carrying ordinary things, syringes, bags of flour, some gum she needed to fix a crack in a table. Meeting her like this, we felt that the marvelous air she breathed, the life she lived, was accessible to us, close. Best of all was seeing her brother in church: a short dark man with a heavy beard who once showed us the knife he kept in the side of his boot.

Why is it that when I write these memories down, they swell until they seem to contain my whole body? Miss Snowfall and her brother in the churchyard, convulsed with laughter as Bishop Gloss walked by with crumbs in his beard. Bishop Gloss was the most terrifying man in the village, the head of every meeting, a brooding presence at every disciplinary discussion, he had driven Brother Lookout out of his mind, it was said, he had come to our house to reprimand our father for keeping a dirty henhouse. We couldn't imagine laughing at him even if, at the fellowship meal that followed the service, he had bathed his whole head in soup. But Miss Snowfall and her brother stood frozen with suppressed mirth at the sight of the crumbs suspended in his majestic beard. Tears started from her brother's eyes; Miss Snowfall crossed her legs just as we did when we laughed too hard. She pinched her brother's arm harshly, like a child. At that the air came slowly out of his nose with a high-pitched whistle like the sound of the ancient brakes on his bicycle . . . Memories sparkling palely in the dustyard. The way Miss Snowfall lifted her chin when she said to Temar: "You may keep the hat." The hat, a knitting project, certainly should have been unraveled when it was finished, the thread returned to the box. But Temar had picked out all the black threads with such care, knotted them together so cleverly, even the hair and wire. And Miss Snowfall, with a strange redness around her eyes, said: "Keep the hat." In the same way she said to me, a year later: "You can be a writer." Another excessive gesture, the jutting chin, the red, sore-looking eyes. The other children snickered; Temar ducked her head, embarrassed. But Miss Snowfall said firmly: "Writing is a noble pursuit." The words sounded awkward, as words do when they have never been said before.

Perhaps this is why my memory of her is illuminated, enveloping: because, as much as we loved her, she dwelt among us like a stranger. I see her standing by the chalkboard, her arms crossed, rubbing her sleeves as if to keep off a chill, her face closed down, inert. Miss Snowfall could not bear discipline. If her pupils interrupted her—Markos and Elias were the worst offenders in our class, scuffling in the back—she simply stopped speaking. She would retreat into herself, go to the window, press her handkerchief to her lips. The first time this happened we were entertained, we wondered how long it might go on, and an evil spirit seemed to seep into the room, the cruel, gloating twin of the spirit of happy permissiveness that surrounded us when we spent whole afternoons building cities from empty jars. The chatter grew louder; Little Yosef laughed his braying laugh. Then Temar got up and strode to the back of the room. "Shut up!" she shouted at the boys. "Yes, be quiet!" I echoed, running up behind her, and some of the others joined in: "Let Miss Snowfall talk!" Temar's fists were clenched, her whole body shook, the air was charged with unbearable energy, and Elias looked us up and down with his slow gaze, a sneer spreading on his face, and I felt that something terrible was going to happen, when Miss Snowfall shocked us, shattering everything.

"No, no!" she cried breathlessly, rushing toward us in such haste that her hip banged against a desk. "Don't, please don't!"

She was speaking to Temar and me. Temar's eyes widened, amazed and hurt, and I felt a pang, for weren't we Miss Snowfall's defenders?

"Don't, please," Miss Snowfall repeated, trembling.

The class fell silent. Gloom covered us. Temar and I returned to our seats. Tears were trickling down my cheeks; I buried my face in my sleeve. When I looked up Miss Snowfall was paging roughly through a book, trying to find her place. She dropped her chalk on the floor, where it broke. Although I could not have expressed the thought at the time, I understood then that she had a horror of the exercise of power, not only the obvious sorts of power—the rod, the shout—but the type we knew most intimately: the power of the group. She had a horror of the downcast eye that waits for others to act, of the elders appearing at houses because someone, claiming to defer to their authority, has summoned them, of the public prayer that flays a member of the congregation in coded language. In other words, a horror of Fallow.

When Miss Snowfall was removed from her position, I had not been at school for two years. It was a difficult time for my family: Temar was working at the Castle and often refused to come home for the weekend, a source of great tension. As I recall, my sister was not at church when the special prayer for Miss Snowfall was held. I remember the heat of the sanctuary, the windows full of light, the grimy feel of the metal pew as I gripped it and scratched at its underside with a fingernail, discreetly, careful not to cause any noticeable vibration. Of course this sensual memory might have been lifted from any Sunday. From that particular day, I remember a sag of the heart as the bishop announced that Miss Snowfall was leaving the school, a feeling of guilt as he described her errors—the "haphazard" and "unorthodox" methods I had loved—and an immediate anxiety about what Temar would say. Then a long, circuitous prayer. Those in Miss Snowfall's vicinity were invited to lay hands on her, but I was too far away. I could only see, at the distant front of the church, the rustling bulge of bodies surrounding her until she entirely disappeared.

Afterward, at the fellowship meal, I remember thinking she looked scrubbed, almost scoured, as if she had washed her face too hard. Her eyebrows were sparse, her hair faded to gray. She gazed down at her plate with her head tilted, wearing an odd little smile. Several of the children were crying and had to be taken away. The truth is, it was a scene of woe. People were greeting each other, shaking hands, finding their seats. Before starting the meal we sang "The Beautiful River":

Oh, will you not drink of the beautiful stream,
And dwell on its peaceful shore?
The Spirit says: Come, all ye weary ones, home,
And wander in sin no more.

O seek that beautiful stream,
O seek that beautiful stream.
Its waters, so free,
Are flowing for thee,
O seek that beautiful stream.

The next time I saw Miss Snowfall, Temar was gone. I had been walking for some time. I had set out at dusk, carrying the lantern, and walked along the edge of the pasture all the way to the grain corridor before the light in my hand began to flicker. On Fallow there is always

a subtle sense of being closed in. I put my hand on the wall of the
corridor; it was freezing. Behind that wall, which reached all the way
to the sky, humid air caressed our grain and an intricate irrigation
system watered the ground. The water was made at the other end of
the corridor and kept in the reservoir. Pipes transported it all over the
village. I stood in the darkness, breathing hard. We are capable of such
miracles but no one could bring my sister back to me.

My lamp was growing dim. I turned and headed back toward
town, where a cluster of lights gleamed out of the dark. It was like
a great ship twinkling all along its sides with holiday lights such as I
had read about in the stories of Earth. By the time I arrived among
those lights I could no longer feel my feet. I stopped and glanced up at
a shadow in one of the windows. Someone stood there, looking out.
I wondered if the person could see me. Then the figure vanished and
the window shone clear.

I was turning away when a door opened and Miss Snowfall came
out into the street. "Who's there?" she cried, peering into the night.

"Agar, Temar Black Hat's sister."

"I saw your light go out," she said.

I looked down at the lantern in my hand; it was dead.

"Look at that," I said. I found it hard to work my lips, they were
so cold. "Do you know, I was just standing here thinking about ships.
Coming into the village I thought the lights looked like the lights of
a ship but they really look the way I think the lights of a ship must
look. Must have looked, I mean. Or perhaps they still look that way,
on the green seas of Earth, with the seagulls winging overhead. Do
you think there are still ships?"

Miss Snowfall seemed to consider. Then she said: "You'd better
come up and charge that light."

Her room was surprisingly bare. As a child, I had imagined it
stuffed with treasure—a more splendid, more glittering version of
her junk collection in our classroom. But it was simple, like anyone's
room. Bed, worktable, chair, gas stove, a lamp shaded with yellow
roughcloth. There was a ceiling lamp too, but it wasn't on. Of course

I thought about that later. I thought so much about Miss Snowfall's room, the big shadows thrown by the lamp, the chair covered with something shaggy, perhaps an old coat, where she made me sit. She knelt and tugged off my boots. Her hair was thin, wide tracks of scalp between the braids. She stripped the quilt off the bed and wrapped it around my feet. There was a photograph on the wall, a ghostly deer among weeds. "Oh, Miss Snowfall," I said, "my sister has run away."

"Yes," Miss Snowfall said quietly, and a charge went through my chest, everything coming up, my face swelling and twisting from the pressure, the pressure of my rage, this useless rage that had nowhere to go, and I broke, I sobbed in her chair, I bawled like a calf.

Miss Snowfall pulled off my gloves. She rubbed my hands. When I was calmer, she made coffee. My lantern, plugged into her outlet, had begun to glow. She put a cup of coffee into my hands and sat on the bed with her own, regarding me with frank, unhappy eyes.

I sipped the coffee shakily. "That's nice," I said, nodding at the picture of the deer.

Miss Snowfall lowered her gaze.

"I mean, I don't care," I added quickly, realizing that the picture could only have come from one of the Council schoolbooks, that it was stolen.

She looked up at me and smiled. For the first time, I noticed the tremor in her lips. Her lips jumped and twitched when she was not speaking. I saw how she tried to disguise it by holding her cup in front of her mouth or drumming her fingertips against her chin. I thought of her old habit of pressing her handkerchief to her lips. I wondered if she had always had this tic, or if, when I was a child, it had been only a vague sensation, a premonition underneath the skin.

I dried my eyes on my sleeve and blinked. "Is it an Earth deer?"

"Yes," Miss Snowfall said, turning to look at the photograph. Her cheek quivered, but the rest of her body seemed filled with a deep stillness like the otherworldly stillness of the picture. The deer looked into the room where we were. In the photograph, too, it was night. The deer stood motionless, pale, its perfect antlers etched against the dark. Its eyes were globes of molten light, symmetrical and clear. A night camera had captured it, Miss Snowfall said.

"It was wrong to take it," she added, "but I was angry, and I wanted something."

"It's not wrong to be angry."

She looked at me with some of the old amusement. "No?"

"No. Even Job was angry with God."

"Yes, but he yielded, he didn't go about tearing the pages out of books."

We laughed, then Miss Snowfall sighed and looked at the picture again. She told me it came from one of the fallow regions of Earth. A place abandoned by human beings because they had poisoned it, ruined it. And slowly, once they had gone, the animals crept in.

"I guess all of Earth will be like that one day," I said.

"That's the idea."

I was startled by the harshness of her tone. When I left, she made me take the picture. I folded it up and put it in my boot. It was the last time I saw her alive.

I once heard a beautiful story. I suppose that's why I write: because once somebody told me something beautiful. I have already submitted all the beautiful stories I know, so I have had to begin on those that are merely luminous. I was at home, washing dishes, when Selemon burst in to find me. He was wretched, panting, so heated with his run the steam came off him. "Hurry, hurry," he said. He seized my hand and dragged me out into the road where the sky had just crossed over the milky hour of noon. Selemon was working delivery then, and he had left two days' worth of meds outside Miss Snowfall's door, because she hadn't come to the dispensary. Now it was the third day. He had knocked at her door and called and then, thinking she might be ill, he had kicked his way in. Oh, I know what people say. They say Miss Snowfall was weak, unsuited to the grand task of being human, they say she taught children nonsense, anything that came into her head, she had no plans, she allowed an evil spirit to enter into her heart. I know, I know. Old Sister Nimble was standing in the hall and Selemon roared at her to get out, get away. Part of the clay wall had broken off when he kicked down the door, the doorway was jagged, the door itself had fallen in and smashed the lamp. "Help me, help me," he said, and I understood everything. We climbed on the bed and he lifted the body while I worked at the knot. It was too tight, I had to climb down and find a knife, there was one inside the cold oven. In the hall Sister Nimble was ordering someone about, probably children. "Fetch the bishop," she cried. I cut the rope and Selemon staggered. Pain is the heaviest thing. I cradled Miss Snowfall's head as he laid her down. I know what people say but I am saying Miss Snowfall practiced, better than anyone else in the village, our highest value, what we call *yieldedness*. She yielded and yielded until there was nothing left. In the room we found boxes of meds, potatoes, jars of sour milk. The food was just a few days old, but it was months since she had taken her injections and her body, Yodit told me, was worm-eaten with radiation. Yodit assisted the examining physician who determined that this body was too contaminated to be returned to the grottoes. I know that people consider this the truly unpardonable sin, worse than suicide: the selfishness of withholding one's body. But Miss Snowfall's body was truly a humble body, a body of Fallow, one that had given up Earth and submitted to this place. Because she had yielded so fully, she was buried in the dustyard. Very few came. I was there, and Selemon, and a few of her other students. Sister Wheel came, looking tense and strange so far from her own yard, and Miss Snowfall's brother arrived on his bicycle halfway through the service. He dropped his vehicle in the dirt and stood with the tears running into his beard. He would die himself, only a few weeks later, under mysterious circumstances. He was found in a tunnel, lying on his back with a handkerchief over his face, and the miners said that a ghoul called a Fetch had carried off his soul. The Fetch is a particular legend of the miners: they say she looks like a woman in a green dress, and that some, in the depths of the caverns, have taken her for a flame.

Anyway, I heard Deacon Broom had to go out there and reprimand them for their superstition and pray over the place. And now I think I've filled this slate to the edge—except, of course, for the photograph of the deer, which I include here, with apologies for keeping it. It's seamed and worn, but you can still see the searing look in the animal's eyes, that naked clarity, the look Miss Snowfall wore at the window after school, the expression of one who awaits the blue radiance—deep, pure, and tranquil—that only comes in the aftermath of a conflagration.

2. Brother Lookout

There was no open vision

I was five years old when my cousin Hana took me to see the Earthman.

At the time, Hana had just turned fourteen: a sly, romping, adventurous girl, part of a group of friends who had been publicly censured for stealing and wrecking a handcart. Temar and I thought she was marvelous. My mother, I knew, was afraid of her, as she was afraid of her own sister, Hana's mother, our Aunt Salt. "Watch her every minute, and keep off the tracks," Mother told Hana anxiously in our kitchen, fastening up my coat.

"Leave it alone, Diborah," Aunt Salt said irritably from the sink where she was banging the plates about, cleaning up after the evening meal.

"Don't worry, Auntie," Hana said. "I'll just take her for a little walk, to the dispensary and back, and then put her to bed."

Mother straightened, her hand at the small of her back. Heavily pregnant with Yonas, she looked tired, her face clammy and drawn. Half concealed behind her, Temar stuck her tongue out at me; she was angry because she had to stay behind and help with the preserving. At seven, she was no longer a baby and could work. Hana saw the ugly gesture and grinned. I knew that Hana liked Temar better than me, and determined right there that I would not complain, no matter how far we walked.

In the end I had to complain, because Hana took me far beyond the dispensary, through the empty streets of the dimly lighted town, through the surveyors' camp, past the school, into the North District, until I feared she was taking me all the way to the mines. "Come on," she coaxed, "it's such a nice night." And it was, the air a few degrees warmer than usual, the sky set to the cool green glow of preserving season, a glow that would last for half the night. Big vats bubbled in country yards, figures rushed to and fro, the whole world smelled of jam. Still, I felt as if my legs were dropping off. I began to cry, and Hana carried me on her back. "Quiet," she panted, taking me through a strange deserted yard toward a house on a rise. "Don't you want to see the Earthman?"

Bent almost double, she carried me up the slope. We knelt at a lighted window. Others were kneeling there too, and we pressed ourselves between them. "Hey," hissed Hana, "I've got my little cousin here. Let her see." The others, teenagers, pushed me forward against the pane. The window was made of clear wrap and bowed outward slightly. It was warm from the room inside. I was looking down into a basement. There was a stove, a few people standing around, including the village doctor, a bed heaped with quilts. In the bed lay the Earthman.

"Is it a boy Earthman?" I whispered.

"Shh! No, it's a girl!"

She was very pale, with white streaks in her black hair. Her face looked creased. Tubes led out from under her quilts and connected her to a kind of stand. On the stand lights flashed and a bag swelled and shrank. If you listened carefully, you could hear the grownups talking around the bed. One was the bishop's wife, Sister Gloss. "We were happy to take her in, brother," she said, "but you see how it is. We can't manage her if she's fading."

"Oh, I expect she has many years yet," the doctor said cheerfully, the way he had said, when he set my arm: "This won't hurt a bit."

The third person standing beside the bed was cleaning a pair of spectacles with a handkerchief. He was thin, clean-shaven, neatly dressed. He frowned as if considering the doctor's words. "I'd like to continue my sessions with her," he said. "Will that be possible at the infirmary?"

"Very difficult, very difficult," said the doctor. "Sterilization, you see. But the point is, she doesn't require that kind of care! Only the occasional tonic. Sister, if you keep the equipment on hand, then whenever—"

"I can't be watching her all the time," snapped Sister Gloss.

The Earthman whose fate was being decided floated in a deep silence. I tried to guess at the contours of the body underneath the quilts. She seemed taller than ordinary people. Her face was broad and strong; her parted lips formed a bloodless triangle. On the way home, Hana would explain with relish that the Earthman had been shunned. On the surface, her suit had cracked and one of her arms had died. She had repented and returned. At the Castle they had cut her arm off, but it wasn't enough to stop the ice flowers creeping toward her heart. Eventually, right here in the village, the Earthman would die of exposure, killed by the distant moment when her suit had been damaged. It was like a parable about sin. What struck me at the window, before I knew all of this, was the fact that no one was praying. It was the first time I had seen someone so ill and so alone. Only the thin man seemed aware of the Earthman as a kind of person. He put on his spectacles, looping the stems around his ears. "I'll take her," he said. "She can stay with me."

The teens at the window giggled and shushed one another. The doctor and Sister Gloss exchanged a glance. Then the doctor said: "Well. That would be a help."

The thin man nodded. "Have you got a barrow?" he asked Sister Gloss. "She'll have to be transported with the monitor."

"I'll see," she said. "We may have loaned it out for the preserving."

As she left the room, the audience at the window broke and scattered. Hana clasped my hand as we ran downhill. Walking back through the village she was exuberant; filled to the brim with what she had seen. She didn't scold when I yawned, she even carried me on her hip. It was then that she told me the story of the Earthman. For a long time this Earthman, whom I never saw again, was a figure of terror for me, a kind of Fetch. The pallor of the Earthman's skin, her terrible solidity, seeped into my dreams. She seemed to be made of surface. If I craved sensation, I only had to whisper *ice flowers* in my bed at night and my body would seize up, strangled with fear. When I return to this memory now, however, it's not the Earthman who startles me, but the thought that the thin man in spectacles, so capable and neat, this man with the steady, reasonable air, is the same person I knew later as the shambling village street sweeper, Brother Lookout.

I discovered Brother Lookout's story accidentally, when I was doing research for my senior project. The senior year, taught by Brother Pike, culminated in a presentation for the whole village, at which each student discussed some aspect of one of the Debates. Each of us began by choosing a set of Debates to work on. Temar, who finished school before me, had chosen the Covenant Debates. Selemon chose the Digital Debates. I chose the Separation Debates, and ended up studying the Young Evangelists.

"Bunch of idiots," Father said, when I mentioned this at supper.

"I know," I said. "I'm going to show that."

"I think it's great," said Temar.

Father ignored her, fixing me with a look of exasperation. "Show what? Everybody already knows."

After that I stopped discussing my project at the table, but I became, if anything, more attached to the idea. I see now that this had a great deal to do with Temar—that is, with the chance to please her by displeasing our father. Temar had done unexpectedly well, in fact brilliantly, at school, and was now employed in the water mines of the Castle, something which put our father past his patience—not that he had ever been particularly patient with my sister. One would think he would have been pleased with her success: of all the children who went to school with us, she was the only one who managed to get into the Castle, excepting Markos and Elias, whose parents worked there, and whom everyone had expected to take that path. Temar had been expected to work with cows. Now, in the mornings, when she appeared in her narrow jacket with the blue stars on the lapels, our father could not resist a sneer: "Oh, very pretty," he'd say, or "Oh, very fine," when she bent down to pull her regulation boots over crisp white trousers. Far from pleasing him, her accomplishments goaded him to fury as much as her "proud looks" and "defiance" had ever done. "Oil and water," my mother used to sigh, in reference to the two of them, or, more often: "She just has to wind him up."

Since going to work at the Castle, Temar had begun to seem distant from me. My senior project brought us temporarily back together. We whispered in bed at night, as when we were little. I told her about the sermons of the young Bishop Gloss, which I'd borrowed from the archives. I described his biting eloquence, the way he compared the Young Evangelists to a leprosy broken out of the burning. "He is a leprous man," the bishop had cried, "he is unclean; the priest shall pronounce him utterly unclean; his plague is in his head."

"His plague is in his head," Temar intoned, in such a skillful imitation of the bishop that we had to smother our giggles with blankets.

"It's sad, though," she added a moment later, still under the blankets, in the cave warmed by our breath. "The poor Young Evangelists. If they'd been back on Earth, in the Former Days, they might still exist. They could've formed their own church."

"There's only one church," I said—a shocked reflex.

"You know what I mean. Their own *little* church. Like they used to have on Earth. All these Debates we've had—somebody always has to lose. On Earth they didn't have that, they had schisms instead."

"But a schism is terrible!"

"I *know*." She pulled down the blankets, emerging from our cave, and I followed her into the cold black air of the room. It felt even colder after being inside. I held the blankets close to my chin. "I *know* it's bad," said Temar, "but at least the Earthmen had space. If people didn't like the way other people were doing things, they could leave. They'd go off over the next hill and build their own church. Brew coffee on Sundays to their hearts' content. Wear bonnets with strings or without, as they liked. It was a bigger world."

"More extreme, though," I countered.

"Oh, *extreme*." I could hear her smirking in the dark. "Brother Pike's favorite word."

I retreated into silence, as usual. I couldn't bear fighting with her. And, as usual, she went on arguing alone into the night. She demanded to know what had happened to the lukewarm being spat out of the mouth of God—had we forgotten about that? Now all we talked about was moderation, moderation, the middle path, keeping the balance, biding our time. "We think we're preserving the church," she said, "but the Earthmen wouldn't recognize us. They wouldn't even recognize our coffee."

At last she too fell silent. She wriggled a little closer to me, so that I would feel her warmth and know she was not angry. For all her sharpness, my sister had a great delicacy of manner. Soon her breathing lengthened; she was asleep. I began to drop off too, thinking of Brother Pike, of his scrawny, excitable limbs, of the way he did, in fact, dislike anything "extreme," of the classroom, the benches, the curtainless window letting in the low gray sky, of the tinge of green in the air before the bell rang, the thudding of boots, of Selemon's curls, the graceful curve of his lip, the intense shyness of his eyes, his voice, his tenor voice at the youth revival meeting, the way our voices mingled, sharing a timbre despite the difference in our ranges, of the slow walk home, the whiteness of the road, and just as I was drifting off my sister's words came back to me, the word "coffee" must have come back, for otherwise I cannot account for the turn of my thoughts, and with a jolt that made my eyes spring open I realized what I was going to do. I would speak with Sister Wheel.

❦

She lived in a low mud house near the center of town. She was a widow of sorts: she had once been in covenant with a woman who had died of cancer. With her steel-gray hair, her profile slowly collapsing from loss of teeth, she ought to have been moved into Elderly Housing. But a strange aura of remoteness surrounded Sister Wheel, as it had Miss Snowfall, too, making it impossible for anyone to speak to her on the matter, and she kept that little house until her death, when it was torn down and replaced with a larger building housing four families and a glazier's workshop. This building occupies not only the site of the house, but also the bare, stony yard where Sister Wheel was accustomed to stand for hours. Her rickety metal table is gone, her apparently untouched cup of coffee, her whole atmosphere of gloomy agitation. This atmosphere only exists now in the memory of a few people. I am one of them. I remember the superstitious tingle as I stepped into her yard, an act which, according to the stories we exchanged in childhood, would turn one into a pillar of salt.

As a protective talisman I carried a loaf wrapped in a cloth. "Good morning, Sister," I said, advancing with a show of bravery. "I've brought you a little loaf from Sister Stalk."

Sister Wheel, true to form, fixed me with burning eyes and barked: "Hello!"

I had feared that *Hello* more than anything; once it had passed, I felt better, though my heart still fluttered. I stepped closer to her and set the loaf on the table. Strengthened by thoughts of Miss Snowfall, who had once gotten a whole sentence out of Sister Wheel, I said: "I'm Agar. I'd like to ask you about the Young Evangelists."

It was Saturday; the town was full of people; bicycle bells jangled behind me, and children chased each other, shouting; but it was still horrible when Sister Wheel, who had been looking down at the loaf, turned toward me as if electrified.

"The . . . Young!" she whispered.

"Yes. It's for my senior project. I'm Agar, the daughter of Brother—"

"Shh! Come inside."

"What?" I said. I had never known Sister Wheel to be anywhere but out in her yard, from morning until night. Now, however, she was picking up her cup of coffee and the loaf I had brought for her with surprising swiftness. "Bring the table," she commanded over her shoulder. And I took it up and followed her to the door, and into the house.

The story she told me emerged in fits and starts over a number of Saturdays. She spoke in difficult bursts, like a clogged pump. I took notes on my school slate, which I later transcribed in the classroom onto the precious paper provided for senior students. These notes developed into the presentation I delivered in the fellowship hall, my voice frighteningly magnified by the speakers, my body limp and trembling as I spoke into the thick silence that greeted my introductory words: "The Young Evangelists." The silence of a large group is extraordinarily solid. I felt as if I'd been buried alive inside a wall. Rows of faces watched me from the tables where, on Sundays, we ate our fellowship meal in noisy comfort. The silence was not distant, but close, excruciatingly attentive, lying in wait for me, alert for any mistake, and it had a burning quality, too, the heat of the shame of my parents who sat with lowered eyes, my father rhythmically clenching and unclenching his fist. Writing this I grip the seat of my chair with my free hand, I scratch it with my nails. Temar was not there. I had undertaken an act of defiance for her and she had not come, she was at the Castle. Oh, how I hated her! Tears stung my eyes, the sound of my own voice cracking filled the hall, reverberating unbearably back through my body, and I rushed toward the end of the presentation, jabbering more and more quickly until I could step away from the podium at last. To stop talking, to join the silence around me, was an immense relief. And yet that larger silence was not mine. On our way home, no one said a word. As we entered the house, Father was overcome and shoved me so that I banged my head against the wall.

And yet I had said so little. I had done as I'd promised Father: I had shown that the Young Evangelists were foolish, unbalanced, extreme. I had compared them to some of our misguided prophets of old Earth: Jan van Leyden running naked through the streets of Münster, Claas Epp who heretically predicted the day of Christ's return. It wasn't my argument regarding the Young Evangelists that had produced the silence, but the impropriety, the sheer unseemliness of the topic. This episode in our history was a wound; the cells of the body sprang into action when it was touched, closing about it, closing it down.

"I didn't do anything wrong," was my silent refrain as I curled around my despair in bed that night, wracked with sobs I would not reveal by the slightest sound, the cords of my throat swollen and aching with screams that were nothing but air. *"I didn't, I didn't! I didn't do anything wrong!"*

Of course, I had known that my choice of subject was a daring one: that was the attraction of it. But I had planned to skirt the abyss without falling in. I had tried to flirt with danger, yet escape its embrace, and everyone had seen through me. I writhed in bed, scalded by shame.

Now I feel differently. Now Sister Wheel rises up from the dust-yard, as clear as if her image were etched behind my eyes. Her big, nervous hands, the flickering lamp, and the dirty dishes stacked in the gloom of the counter seem to hold something immeasurably precious. The windows are covered with blinds shutting out the day. The lamp makes a small buzzing sound as it flickers: there's a bad connection somewhere. Her face is large, anguished, imploring, the eyes like liquid gems. She tells me that her life is a life of guilt. She tells me this with a reckless openness, something beyond generosity. She'll tell anyone. Every day she waits for someone to ask. She tells me that she was born with this feeling of guilt, that all the Young Evangelists were, and their inborn guilt led to further guilt, sin upon sin. I'm taking notes. My hand quivers with excitement, the chalk squeaks. I'm in a cave, the closest thing on Fallow to an ancient tomb. Fallow is old, but not ancient; its age has no meaning; its sands and radioactive stones are alien, cold, untouched by human history. But in this kitchen, history is alive. Something has happened here. Once this room was crowded with impatient, warm young bodies. The thick spectacles that had given Brother Lookout his name filled up with fog when he walked in with his Bible under his arm. He also carried a sheaf of papers borrowed from the archives. Laughing, he greeted everyone with the Kiss of Peace. Then he sat on this very counter, his long legs dangling, and read. "The spread of His glorious Gospel . . . the extension of His Kingdom from shore to shore . . ."

The idea was simple. We belong to Earth, Brother Lookout explained, but we have abandoned it. We have cared only for our own salvation, our removal from the wars that blaze across its suffering continents, our preservation from its plagues and floods. Like the priest and the Levite, we have passed by the dying man in the road. Unlike true Christians, we have given no thought to our neighbors. We have not considered those who have perished since we departed Earth long ago, their souls crying out for peace. How many have been born since our departure who, had they only been alive at that time, would have joined the trek? Are they to be punished simply for being born too late? How can we receive Gabriel's reports so complacently? Every quarter century produces a catalogue of horrors, yet we sit here— Brother Lookout struck the counter with the heel of his palm—we sit here like the carrion birds, the eagle and the ossifrage, waiting for others to die so that we might inherit the Earth.

Someone objected that, however much we might want to help the Earthmen, we are unable to communicate with them.

"Not so," said Brother Lookout, his eyes gleaming behind his spectacles. And here he called on one of the gathering, a certain Brother Pin, to speak. Brother Pin worked at the Castle. He was a slight, sallow creature; the attention of so many people brought tears to his eyes. Twisting his fingers together, he spoke of the Earthmen who arrived in ships from time to time and were shut up in the Castle.

A communal gasp, then silence. The room throbbed like a stove. "Tell them," Brother Lookout said quietly. And, weeping, Brother Pin went on. He said each Earthman to arrive was locked in a room, instructed in our language, and questioned. Eventually, if they survived (and many did not, being worn down from the journey they had made in ships much smaller, though indescribably faster, than our Ark), they were taught the rudiments of prayer and set to work at menial tasks in the bowels of the Castle. Those who refused either work or Christ were shunned.

"That's what they do," whispered Sister Wheel. "They give them suits and enough food and oxygen for thirty days, and shun them."

Of course, I knew this. I belong to the generation after Sister Wheel's, those who have grown up knowing of the Earthmen occasionally coughed up onto the deserts of Fallow. I also know the arguments that justify their treatment, the essence of the Separation Debates. I would repeat these arguments in my presentation at the church. We are the last survivors, humanity's hope. We are the angel of the church in Philadelphia, who have a little strength, and have not denied His name. We cannot allow the Earthmen who discover us to depart, or, with their miraculous speed, they would surely return to Fallow with an army. Nor can we permit them to enter the village, sowing discord. This position is now set down in our schoolbooks. I learned about it in Miss Snowfall's class. I remember the curious deadness and remoteness of her face as she led the prayer after the lesson. This prayer was written in the teacher's book. She spoke the lines, and we repeated them. *For the Lord knoweth the way of the righteous: but the way of the ungodly shall perish.* Some of us wept. It is hard for children to accept the idea of separation. For the Young Evangelists, it was impossible. They were going to welcome the lost Earthmen to the village. They were going to learn their languages and use Gabriel to send messages back to Earth, inviting everyone who desired peace to our refuge. If Gabriel could not be used in this way—nobody was sure—they would go to Earth themselves, using the Earthmen's ships. They would cry out like the prophets of old: "Seek ye the Lord while He may be found, call ye upon Him while

He is near." The heat in the room was unbearable. They opened all the windows. Someone began to sing. Harmony filled them, as in a revival meeting. In the coming days, their passion would spread. They would go from house to house, eagerly preaching the truth, demanding others' support. And they would be victorious. No contrary voice could conquer them. "We were *right*," said Sister Wheel, her mouth working. They would receive permission to bring an Earthman down into the village, provided that Earthman accepted Christ. The first one, and indeed the only one they were ever able to bring, was the one I saw that night with my cousin Hana, her great prone body battered by the sands. Her name was unpronounceable. They called her Sister Earth.

When Brother Lookout was disciplined, it was discovered that he had hoarded a great deal of paper in his rooms. A little paper factory was set up in the kitchen, with two broad vats on the floor and drying screens on the counters. There were more screens underneath the cot where Brother Lookout slept in the musty smell of the slurry composed of kitchen scraps and his own used paper, and stacks of paper were piled up everywhere, a resource that certainly should have been returned to the archives to be pulped or filed.

Most of these papers are records of what Brother Lookout called his "sessions" with various patients. He was the first and last psychologist in the village. He had discovered the field of psychology as a young man, Sister Wheel told me, during a brief period working in the archives. Later I learned from Ezera that there are several books concerning this science in the archives, but they are kept in restricted files. Brother Lookout's papers are restricted, too, but Ezera allowed me half an hour with them in a back office. Page after page, in a handwriting that is sometimes small and fluid, at other times larger and strangely angular, as if carved with a knife. There are only ever two speakers: "D"and "P," the former indicating Brother Lookout, the "Doctor," the latter his patient for the day. Everything is dated, but there are no names. Apparently, Ezera says, Brother Lookout kept a calendar on which he recorded the names of his patients, a key to the records and the shifting identity of "P." The charred remains of this calendar were discovered in his stove.

> D: What is your first memory?
> P: Fog.
> D: What is fog?
> P: Something that makes it hard to see, like a veil.
> [P. takes my glasses and smudges them with her thumb.]
> D: And what can you tell me about this fog?
> P: It was autumn, and they were burning the rice fields.

I wrote these words on my hand. It's the earliest entry I can link to the Earthman. It's in the small writing, from the days when Brother Lookout seemed in control of his pencil. Afterward came the big, boxlike writing, as if he were trying to construct a room the words could fit inside.

I pieced together the story of Brother Lookout over some time, from a number of sources. From Sister Wheel, I learned of his leadership role among the Young Evangelists, although, she added, clasping her hands together on the table, he practically dropped out of the group after the Earthman's arrival. It was at that point that she and her partner in covenant, whom she referred to only as Rahel, became leaders, holding long debates in the fellowship hall, petitioning the Castle unsuccessfully for clearance, and meeting with the old bishop and then, when a new one was chosen, with Bishop Gloss. "People began to laugh at us," she said. Her frown deepened; her eyes flashed, roving alarmingly from side to side. "What about Brother Lookout?" I said, to distract her, and she froze.

"He was—he was with the Earthman," she stammered at last.

He was with the Earthman in his rooms behind the archives. She slept in the bedroom. He had made up a cot in the kitchen. Sometimes she was strong enough to come out and sit at the table. She ate the breads and pancakes prepared by the women of the church. At first these charitable women were allowed in. They would leave the food they had brought on the table and sit down with the Earthman for a while. But soon Brother Lookout began to stop his visitors at the door. "Thank you," he would say, standing in the doorway, taking the food.

At this point, Sister Wheel lost the ability to follow the thread. She veered away from the story, she went back in time. She told me that Brother Lookout was the middle child in a family of three sons. He was the weakest and the most intelligent. Something in the way she fixed her eyes on mine suggested that she was pleading. "You know how he walks," she said, demonstrating by swaying in her chair, thrusting her head forward and shaking it in Brother Lookout's manner. "He used to get like that sometimes, even then."

Her story began to disintegrate. She told me about the marvelous humor Rahel preserved during her last illness. The way she would describe Sister Wheel's stews, which grew worse and worse under the stress, as "fearfully and wonderfully made." "And you know," Sister Wheel added, as if the connection between the thoughts were obvious, "I was a cart driver. I was the best cart driver in the village." She carried the most precious things, medicines, plastics, rare wood from the grottoes. "I can't believe," she said, "they took my job away."

The day she said that was the last Saturday I went to her house. I did not learn, from her, the story of the fall of the Young Evangelists. I remember running outside, chalk and slate rattling in my satchel, and pausing in her yard for a gulp of air. The light slanted toward dusk. The air was saturated with dust; in the distance the Castle door threw down a tremulous golden ray. I did not learn, from her, of the suspicions of the church women, the curious dank smell that seeped under Brother Lookout's door. I learned only that he loved Earth, that he wanted to save every soul in the universe, that he was a middle child, that he was intelligent, shy, weak, a gifted preacher, that his trousers were always an inch too short, that he studied a lost philosophy, a science of dreams, memories, comfort, and terror. "What is your first memory?" I don't know. Before I left her, Sister Wheel put her hands over her face. I ran outside, panting. In the sky a ray of gold. It was from Ezera that I learned how the Young Evangelists fell. It was after Temar was lost. I was drowning, gasping for life, and everyone knew it. Ezera, my old school friend, couldn't refuse me anything. He unlocked a back office and brought me restricted files. Brother Lookout's papers, the long dialogues between "D" and "P." Such a strange faith, this psychology. A belief in the power of memory. It is outlawed now, stamped out with the Young Evangelists, shunned like the Earthman who was taken away from Brother Lookout's rooms, cringing in the metallic light of day. This part of the story I learned from my cousin Hana, who, with a group of friends, ducked out of school early, having heard a rumor of some excitement in town. "She was as ugly as rock," Hana exclaimed. "Her dress rode up—do you remember that, Yosef? Her dress came up in the middle of the street!"

"Bullshit," her husband, Yosef, called laconically from the next room.

"It did, I tell you!" said Hana, yanking up her own skirt where we sat in her kitchen. Her baby girl, who sat on the floor trying to eat a potato, looked up curiously. "Slabs!" said Hana, slapping her own thigh. "Great white slabs of flesh they were. Ugh! Her legs kept crumpling, and the flesh kept jiggling. But some of the boys said she had nice great shaking breasts, too! I used to run with a nasty crowd, and Yosef was the worst of them!" she concluded, laughing heartily.

Deacon Broom and Brother Wick, two Council members, pulled the Earthman into the street. They dragged her onto a cart and took her away. And so the Earthman was shunned a second time, and it was decided that Earthmen would never be admitted among us again. Ezera let me see some of the records pertaining to the issue, most of them written and signed by Bishop Gloss. It was Bishop Gloss, too, who spoke at the evening meeting. "And now, O our God, what shall we say after this? for we have forsaken Thy commandments."

It was the end of the Separation Debates. Sister Wheel sat with her face in her hands. I ran outside, chalk clacking in my satchel. In our schoolbook it said simply, "The Earthman could not adjust to life in the village. The Young Evangelists confessed their error and were reconciled with the church." That was how I would end my presentation. Now I stood in Sister Wheel's yard, drinking in the chilly air. The light slanted. It was preserving season, and there would be a long pale night, shadows etched on all the roads. I was young. Sometimes it's hard to remember how very young I was. Strength coursed through me to the ends of my fingertips. I would never be a bitter, dried-up woman like Sister Wheel, or pace the streets all day like Brother Lookout. I would go home, feed the chickens, eat my supper, bring in the wash, and go to the youth revival meeting to pray and sing, to stand beside Selemon, to kick his ankle when he kicked me, to pass a slate bearing a caricature of the youth leader, Sister Small. More and more, I see this writing project as a kind of rescue. I don't want to forget the dimness of the sanctuary, how different it looked at night without the Sunday light streaming through the windows, how different it sounded with so few of the pews filled. When people ran in late their footsteps echoed. Sister Small was stocky, harassed, with straggly brows and a shiny nose. Only a true spirit of sacrifice could have induced her to put up with us as we tussled and writhed with laughter. Anything could set us off. Elias stood up and, for no reason, cracked Ezera across the head with his hymnal. Yodit's stocking tore. "Oh, pins," she said. Even the hymns made us laugh, the boys winking as they boomed out the line: "Here I raise my Ebenezer." Naomi was my best friend then. I pinched her thigh when she made me laugh too hard; she drove her fist into my hip. The world was made of her soft brown body, the slippery pew, the shadow of Selemon's cheek, the odors of coats, cowshit, boots, a child's sickness cleaned up long ago. Holy smells. The deacon dragged the Earthman to a cart. Bishop Gloss stayed upstairs in Brother Lookout's room. "The brother remained defiant," he wrote. He recorded everything he found in the rooms: the hoarded paper, the vats of slurry, the burnt calendar. "The brother could not be persuaded to see his error," the bishop wrote. "It was necessary to bring him before the congregation." It was necessary to bring him to evening meeting, which the children did not attend. It was necessary to display some of his papers. It was necessary to display the drawings of the Earthman and the drawings of the Earthman and Brother Lookout together. It was necessary to display the drawing of Brother Lookout with his hands tied and the plastic tube that was used to do the tying. After revival, we would go to somebody's house to help with the preserving or the hog killing, if there was one. Sometimes one of us knew where to go, sometimes we merely followed the sound of voices or the mouth-watering odors of sugared fruit and smoke. Always there were places to get lost along the way. There was a recess in the alley between the infirmary and the dyeworks. There was a shed with a broken door behind Brother Blunt's. The best place was the old surveyors' camp, with its trackless wastes, its sheltering piles of stones. In the camp you had the feeling of standing at the edge of the world. There were caves, too: you could go in and touch the wall where the village ended. We were supposed to stay out, because of the radiation. "I don't care," I said. Selemon pressed me to the wall and his hat fell off. It was necessary, wrote the bishop, to display the bruises on Brother Lookout's wrists, to remove his shirt and reveal the stripes on his back. At this point, the brother began to show himself more tractable: he stopped demanding to know the whereabouts of his partner in sin. Unfortunately, he still refused to pray or to repent. Hands were laid upon him, and the people began to sing. The caves at the surveyors' camp were the site of such intricate negotiations. Can I undo this clasp? *Yes.* This one? *No.* Selemon took off his shirt, his breath smoked, I feared he would freeze. He had the body of a waterbird of the grottoes. So graceful, shivering, thin. At last, wrote the bishop, the brother repented. The poison of the Young Evangelists was removed from among the people. "They knew," whispered Sister Wheel before I left her. "They planned it all. They knew something would happen. All they had to do was wait." At the time I didn't know what she meant. I slipped out of her kitchen and into the yard, where the light was changing, the Castle door diffusing its golden ray. That night I would go with Selemon to the old surveyors' camp. A rescue project, yes—that's what this writing is. I know I'll be accused of trying to stir up dust from the dustyard, but it's not true. I want to save everything, everyone. I understand the Young Evangelists, who wanted everyone to be saved. And Brother Lookout sweeping the streets of the village so carefully, collecting what we, even we, who prided ourselves on our frugality, let fall in the course of a day: threads, bits of chalk, needles, hair. From gazing beyond the sky he had turned to peering at the ground but he was still what he had been, a collector whose first impulse was to preserve. He was the one who gathered the black threads for Temar's hat. Boys used to push him down, seize his bag of trash and empty it in the street. "Look out, Brother Lookout!" I want to save everything, pick up every hair from the dirt, save the boys too, their chapped cheeks, their fresh and panting breath, these boys who would grow into men who disciplined others and ruled the village with a heavy, brutal, joking confidence. "We're at our best," Temar once remarked, "when the generator is broken." The men had worked on the generator for twenty-four hours. The women kept fires going around them, heated gloves and boots, conjured up steaming bowls of potato soup. Afterward Father laughed so hard in the kitchen with our uncles, remembering who had fallen, who had dropped a wrench on someone's head. He fell asleep at the table, his face soft and golden like a child's. Temar put her finger to her lips and knelt to untie his boots . . . This was Temar, who only a few days later, sitting at supper with a swollen lip, said brightly: "You know, there's one thing I don't understand! How can a man call himself a pacifist while he beats a girl with a hose?" Yonas burst into tears. Father stood up. He seized Temar by the hair . . . And Brother Lookout died in the old surveyors' camp, lying frozen in a shallow depression almost like a grave. It was the third time he had run away, I learned from Lia, who used to work at the desk in Elderly Housing. When they moved his bed out, they found the floor underneath it covered with writing. He had been collecting verses from the Bible. Strange verses—"and the sound of a shaken leaf shall chase them," "then thou shalt take an awl, and thrust it through his ear unto the door." As if he were assembling the pieces of a secret message. He only got as far as the first book of Samuel, ending with the words: "And the word of the Lord was precious in those days; there was no open vision."

I had my own boat. I'd paddle down the canal. The buffaloes up to their knees in water. Very far in the distance, the train. Words lifted from Brother Lookout's notes, images that could only have come from her, from the Earthman. Sister Earth. I wrote them on my hand, taking a sentence or two at a time. I thought of how they had been carried to Fallow from a distant planet. They were carried to the Castle and then, when she was shunned, to the surface. Then they came back to the Castle, and then down to the village. And Brother Lookout received them from her in the tiny, musty apartment behind the archives, in the odor of rotting husks. He received so much from her in those isolated days. I see him helping her to sit up, placing a pillow behind her back. I've never seen the pictures he drew, I don't even know if they've been preserved. I didn't ask. I don't know how D. and P. progressed from speech to touch. I know that he took her words and wrote them down, and I carried them out of the archives as communion wine is carried to the church. I don't want to spill a drop. *The carpets everywhere, in every street. Everyone ate meat on that day, even the poor. What I remember most is the smell of burning leaves mingled with the smell of exhaust. And the old men stretched in the grass beside the road.*

Shunned. I see her walking out onto the surface, immediately thrown down and tumbled by the wind. She has to crawl on her belly. Oh, the delicate mask of her helmet. She squirms on, waving her arms in front of her, seeking some sheltering crevice. The dust makes a hard pattering sound on her helmet, the wind roars, she rises to her knees, fighting the storm, she turns to look at the Castle. It rises nobly through the murk, a cold and distant mountain, and watches her mournfully with all its lights.

I think of her weight, her body accustomed to slightly weaker gravity, her long back. This time, she will survive. She will make her way back to the Castle at last, one arm flapping uselessly at her side. She will say: "I repent, I yield." But what of her second shunning? For a long time I was tormented by the thought of the Earthman sunk in some hole, her chest straining for breath, her face blackening as her oxygen ran out. I used to pray: "O Lord, forgive us." Then one day I happened to mention her to Aunt Salt. I was visiting my aunt and my mother in the lounge at Elderly Housing. I had brought them some quilting stuff, which delighted them. I sat with them to work at the quilting frame. With age, they had come to resemble each other more closely than ever, and now looked like two gnarled and tufted twins. Aunt Salt still possessed the brighter eye, however, and the quicker tongue. She looked up sharply when I mentioned Sister Earth. I was recalling for the two old women, as an amusing story, the night Hana took me to see the Earthman.

"And she was shunned in the end," I said with a sigh.

"Nonsense!" snapped Aunt Salt.

I glanced at her, tugging my needle through the cloth.

"She wasn't shunned. They put her in the grottoes, behind the apiary. She kept bees for twenty years."

I smiled.

"Don't grin at me in that foolish way," said Aunt Salt. "Ask at the grottoes if you don't believe me. Didn't I pass her every day for years, on my way to the salt lab? She stood there like an archangel, all in white."

I will not record the arduous process of getting clearance to the grottoes. Eventually I was admitted, and visited the apiary, where a pair of workers moved through the air with slow, deliberate movements, swathed in white, just as Aunt Salt had said. No, they had never heard of Sister Earth. But there had been, for quite some time, a worker who lived there in the grottoes. One of them gestured toward a nearby shed with a luminous glove. The worker had lived there, in a single tiny room. She was understood to be suffering from some disorder of the spirits, and they took it in turns to bring her a daily meal. She never appeared outside without her full uniform and mask of spotless gauze. She was tall and thin, and did all her work with her left hand. She was the most dedicated of the workers, the most solitary and silent. "Often," said one of them, "when I arrived in the morning, I would find her already among the hives, a tray of honeycomb in her hand and bees encircling her head like a halo." They called her Sister Keep.

It remains only to report that I did try to speak with Brother Lookout once, though he had a reputation for never talking sense. It was while I was working on my senior project. I was on my way to revival when I saw his unmistakable silhouette bent over the steps of the dispensary. No time like the present, I thought. "Brother Lookout," I cried, running toward him. He glanced up, looking both affable and cowed, as if he expected to be tormented and was resigned to it in advance. "I want to ask you about the Young Evangelists," I said.

He smiled, his spectacles catching the stray light from a nearby window. I don't know why my memory of certain people is illuminated like this. Miss Snowfall teetering through the streets on her borrowed bicycle, Brother Lookout's glasses reflecting the light. Sister Wheel, too—sometimes when I pass the glazier's workshop I see her so clearly, standing in her yard as if guarding us all from some invisible threat, and it seems right to me that glaziers work there now, creating lenses through which, perhaps, something of reality might be perceived. I remember that Brother Lookout's face brightened when I spoke to him, and he answered in tones of unexpected vigor. "It is wonderful that you should ask that, sister," he said, "since only last night I dreamt I was crossing the river on a ferry. I wore a student's coat—I was certainly on my way to join the seminary—and a heavy woolen scarf against the cold. Although the sky was dark yellow, and the waters rather turbulent, I felt sure that we would reach the other side."

SOFIA SAMATAR

3. Temar

This world is not my home.

I had hoped to complete these recollections without speaking of
Temar at any length. Yet it seems impossible to conclude without telling her story. Caught between the necessity and the pain of writing
about her, I have not written anything for weeks. It was yesterday, as
I was coming home from a visit with Yonas at the old place, that a
solution occurred to me. Yonas had taken me out back to see the hens,
and at the sound of their subdued voices and the smell of their feed
I was overcome, as often happens, by the memory of the past. Suddenly I saw my sister standing by the coop, with her particular slouch
that expressed disillusionment with everything around her, the big
black hat casting a lumpy shadow on the wall, and her gaze, sharp,
sober, and appraising. She was looking at me precisely as she had the
day before she ran away. I remember she told me: "You're one of the
innocents." The "others," she went on, clearly classing herself among
this group, have only three choices: "Fade, fester, or run."

As I walked back to Housing, Temar seemed to hang beside me,
glittering softly. Her voice blossomed just inside my ear. I entered my
room, turned on the lamp, closed the door, and took off my coat and
boots. She was still there, like the light on a page. I don't know why
she seemed to me like light on a piece of writing. But for the first time
in years, I opened my trunk and took everything out. The good dress,
the extra quilt and towel, the half-finished scarves and mittens, the
mug stamped "Trust in the Lord" that Father left me when he died.
At the very bottom, a sheaf of papers tied up with green thread. It
took me a long time to undo the knot. My legs ached from kneeling
on the floor beside the trunk, but I wouldn't get up. It was as if I were
caught there, engaged in a struggle with something. This was a battle
and I must see it through. I took off the string and smoothed the
papers on my lap, I gripped their edges. Jacob wrestled the angel by
the waters of the brook and said: "I will not let thee go except thou

248

bless me." Temar, I thought, I will not let thee go except thou bless me. And I realized that rather than writing about her, I could include her own words in my writing, this long letter she left me and which I have kept in the trunk, hiding it like a sin. *Dear Agar I am going away for good.* I read it once, then put it away for years. Forgiveness takes so long. I wonder, who is the angel—Temar or me? Which of us has the power to bless? Which will not let the other go?

Dear Agar I am going away for good. I'm not the writer in the family but I am leaving you this letter to say good-bye. There's so much I want to tell you so you can understand a little bit and not hate me too much—at least not more than you have to. I couldn't tell you any of this before because of the Rule of Mary—one of the things I hate the most. We're supposed to keep everything that happens at the Castle and ponder it in our hearts. Don't Tell Anybody, is what it means.

Well I never told anybody but now that I am leaving I guess I can. I'm so lonely, I want to take you up to the Castle. I want to take you up on the ladder into the blue hall with the white steps leading up in eight different directions. Look, you're going up Staircase E. It already smells like salt. You hang up your coat and hat on the rotating rod. It's amazing how poor the village things look there, how drab and dirty. Through the big windows comes the day. You kneel down with the others and say a prayer. Nobody introduces or leads this prayer, it just happens, it's a tradition. It feels good to kneel down and close your eyes. Sometimes people put their heads all the way down on the floor. I've done that a couple of times. It's just the day is so big. Especially the first time you see it, it's hard. It's the surface. It can make you a little sick. Like going into the grottoes, but different. You feel like there's nothing holding you down, like God's going to snatch you right up into the sky. What we call a sky down in the village is not a sky, it's just a roof. In the Castle you really see the sky. It's moving and coiling, full of dust. Or sometimes it's perfectly still, a low pink color or a whiteness that never ends. The really scary thing is that you want to run out in it. That's why we kneel, I think. We're trying to keep ourselves down. You're glad those windows are so thick and protected with layers of clear wrap because you want to burst through, to throw yourself onto the surface. It's a little bit like looking down a stairwell. You know you shouldn't jump, you'll break something, but the pull to jump is so strong. The truth is, people want to fall. Markos used to call it the power of Satan. Sister Glove, our superior, called it vertigo.

You're going down a hall. You have a blue tab on your jacket because you work in water and you follow the blue arrows on the walls. The smell of salt grows stronger, the air heavier, your hair springs. It's hard for me to tell you what you see. Like the church, I guess I can say. The high ceiling and the light. There's scaffolding you can climb on, but you have to be careful. Everything's dripping. It's very warm. Salt crystals have formed underneath the tanks. You can feel the distant vibration of the drills. My job was cleaning. I cleaned the fixtures, the tanks, the walls, the floors, the hallways, the windows. You probably thought I was doing something more exciting. I'm sorry for letting you think that, now. I wasn't a scientist. I carried a bucket and rags. I wore gloves because the solution can rot your hands.

You can imagine—after some time—the empty halls— the stillness of the tanks—the hums and clanking making the stillness even deeper—the routine, knowing what time the inspectors come, and Sister Glove—yes, the routine— after a while you start to break it. You start to know the blue arrows. You can turn left instead of right, following a red or green arrow, and catch up with the blue ones later on. There's a moment when you're in the wrong hallway, following the wrong arrows, you know you're lost, you're going to get caught, and everything stiffens. Your chest is so tight it's like being pinned to the darkness of that hall. The smell. Something cooking—you must be near the kitchens. And maybe a laugh comes down the tunnel, or voices, somebody singing, and the excitement is so much your knees shake. Then you come into a grayish light, gasping. It's a blue hall. You're so relieved. You know exactly where you are. Everything softens now, and it's a kind of happiness. It doesn't last long. Something pierces it. Regret . . .

My defiance, Father used to call it. That feeling of longing. It made me strange, I know. Mother used to ask me: Why do you wind him up? I was so sorry to hurt her, I'd cry as if the world was ending while she dabbed my ear or bandaged a cut on my elbow. That was in the cool room. I know you were waiting outside, so maybe you heard. It always seemed funny to me that that was where everything happened. The cool room was where Mother brought the disinfectant and towel to clean you up and it was also where Father sent you when you were really in for it. The smooth hard floor and the jars on the shelves. The sliver of a window up near the ceiling, partly covered with tarp. A piece of sky. The freezer where I hit my head. The pile of potatoes where I fell. They rolled everywhere. Believe it or not, me and Father both started laughing.

This isn't what I meant to write but I guess it's all the same thing, really. My life. A feeling of being pierced. I used to cry so much and I used to hate you, and Mother, and even little Yonas, because none of you had that feeling. Of course I hated Father most of all, even though I believe he had the feeling too, maybe even worse than me. I hated him and I loved him, like David loved and hated Saul. I used to imagine Father as Saul and myself as the boy David. I was the Lord's anointed and Father was chasing me to kill me, he was pursuing me into the wilderness of Ziph and the wilderness of Maon. I'd pray: Let not my blood fall to earth before the face of the Lord; for the king of Israel is come out to seek a flea, as when one doth hunt a partridge in the mountains.

Maybe my trouble was the power of Satan. Maybe it was vertigo. Whatever it was, it pierced me. I felt it even in the Castle. That made me sad enough to die, because all the time I'd been thinking, if only I could get into the Castle, everything would change. It did seem changed for a little while. There was a happy time, but it didn't last. Soon it was just blue arrows, a bucket, and gloves. The long blank halls, the glaring sky, the maddening feeling of something better happening somewhere else. It was like an itch. I felt myself getting quieter. I knew it wasn't good, but I couldn't help it. Every day the same low chime, the signal for lunch. In Water we had our own dining hall. Sandwiches came on a cart. Sister Glove ate carefully, primly, her hands covered with scars. And Markos would make jokes with me about cows. He kicked my feet under the table. Once he cornered me by the tanks and tried to kiss me. I dashed him with my whole bucket of solution. I didn't hit his face, but not for lack of trying. It was good he was wearing a suit. And then we'd go home for supper, for prayers, for Saturday shopping, for church. Do you see what I mean? I'd seen everything, and that's all it was. I told myself: that's it, there's nothing more. But I knew there was something more. I believed in it like I believe in God.

You're going down a hall. A glance behind you. No one's there. You turn down an ill-lit corridor, carrying your bucket and rags. You wander around corners, chasing green arrows, yellow ones, red, in no kind of order. Eventually all the arrows are black. And when you get deep enough, there are no arrows. Sometimes a small light blinks in the darkness. That's frightening, because it might be an alarm. There are places so dark you can only guess at their shape by the sound of your footsteps and the taste—either dry, or foul and suffocating—of the air.

These abandoned caverns and tunnels became my playground. Of course I couldn't go where people were—after the white arrows, for example, into the busy halls, toward Gabriel. But I grew bolder and bolder in the tunnels. I even took out my torch. The light jumped around because my hand was trembling. But there were marvels down there. Hundreds of doors that wouldn't open. Some had windows. I'd shine my torch in and see shapes standing in the dust. Things that looked like consoles and stoves. There were rows of empty cages. It made me remember that a good portion of the Castle was once the Ark. I saw beds in some of the rooms. I thought of people traveling through space, praying and singing. *Unser Zug geht durch die Wüste. Hisboch hoy, des yebelachew, igziabeherin amesginu!* It made me feel close to something. We have a history, Agar, after all.

Well, it happened. I came out of the tunnels into a dim gray hall. I switched off the torch. I thought I was back among the blue arrows, or at least green. But no. There were no arrows at all. The walls were blank. It gave me a queasy feeling. There were lighted panels set into all the doors. I'd never seen anything like it. I made to turn back, but I heard a sound. Somebody was shouting. I went along the hall and listened at all the doors. My hands were sweating inside my gloves. When I found the door with the shouting behind it I pressed the panel and the door slid open.

There was a man inside. He was on a bed. The thing I remember most about him is the blackness of his nostrils. His nostrils were full of dried black blood. His face looked very white. He stared at me, panting, and I knew he was an Earthman.

His name was Moan. Lugran Moan, he said, though he didn't tell me that right away. Instead he asked for water. When I entered the room and set down my bucket, the door closed behind me and a light came on, so bright I thought I was caught. I froze for a moment, but not long. I was too angry to be scared. There was a cup with a lid on a sink and I brought it to him. His wrists and ankles were strapped to the bed. One of his wrists was bandaged too. I helped him sit up and drink, and that's how it started. That's how I came to be writing this letter now. Moan smelled funny. He smelled human like piss and alien like hay. His hair was like black feathers. He was shaking. Some kind of animal. He didn't know how long he'd been in that place, he said.

It was long enough to know our language, even though he spoke it kind of funny. Don't, he said, when I started undoing the straps on his wrists. He said it was no good without a plan. He needed a map, he told me. A map to his ship. It was somewhere in the Castle.

Writing this I'm afraid you won't understand. You'll think I've run away after a man or just for fun, as if on a dare. It's not true. The light in the room was white. There was a tautness to it. The tautness of Moan's throat as he swallowed. After he had drunk he lay down quietly like a child. Who are you? he asked. His voice was hoarse. I told him my name. He repeated it several times, as if to fix it in his memory. Later he told me he was afraid of losing his mind. Since I couldn't undo his straps I just knelt there with my hand on his arm. I'd taken my gloves off. He lay with his head turned on the pillow and looked at me. How was it possible? He told me that every day the bishop came in and talked to him about the path of Christ. The walls had a strange gleam, like silver paper. Moan said he was being treated for something, but he didn't know what. Was it the adjustment to our planet that made his body so tired, or was it, as the bishop said, the state of his soul? Every day he was given sermons and injections. They said they would let him go when he was well enough. If he accepted Christ he would be given a job in the Castle. If he remained stiff-necked he would be shunned. Shunned means killed, I told him. I know, he said. He was afraid we would kill him anyway, no matter what he did. He was afraid we were lying to him, using him for something. His blood had been bottled. With a thin instrument, a nurse had scraped the inside of his mouth. When he said that I put my head down on his chest. I couldn't look at him anymore. I listened to his heart. The walls were strangely silver like the walls of the church decorated for Easter with the silver birds we made in Miss Snowfall's class. Do you remember those silver birds? They hung near the ceiling, glittering. There was a feeling of enchantment. A smell of oranges. Each of us got an orange after church, fresh from the grottoes. The flesh was sweet, the rind bitter as gall, delicious. Moan's heart beat underneath my cheek. His breath was in my hair. Help me, he said. If you could take the magic of a childhood Easter, and put it together with all the sorrow we have learned since then—then, Agar, you might understand how I felt. All I can tell you is that I was born again. Was it his face, his mask-like face with the black nostrils? Was it his tender throat? His heart? He was talking because he didn't understand that already I had crossed over to his side, that I was going to save him. He told me that he was a transporter. He carried materials between the cities—cities, he said, that orbited a dead planet. He had never been to Earth, but his father was born there. Sometimes he picked up Earth materials and transported them from one city to another. Only the bravest transporters visited Earth, which was on fire. He was not one of the bravest. He was lost. He told me that space was full of pathways, and sliding through one of these pathways he had been cast into the galaxy of Fallow. Then he had noticed the Castle and stopped, curious. He had not known that there were human beings so far from the cities. And now he was strapped to a bed. But if I would help him to find his ship he would take me anywhere. He would let me look at his collection of Earth things. I will show you a piece of amber, he said. I will show you a beetle's shell. But for these things, Agar, I would never leave you. Nor would I leave you for Moan himself. But a falling star means space is real. A fallen angel means there is a Heaven.

Do you remember the story Miss Snowfall told about the two old people? The ones who tried to get medical help at the Castle. The brother was dying and his sister was carrying him around. You liked it so much, and I thought it was garbage. I hated that it was supposed to be sweet and maybe even comforting but the old people couldn't find anybody to help them. There was a long middle part about the sister going from room to room getting turned away. It should have been just boring but it was worse. Well I have been that unhappy sister. I went looking for Moan's ship through the Castle. It's so bewildering, so big. An impossible place. Twice I got caught in the wrong halls. The second time it was Elias from school who caught me—he works in security now. I was lucky it was him because he wrote off my second offense. He didn't report it. If he had, they would have suspended me for two weeks. On the third offense they kick you out. Thank you so much, Elias, I said, beaming at him, this schoolyard bully, this thug. He still has that way of looking you up and down slowly, that hateful grin. He beats Lia, you know. She told me he beat her for leaving his shirts on the line. After smiling at him in that winning way I wanted to wash my face in solution. I knew I couldn't afford to keep getting caught. Then one week we had a big job. Drain the tanks, take them apart, clean each individual piece, put them back together. It was an urgent job and because we didn't finish on Friday we had to spend the weekend in the Castle. That was when I knew it could be done. There was a room full of cots where we slept. Cupboards with dried food you could eat after adding water. Of course I left in the night. I ran to Moan. The halls were weirdly empty and dark. I went much faster, with no bucket, my torch alight. I had trouble finding him though, because I always got turned around in the tunnels. There was always a moment when I thought: I can't do this. I'm lost. Or I'd come into the gray halls but not find his room. That was worse because I was so afraid he had been moved or shunned. I was afraid I'd never find him again. Running along the gray corridor, flashing my light, slamming the door panels, shouting. I didn't care about being caught then. The sister in Miss Snowfall's story was lucky, she got to carry her brother on her back. If only I could have carried Moan. Then, very faintly, I'd hear his cry. I ran to him. I never found anyone else in the gray halls. Earthmen must not come to us very often. That's why I'm grateful—awed by grace. That's why I consider myself blessed.

I found him on Friday night and again on Saturday. On Sunday I went looking for his ship. I didn't find it that night. The Castle's too big. So many silent halls. Strange places. The labs. A ghostly room full of empty cribs. I failed, but I began to find excuses to stay at the Castle. Unfinished work. Sometimes I broke things, nothing serious but enough to let me stay. And I found the ship. I saw it through a window. There are other ships too, abandoned in the distance, half buried in sand. Some are half ruined, broken apart, pieces scattered around them, as if people have been mining them for parts. Moan's ship is the newest one, still whole. He laughed when I told him, his eyes bright. He guesses we've been trying to get in, but only he can open the door. Only he knows the code. He told me the other things I needed to find, the suits we have to wear, the door to get out. That door, I am sure, doesn't have a secret code. It won't be locked. Why would anybody want to get onto the surface? But I can feel vertigo pulling me. It's pulling me outside. It's pulling me toward the moment when I will set the prisoner free. To unbuckle the straps on his wrists, his legs. To see him stand up and walk. The flesh unbound. Everything feels alien to me, but also very beautiful. Oh Agar. The most I can say is that I love you and I am sorry. But I have always been a stranger in this place. At least now I will be a stranger without the pain of having failed to belong. For as the hymn says, this world is not my home.

Temar

Do you remember the way to the Castle? Its door glimmers above the village, pale and opalescent like a sun. I have realized of late that the Castle door is, even more than the church, the center of our life. That radiant disc beams down on us with a soft, embracing gaze, overseeing everything: the wedding processions going to the church, the coffins borne toward the grottoes on carts, the gossip in the dispensary line, the small battles, bargains, kindnesses, and contracts. Without it we should be worms. A door is so precious, even if one never steps through. I think of this, walking with Ezera and Sheba after church: how the presence of that door subtly brightens the atmosphere of the village, making us feel humble, yes, and ignorant, but also protected, saved. I sit at the table in Ezera and Sheba's kitchen, surrounded by their irrepressible children, who call me Aunt Hat. They snatch the rolls from the central bowl; Sheba dispenses scoldings and flicks the eldest son, her favorite, with a napkin. Eventually the children run outside, calling each other in the raw air. They play a game called "cows," using corncobs for hoofs. They swing on the gate, singing a nonsense song. "Deedy-daddy-doe," over and over. We are the saved. We have survived.

I lost my sister, I lost my teacher, we all lost the Young Evangelists, the openness and vibrancy of their ideas, but we still have this: our survival. Ezera and Sheba take care of me. Sunday afternoon is mine; I never have to worry that Sheba's sister Naomi will stop by. Naomi and I have not been close since she married Selemon, and though I am no longer angry, our meetings are unnatural and stiff. But Naomi and Selemon never visit her sister after church, and in this way they take care of me, too. At four o'clock Sheba walks me out to the road. "Good grief!" she exclaims every time she realizes she's still wearing her apron. This is when she tells me about her struggles with the children and even with Ezera. In the green afternoon, with coils of hair escaping from her cap, she looks just as she did at school. There is no end to writing, I think, no end to the project of rescue. I realize that Sheba, too, is illuminated. She too deserves to be saved from oblivion, this quiet friend whose face, though lined, always looks burnished as if rubbed with butter. I have left so much out of these pages. I ought to have mentioned Sheba's kiss at the crossroads, her vigorous hug that almost knocks me over, the jar of pickles she gives me for Lia, whose house I will pass on the way, a jar miraculously concealed until the last moment. I ought to have mentioned Lia's smile, her capacity for delight, the way she insists I sit down and try some pickles, goes to the coolbox for eggs, and prepares a dish for Elias who, since his accident in a Castle fire, lies immobile in the bedroom. It's always the same plate, painted by Lia herself with tiny buds. I ought to have mentioned their daughter, with her halo of dense black hair, a child beloved by all the village and already nicknamed the Spark, who sits on my knee and sings while Lia feeds Elias pieces of egg. I ought to have mentioned the burst of dazzling harmony on the road outside, young people singing their way to Bible study. They are preparing for the Christmas service. I ought to have mentioned "Lo, how a rose e'er blooming." I ought to have mentioned that we are happy.

When, in moments of anxiety, I scratch the underside of whatever I happen to be sitting on with a fingernail, I know that I am engaged in a process of grounding, which, it seems to me, is similar to the process of writing. In this manner I hold myself down and remind myself where I am. Walking from Lia's to the old place, I think of gravity. When our ancestors chanced upon Fallow, this bleak and poisonous piece of rock, it had almost nothing to recommend it but its gravity, near kin to that of Earth. I think of how, in our displacements throughout history, we have always tried, with a poignant doggedness, to replicate what we have lost. So the hills of Pennsylvania replaced the lost hills of Germany and the wheat fields of Saskatchewan those of Russia. Now, on Fallow, our grain corridor holds yellow-green fields of teff. We are that heart-breaking paradox: wandering farmers. I walk to the pasture, knowing that Yonas will still be with the cows; he has inherited our father's affinity for them, and also—thank God—our mother's cheerfulness. And there he is, putting the cattle into the corral. I approach him through the rich, mellow air of the pasture. He is worried about the ventilation and immediately begins talking about it as he settles the animals for the night. I have always been afraid of cows, but my brother moves among them with ease, often laying a hand casually on a flank—perhaps his form of grounding. Once he told me, in a moment of uncharacteristic pensiveness, that to look into a cow's eyes is to look on paradise.

He is probably right, I think, as we leave the pasture for the dust. The kitchen light is shining from the house. This house has belonged to Yonas since our father died, while I moved to the Henhouse and, after some years, our mother went into Elderly Housing. Mother will be home now, as she always visits Yonas on Sundays, teaching her grandchildren to play cat's cradle. Her years and even her sufferings have endowed her with the dignified grace one sees in so many elderly people of Fallow. This grace manifests in an almost physical way, like a shining underneath the skin. I kiss her cheek. Do you see what I am trying to say? I am saying that for some of us there are only three choices—fade, fester, or run—but others have a fourth choice: to endure. I am saying that our father could not bear the loss of Temar, his heart went out like a blown match, while our mother took control of all the funeral preparations, even unscrewing the door herself to make room for the coffin. Which of them yielded? I kiss her cheek, I pat my niece's back, I look up as my nephew tugs my arm, wanting me to toss a ball with him, this boy of nearly eleven years old, handsome and tall like my father, who still sleeps in his parents' bed because he's afraid of the dark. I am saying we live a life defined by the loss of paradise, structured spiritually by the Castle in the sky. Each of us must decide how to respond to the idea—the comfort, the torment—that there is another world.

And these figures that have passed so close to me without touching—what do they mean? I am speaking of the Earthmen. What does it mean for our survival that others have also survived, that we are not the only souls plucked from the flames? Sometimes at night their names run through my head. Earth, Patient, Keep. Moan. No, I will not reopen the Separation Debates. I see the Earthmen rather as signs that appeared and then dissolved, like communications from Gabriel or writing on a wall. They came to say: Not yet. Earth is not yet for you. Keep patient. And I do keep patient, but I can't help moaning. I moan like any exile, full of longing for the lost homeland. By the dustyard of Fallow I sit down and weep. For there is another world. There is a world of apples and flowering trees, a world where the fig tree putteth forth green figs. There is a world where goats appear from Mount Gilead, where flocks of sheep come up from the washing, each one bearing twins. Please accept these pages. Accept, this time, my submission to the archives. Accept my absolute submission. If I have written of shame and sadness, I have done so out of reverence for the story we fight to preserve with every breath. I have done so in the spirit of one who endures, in the spirit of those who built the Ark, who set off knowing that, for them, the waters would never subside, who took on self-preservation as a duty and a vocation, who survived for the sake of the sacred human story. For there is another world, a future Earth. There is a land called Canaan. There is a land flowing with milk and honey. There is a country of turtledoves, a garden of pomegranates, of saffron, of camphire, of myrrh. And we will never go there.

The Red Thread

Dear Fox,

Hey. It's Sahra. I'm tagging you from center M691, Black Hawk, South Dakota. It's night and the lights are on in the center. It's run by an old white guy with a hanging lip—he's talking to my mom at the counter. Mom's okay. We've barely mentioned you since we left the old group in the valley, just a few weeks after you disappeared. She said your name once, when I found one of your old slates covered with equations. "Well," she said. "That was Fox."

One time—I don't think I told you this—we lost some stuff over a bridge. Back in California, before we met you. The wind was so strong that day, we were stupid to cross. We lost a box of my dad's stuff, mostly books, and Mom said: "Well. There he goes."

Like I said the wind was strong. She probably thought I didn't hear her.

I think she's looking at me. Hard to tell through the glass, it's all scratched and smeared with dead bugs. I guess I should go. We're headed north—yeah, straight into winter. It's Mom's idea.

I've still got the bracelet you gave me. It's turning my wrist red.

Dear Fox,

Hey. It's Sahra. I'm at center M718, Big Bottom, South Dakota. That's really the name. There's almost nothing here but a falling-down house with a giant basement. They've got a cantenna, so I figured I'd tag you again.

Did you get my message?

It's crowded in here. I feel like someone's about to look over my shoulder.

Anyway, the basement's beautiful, full of oak arches. It's warm, and they've got these dim red lights, like the way the sky gets in the desert sometimes, and there's good people, including a couple of oldish ladies who are talking to Mom. One of them has her hair up and a lot of dry twigs stuck in. She calls me Chicken. It's embarrassing but I don't really care. They've got a stove and they gave us these piles of hot bread folded up like cloth. Are you okay? I'm just thinking, you know, are you eating and stuff.

Big Bottom. You won't forget that. It's by a forest.

Don't go in the forest if you come through here. There's an isolation zone in there. We even heard a gunshot on our way past. Mom's shoulders went stiff and she said very quietly: "Let's pick up the pace." When we got to Big Bottom I was practically running, and Mom's chair was rattling like it was going to fall apart. It's cold enough now that my breath came white. We rushed up a sort of hill and this lady was standing outside the house waving a handkerchief.

She took us downstairs into the basement where everybody was. The stove glowed hot and some of the people were playing guitars. The lady gave me a big hug, smelling sour.

"Oh Chicken," she said.
Oh Fox. I miss you.
We're still headed north.
Tag me.

Dear Fox,

Hey. It's Sahra. If you get this message—can you just let me know if you left because of me? I keep on remembering that night in the canyon, when we sat up on that cold, dizzy ledge wrapped in your blanket. You tied a length of red thread around my wrist. I tore off a piece of my baby quilt for you, a shred of green cloth like the Milky Way. You said it was like the Milky Way. The stars rained down like the sky was trying to empty itself, and when you leaned toward me I emptied myself into you. Did you leave because of the fight we had afterward, when I said my family belonged to this country, we belonged just as much as you? "Don't embarrass yourself," you said. Later I said, "Look, the grass is the exact color of Mom's eyes." You told me the grass was the color of plague.

You were her favorite, you know. The smartest. The student she'd always longed for. "Fox-Bright," she called you, when you weren't around.

Well. We're still in Big Bottom. Mom wants to get everybody out of here: she thinks it's too close to the isolation zone. Every night she lectures and the people here argue back, mostly because they have lots of food: they farm, and can fruit from the edge of the forest. The lady who calls me Chicken, who seems to be the mom, opens a jar every night with a soft popping sound. She passes it around with a spoon and there's compote inside all thick with beet sugar. This one guy, every time he takes a bite he says, "Amen."

Sorry. Hope you're not hungry.

264

Anyway, you can see why these people would want to stay in Big Bottom and not try to haul all that stuff somewhere, including sacks of grain and seed that weigh more than me. "We've wintered here before," said the Chicken lady. "We've got the stove. Stay with us! You don't want to go north with a kid and all."

Everybody was nodding and you could see the pain in Mom's face. She hates to be wrong. She argued the best point she had. "Sooner or later they'll come after you," she said. "You're too close. You've got kids too." She said it was a miracle the isolation folks hadn't already attacked Big Bottom, with all that food. Then everybody got quiet, the Chicken lady looking around sort of warningly, her eyes glinting, and Mom said, "No." And the guy who says "Amen" over his compote, he told her they'd already been attacked a couple of times.

Mom covered her face.

"We do okay," the Amen guy said. You could tell he felt bad about it.

Later I got in a corner with the other kids, and I asked about the attacks and one of them, a boy about my age, pulled up his sleeve and his wrist had a bandage on it. He didn't get shot or anything but he twisted it hitting somebody. With a crowbar.

When Mom uncovered her face she said: "That's not the life." She said: "That's not the Movement." She said standing your ground was the old way, not the new, and the Chicken lady said: "Honey, we know."

After I'd seen the boy with the bandaged wrist, I helped Mom to the toilet and back and we both lay down on the blankets. "We've got to get out of here," she muttered.

"Okay," I said.

"You know why, right?" she said. "Because we never stand. We move."

"Sure," I said. Sure, Mom, I thought. We move.

We move when and where you want, Mom. We've sailed back and forth over the ocean. We've slept in the airborne beds of Yambio and the houseboats of Kismaayo. And now you've decided to go to North Dakota when winter's starting, through country dotted with isolation zones, leaving all our friends behind. I had such a good art group back in the valley—you saw our last project, Fox. A slim line linking the tops of twenty trees. Wires and fibers twisted with crimson plastic, with cardinals' wings, making an unbroken trail, a gesture above the earth. It seemed to pulse in the morning light. You said it reminded you of radio waves, of a message. We called it *The Red Thread.*

I'll probably never see it again.

Such gentle light here, but it couldn't soften Mom's smile when she saw me crying. "You don't know how lucky you are," she said.

Dear Fox,

Hey. It's Sahra. I'm at center M738. Somewhere in North Dakota. The center's in an old church. At night they feed us pickles and beet soup off plastic tablecloths that an old man carefully clips to the long tables.

They set beautiful candles made of melted crayons on all the windowsills. For travelers. For strangers to find their way at night.

"If we could have known," says Mom, "if we could have known this life was possible, we would have started living it long before."

There's a man with a blunt gray face who argues with her. "You're one of those human nature people," he sneered tonight. "The ones who think oh, we've proved that people are good. Let me tell you something, friend. If it wasn't for the oil crisis and the crash we'd be living exactly like we were before."

Mom nodded. A little half-smile in the candlelight. "Sure, *friend*," she said, subtly emphasizing the word.

"And another thing," said the blunt-faced man. "These kids would be in school."

"Or in the army," Mom said sweetly.

Of course the kids *are* in school, because Mom's around. Wherever we shelter, teaching is her way of giving thanks. She gets all the kids together and makes them draw their names in the dirt, she quizzes them on the multiplication table, she talks about the Movement. How precious it is to be able to go where you want. Just walk away from trouble. Build a boat and row across the water. When she was a kid, she says, you could barely go anywhere at all: borders, checkpoints, prisons, the whole world carved up, everything owned by somebody. "Everything except light," she says. "Everything except fire." And if they wanted they could keep you in a dark place. Tonight she told the kids what I already know, that that's where my dad ended up, in some dark place, seized on his way to work and then gone forever. "Why?" a kid asked. "I don't know," said Mom. "Because of his name? Because they thought he was working for terrorists? In those days, they could seize you for anything."

Usually she goes on from here with the story of how the Movement once had another name, how people used to call it the Greening, how the media reported it as an environmental movement first, folks abandoning cars on the freeways, walking, some rolling along like her. She tells of how in the wake of the crash the Greening intertwined with other movements, for peace, for justice, for bare life. Grinning, showing the gaps in her teeth, she uses her favorite line: "In the old days, when I worked in a lab, we called it evolutionary convergence."

Tonight she just stopped after talking about my dad. Her face shrunken, old. And I said: "We might still find him, Mom," because you never know. When the Movement started he could have crawled out of that dark space like so many others, the ones you find on the road, cheerful, wearing pieces of their old uniforms. An orange bandana, a gray rag tied on the arm. Tattoos with the name of their prison, where they were kept before the doors opened, before the Movement. I once had a dream that my dad walked down some steps and touched my hair. "We might still find him," I said. Mom pretended not to hear me.

In the night she woke me with a cry.

"What is it, Mom? What's wrong?"

"Nothing, nothing," she whispered. "Go back to sleep."

I can't go to sleep. Lying there I see you walking along a creek. You're wearing your black shirt and your head's tilted down, with that concentrating look. I think about how I recited the generations of my dad's family for you, there on the ledge, at the cave in the canyon wall. My name, then my dad's, then my grandfather's then my great-grandfather's, back through time. Sahra, Said, Mohammed, Mohammuud, Ismail. I can do ten generations. "Amazing," you said. Your blanket around us and our breaths the only warmth, it seemed, for miles.

"It's like a map," you said, "but it shows people instead of places." You said it felt like the future to think that way.

"Yeah," I said. "But during the war they killed each other over family lines. Like any other border."

Belonging, Fox. It hurts.

Fox it's Sahra. You knew? You knew Mom was sick? You knew and you didn't say anything to me? You knew and you left her?

What kind of person are you? It was like somebody walked up and hit me in the chest with a hammer. "I told that boy," she murmured in the dark room. "I told that boy." And I knew who she meant. I knew it right away. She said she was sorry. She didn't mean to chase you off.

That's why you left? Because you found out someone who loved you was going to die?

I've never seen Mom work with a kid the way she worked with you. The two of you scratching away at your slates while the rest of us leached acorns. You'd kneel in the dirt by her chair and rest your slate on the arm. Leaning together you'd talk about how to make the Movement last, how to keep the meshnets running, how to draw power tenderly from the world, and later you told me that you and I were perfect for each other because we both wanted to draw lines over the land, mine visible, yours in code, but the truth is you were perfect for Mom. You were perfect for her, Fox. "Fox-Bright," she called you. And you left her when she was dying.

You know what? I'm not sorry for what I said the day after we spent the night in the canyon. I'm not sorry I said I belong here as much as you. They picked up my dad and probably killed him because they thought he didn't belong here, an immigrant from a war-torn country. But my dad knew this land, he lived in thirty states before he met my mom, in the days of oil he used to drive a truck from coast to coast. He left fingerprints at a hundred gas pumps, hairs from his beard in hotel sinks, his bones in some forgotten government hole. And my mom belongs here too even though she cries, can you believe it, my mom, someone you'd look at and swear she never shed a tear in her life, she cries because she grew up in the house we're living in now, an old farmhouse crammed with noisy families—this is where she was born. She cries because she wanted to come back here before she died. That's why we're here. She thinks she's betraying the Movement by clinging to a place. She lies in the bed in the room where we found a page of her old Bible under the dresser and cries at the shape of the choke-cherry tree outside the window. That's how much my mother loves the Movement that changed our world, the Movement she worked for, for years, before we were born, losing her job and her teeth. She loves it so much she's going to die hating herself.

I've cut your bracelet off.

It's started to snow. I have to go now. Good-bye.

Dear Fox,

Hey. It's Sahra. It must be six months since I tagged you. I see you never tagged me back.

Today I left the farmhouse. I cleaned Mom's room, the room she slept in as a child, the room where she died. Old fingernails under the bed like seed.

There are good people in that house. What Mom called "ordinary people" or, in one of her funny phrases, "the most of us." They got her some weed, and that made it easier for her toward the end. One night she said: "Oh Sahra. I'm so happy."

She laughed a little and waved her hands in the air above her face. They moved in a strange, fluid way, like plants under water. "Look," she said, "it's the Movement." "Okay, Mom," I said, and I tried to press her hands down to her sides, to make her lie still. She struggled out of my grip, surprisingly strong. "Look," she whispered, her hands swaying. "See how that works? There's violence and cruelty over here, and everyone moves away. Everyone withdraws from the isolation zone until it shrinks. A kind of shunning. Our people understood that."

"Our people?"

She gave another little laugh, kind of secretive, kind of shy. She said she'd grown up going to a plain wooden church, a church where they believed in peace, where they sang but played no instruments, where the women covered their hair with little white nets. I said we'd met some people like that back in California. "They had the peppers, Mom, remember?" "Of course," she breathed. "The red peppers." The memory seemed to fill her with such delight. She said she'd left her old church, her old farm, but now she could see her childhood in the shape of the Movement. "What's isolation but a kind of shunning?" she said softly. "That's what we do, in the Movement. We move on, away from violence. A place ruined by violence is a prison. Everyone deserves to get out. The Movement opened up the doors."

She looked so small in the bed, in the light of the pale pink sky in the window. It does that on moonlit nights, in snow. A sky like quartz.

"That baby quilt," she said, "do you still have it?"

I took it out. One square ripped away, a green one. "Your grandmother made this," she said.

I wonder if you still have it, Fox. That green square. The Milky Way.

Later, I don't know if she could recognize me, but she asked: "Where are you from?" And I said "Here." Because "here" means this house and this planet. It means beside you.

"Are you an angel?" she asked me.

"Yes," I said.

Dear Fox,

Hey. It's Sahra. The snow is melting. The geese are back.

When I leave a place, I also leave a word for you. By now, it's like talking to myself. I leave words like I'd leave a stray hair somewhere, a clipped fingernail. My track across the land.

Movement. Back and forth. The two of us sitting wrapped in your blanket, breathing fog against a rain of shooting stars. I'm thinking today about your excitement when I recited my ancestors' names, how you said it felt like the future, and how quickly I cut you off. "There was war," I said. "Those family lines became front lines." As if your enthusiasm was somehow unbearable. I think of the fight we had later, and how you said: "Don't embarrass yourself." Did you mean I'd never belong? Maybe you meant: "Don't make me into a symbol."

Is it possible to be worthy of the Movement? Of my mom? Of my dad? I just walk, Fox, I meet people, seek shelter, avoid isolation. I make art with kids out of gratitude. I think about Mom all the time. All the time. "Are you an angel?" Her last words.

The night after I slept with you in the cave I woke up cradled in light. My arm looked drenched with blood, but it was just dirt from the floor.

I still have the bracelet you gave me. I carry it in my pocket. I still have a redness on my wrist, as if someone's grabbed me.

Dear Fox,

Hey. It's Sahra. Sometimes I just feel like leaving one word. Even if it's just my name. A single thread.

Dear Fox,

Hey. It's Sahra.

Dear Fox,

Hey. It's Sahra.

Dear Fox,

Hey. It's Sahra.
    I got your message.

Publication History

"Selkie Stories Are for Losers," *Strange Horizons*, January 2013.
"Ogres of East Africa," *Long Hidden: Speculative Fiction from the Margins of History*, 2014.
"Walkdog," *Kaleidoscope: Diverse YA Science Fiction and Fantasy Stories*, 2014.
"The Tale of Mahliya and Mauhub and the White-Footed Gazelle," *The Starlit Woods: New Fairy Tales*, 2016.
"Olimpia's Ghost," *Phantom Drift*, Issue 3, Fall 2013.
"Honey Bear," *Clarkesworld Magazine* 71, August 2012.
"How I Met the Ghoul," *Eleven Eleven* 15, September 2013.
"Those," *Uncanny Magazine*, 2015.
"A Girl Who Comes Out of a Chamber at Regular Intervals," *Lackington's* 2, May 2014.
"How to Get Back to the Forest," *Lightspeed* 46, March 2014.
"Tender," *OmniVerse*, 2015.
"A Brief History of Nonduality Studies," *Expanded Horizons* 36, August 2012.
"Dawn and the Maiden," *Apex Magazine* 47, April 2013.
"Cities of Emerald, Deserts of Gold," *Revelator* 139,1, 2016.
"An Account of the Land of Witches" appears here for the first time.
"Request for an Extension on the Clarity" *Lady Churchill's Rosebud Wristlet* 33, 2015.
"Meet Me in Iram," *Guillotine Series* 10, 2015.
"The Closest Thing to Animals," *Fireside Fiction* 27, 2015.
"Fallow" appears here for the first time.
"The Red Thread," *Lightspeed* 73, 2016.

Some stories here were inspired by or are in conversation with the following works, many of which are in the public domain or whose minimal usage falls within fair use; all other permissions are cited below. A good faith attempt was made by the author and publisher to identify and contact rights holders wherever appropriate and this list will be updated in future editions if rights holders are contacted:

Attar, Farid al-Din, translated by Charles Stanley Nott, *The Conference of the Birds*, Janus Press, 1954.
Baum, L. Frank, *The Annotated Wizard of Oz*. Edited with an Introduction and notes by Michael Patrick Hearn. W. W. Norton & Co., 2000.
The Black/Land Project question, "As a black person in the U.S., how would you describe your relationship to land?" www.blacklandproject.org/218.
Boehme, Jacob; tranlated by John Sparrow, *Aurora*, John T. Watkins, 1960.
Briggs, Katharine M., *A Dictionary of British Folk-Tales in the English Language*, Routledge, 1970.
Dinesen, Isak, *Out of Africa*, Penguin, 1937.
Funk, Joseph, *The Confession of Faith*, 1837.
Hume, David, *An Enquiry Concerning Human Understanding*, 1748.
Iram Wiki: https://en.wikipedia.org/wiki/Iram_of_the_Pillars
Lyons, Malcolm C. (translator), *Tales of the Marvellous and News of the Strange*, Penguin Classics, 2015.
Martensen, Hans Lassen; trans. T. Rhys Evans, *Jacob Boehme: His Life and Teaching, or Studies in Theosophy*, 1949.
Excerpt from *Dakota: A Spiritual Geography* by Kathleen Norris. Copyright © 1993 by Kathleen Norris. Reprinted by permission of Houghton Mifflin Harcourt Publishing Company. All rights reserved.
Oppenheimer, J. Robert, *Physics in the Contemporary World*, Anthoensen Press, 1947.
Schlabach, Theron F., *Gospel Versus Gospel: Mission and the Mennonite Church, 1863-1944*, Herald Press, 1980.
Seaborg, Glenn, 1947 Associated Press interview as quoted on Science Beat: lbl.gov/Science-Articles/Archive/seaborg-quotes-own.html.
Ward, Sister Benedicta, SLG (translator), *The Sayings of the Desert Fathers*, 1975.

Acknowledgments

To the editors who first published the stories in this collection: Thank you for accepting the good ones and rejecting the bad ones. To Gavin J. Grant, who convinced me I had enough good stories to make a book: Thank you for keeping your eyes open! To Kathrin Köhler, my partner in crime: I couldn't have done it without you. To Keith: Thank you again, and forever. To the many living writers whose influence flickers through these pages— Karen Joy Fowler, Kate Zambreno, Dodie Bellamy, Eileen Myles, S. D. Chrostowska, Kuzhali Manickavel, Nalo Hopkinson, Kelly Link: Here we are, together, in a way.

About the Author

Sofia Samatar (sofiasamatar.com) is the author of the novels *A Stranger in Olondria* and *The Winged Histories*. She has written for *Strange Horizons*, *BOMB*, and *Clarkesworld*, among others, and has won the John W. Campbell Award, the Crawford Award, the British Fantasy Award, and the World Fantasy Award. Two of her stories were selected for the inaugural edition of the *Best American Science Fiction and Fantasy*. She lives in Virginia.